MILKSHAKES FOR THE ALMOST DEAD

A HORROR STORY, FOR GIRLS

BY LULU WOOD

ALSO BY BY LULU WOOD

For Parsley, with every bit of my love.

'There is a special place in hell for women who don't support other women.'

Madeleine Albright

~

'You can't hide from a hurricane under a beach umbrella.'

Philip Rahv

~

'They sicken of the calm who know the storm.'

Dorothy Parker

CONTENTS

INTRODUCTION

When we are children, we picture the monsters that lurk in the shadows of our lives, hiding in our wardrobes until the lights go out, curled up under our beds just waiting until we fall asleep, with their fangs and their fur and their pointy claws. Then we grow up and we are told that there is nothing to be scared of because monsters only exist in stories. But that's a lie. Monsters do exist, they just don't have fangs and fur and claws. Mostly they wear expensive suits and have all the money, and they flick at our lives like imaginary specks of dust on their trousers.

A monster thought he'd got me. He thought I was so lonely and desperate that I'd go along with anything. He thought he could steal my life and I'd let him because I was stupid and naïve, and my head was full of romance. Because I wasn't paying attention. Because I was just a *silly, young girl*. But he was wrong.

The knot in my blindfold is too tight and it's digging into my scalp. I sit on my hands, pressing my palms flat into the leather seat beneath me. I could just reach up and untie it, but I don't.

It's better if I don't know.

PART I

1

Dad started losing it again after dinner. He was muttering and twitching.

"Ha ha," I said and rolled my eyes, but he wouldn't stop. At first I thought he might be joking, because of Midsummer...

My dad was born in Lulea, in Northern Sweden, and the sun doesn't set there on Midsummer's Eve. There are these huge open-air parties that go on all night, and a myth that for 24 hours you can do anything you want, and it won't matter. Unfortunately, Grandpa Lind took it literally, so when he stood up in court and shouted, "It was Midsummer!" the judge tutted and agreed with my grandma that it was an unreasonable defense for adultery.

My dad was only five when he and Grandma Lind moved to London. When I was little, I would sneak into her kitchen and dip my hand in to the pouch of her apron where the boiled sweets lived. Grandma Lind died of breast cancer when I was seven. Another one gone.

I stared outside at the sun disappearing between the oak trees in the field. My initials are carved into one of those trees. Dad did it when I was little. He was teaching me how to ride my bike and I'd crashed into Mum's bench, scraping my knees and the palms of my hands. Rosebuds of blood formed at my palms and I wouldn't stop crying. He picked me up, carried me over to the tree and started digging into the bark with his penknife.

"See, DL - that's you, Diana."

Then he carved his initials, TL, and a crooked heart around them both. He said, "Now we'll always be together, somewhere."

Our kitchen is small, white, plastic. A tiny table for two is squeezed in against the wall. Fruit lives in the bowl but nothing too exotic, all just Tesco's oranges and apples, sometimes a banana if I get one at school and forget to eat it. But my dad doesn't trust them. 'They give out a chemical that rots everything else in the bowl,' he says. 'The banana is the terrorist of the fruit world,' he says. I know.

He knocked on my bedroom door just as my eyes were glazing over in front of a Vietnam War mind map. He sat at the end of my bed staring up at the ceiling. After five minutes I went back to studying because sometimes this is all he does, just comes and sits in a room I'm in without actually saying anything. But then he coughed three times and began to talk.

"Sausage, you know that things change and life surprises us sometimes?"

I opened my mouth to speak but he shook his head sadly and continued. "And sometimes those changes are for the good, Diana, but sometimes not. All you can do is... You have to just... I want you to trust yourself, Sausage. And trust the universe, if you can, even if it seems awful. Roll with the differences. Let them take you somewhere. My time will come, of course, although I know young people don't like to think about death. But even then, when it does, everything will be okay for you. So, what I'm saying is, even if something terrible happens, you have to trust me. Because I love you, Diana. Do you understand what I'm trying to say?"

I made an 'uh-huh' noise and smiled. He kissed my head

goodnight and left the room. I couldn't pull at the threads of this new crazy, yet. As soon as my last exam was over – as soon as my summer officially began the following afternoon - he'd have my full attention. It was less than 24 hours.

Nothing truly terrible could happen before then.

2

Dad used to check my windows every night before bedtime. These days I have to promise I'll do it myself, before I go to sleep. "Have you checked your windows?" he shouts before he shuts the door to his bedroom. "Yep," I shout back, getting back up to do it. It's made me paranoid, obviously. I still wake up in the middle of the night sometimes, wide-eyed, holding my breath, convinced I'll hear a stranger creeping up our stairs...

For as long as I can remember I've dreamt that someone watches me while I sleep. Once, when I was younger, I thought I saw him. I opened my eyes and he was standing in front of me with his back to the window, softly pressing his boot down on the squeaky floorboard by my wardrobe. The light from the streetlamp made his hair glisten like it was wet. I couldn't see his face, but he shook his head slowly and whispered, "Go back to sleep, little one."

I don't know why but I did what he said. In the morning, when I opened my eyes again, he was gone. It was just a dream. But the floorboard didn't squeak anymore.

That night, a noise woke me up at 03.23am. Something felt wrong. There was a light on downstairs. Crouching by the bannister, I held my breath and craned my neck to see. My dad was standing in the middle of the kitchen, clutching a letter, tears rolling silently down his cheeks, repeating the same thing, over and over: "Vita. Vita. Vita." Turning quietly, I crept back to my room, re-checked my windows and went back to bed.

3

Aunt Vita sends me a card and a cheque for my birthday every May, and the money for a new school uniform every August. Sometimes she includes a photo of her latest painting - some naked old woman smiling (it's not abuse, *apparently*), all loose skin and age spots, holding an inflatable shark or unicorn or pineapple or something.

"You want to reach out and touch them", she says.

I really don't.

Some of Aunt Vita's work is hanging in the library in Lattering, the random seaside town where she lives on the south coast, half way between Brighton and Bournemouth but a world away from civilisation. 'Eileen Meets Jaws' has got pride of place in the Science Fiction and Fantasy section, apparently.

I've never known anyone write swear words with an actual pen, but Aunt Vita swears a LOT. Just 'bloody' and 'bugger' and 'bastard' and 'Christ', but she writes those ones loads. Dad always says, 'Aunt Vita is one of a kind.' That feels like a nice way of saying someone is terrible. She has lived in Lattering my whole life but I've never seen her house, or the beach, or the town. I've never been invited. Aunt Vita calls herself a 'flag-waving-feminist', but do they have an actual flag? Sometimes her cards finish with a quote from a famous woman to *inspire* me. I only remember one: 'There is a special place in Hell for women who don't support other women.' I liked it and repeated it in my head, until I'd learnt it by heart. Aunt Vita's card and cheque came last month. There was no quote this time, or at least it wasn't attributed. She just wrote: 'Life comes at us Diana. Brace yourself. Vita x'.

I haven't seen Aunt Vita for ten years. I could walk past her in the street and not recognise her. She'd only know it was me because of the photos I send of me in my new uniform each September and the fact that, apparently, I look a lot like Lana did when she was sixteen. Lana is my mother and her sister. Correction: my dead mother and her dead sister. Lana is the reason Aunt Vita isn't a barrister anymore, and my dad isn't a reporter anymore. She left us all and it broke the ones who were old enough to understand. My dad held it together for a long time, considering. He's never met anybody else. I think that part of his heart just gave up when she died.

4

The front door slamming woke me up at 7am. Dad's coffee cup and toast plate were washed up by the sink as usual, which was a good indicator that his episode may have broken, like a fever in the night, and everything was back to normal. I said, "False alarm!" out loud to the kitchen, to the world, to try and convince myself. I told myself the dread in my belly was just my nerves misbehaving before my last exam. Nothing really terrible could happen in six hours anyway, right?

I twisted my hair up with the usual mouthful of clips. I swear it weighs about 5kg on its own, it's surprising I can keep my head up. It's so hot, the hottest June on record they say. The exam hall is going to stink. None of the moderators' wear deodorant. I imagined one of them leaning over me last week (the old lady with the long black witch's plait) with her stinky armpit in my face. My stomach contracted violently, but I couldn't stop.

'Imagine it again,' the voice in my head whispered, 'her armpit hair tickling your face. Her old, grey, wet, pit-hair pressing against the skin by your mouth.' I gagged SO much. I'm gagging now just thinking about it.

Sometimes I picture the most disgusting thing I can put in my mouth until I'm almost sick. I'm not just talking about weird stuff like the dog diarrhoea I saw in the street last week (which I pictured eating, by the way). I mean otherwise normal food, that normal people eat. Greasy things. If you can see drops of oil on a sausage you *know* it will harden into little white balls of fat. What if those balls get stuck to your ribs? How do you get them out once they are in there? Sometimes I'll even put something in my mouth *knowing* I'll gag. It can be healthy food too. I can't eat anything that will burst *while* I eat it. I can't bite down on a grape and feel the liquid oozing out, like a pus-filled boil exploding between my teeth, but I force myself to think about it anyway. I know.

It started when I was seven, the year I got fat. The other kids noticed of course, because kids notice everything, and even the girls that were usually nice to me started calling me Blubber Belly, and Diana the Whale. My dad couldn't afford to buy a new uniform, so my school skirt was held together with a safety pin. He called it 'puppy fat', like it was cute. I might have agreed with him – my belly was soft, and I liked how it squished beneath my fingers - but all the other girls were bullet quick to point out that I was disgusting.

I was sneaking extra food out of the kitchen and hiding it under my bed. Before I went to sleep each night, I'd crawl under my duvet and eat two or three bags of Hula Hoops, popping them in my mouth as quickly as I could, waiting for that tired full feeling. It felt nice, like I'd filled something that was missing. It made me genuinely happy. Then something weird started to happen. Whenever I was about to put something in my mouth my brain offered up fifty different alternatives of what it could be. That burger? That's not actually beef. It's mashed-up penguin or minced-up rat. I'd manage to chew it once, before spitting it out. Then I basically stopped eating.

I'd lost all the new weight by the time school started again, and the mean girls looked genuinely disappointed. Dad took me to see a counsellor anyway. That was the *first* time. Her name was Dr. Sylvia and her room at the clinic was stuffed with sad looking dolls. Dr. Sylvia said my brain was trying to stop me over-eating, in its own awful way, but she was more concerned with *why* of course.

"Are you depressed, Diana?" and "Are you suicidal, Diana?" Those questions started pretty early.

It's never completely gone away - the food weirdness - but obviously I eat now. I'm okay with stuff that I trust, like toast, or most vegetables, or anything I've cooked myself. I still gag a LOT but it's manageable. I haven't told my dad again. I've seen enough of Sylvia to last me a lifetime. Her room reeked, like vanilla and cigarettes, and the smell of smoke still triggers me. Dad gave up after the fire. The investigator said it was an electrical fault with our fridge-freezer, but of course Dad didn't believe him. I'm not saying he's the most paranoid man in the world but he would win in London, *and* I'm including the guy that I see at the cinema who wears that silver cone on his head to protect his brain from gamma rays. Now Dad just has one cigarette a week, on a Saturday night. He stands at the bottom of the garden and blows smoke rings in the air, even when it rains.

5

They were already sitting on the wall when I got to school, running their perfect fingers through their perfect hair. As usual my mouth went bone dry, and I blinked three times. Audrey saw me straight away. She's the worst one.

"Pound Shop," Audrey coughed into her hand. Virginia laughed.

"Everything's a pound," Audrey coughed again. I scanned for Amy, or Betty, or a teacher, or anyone that might help, but I was on my own again...

Audrey is the leader of The Debs. They have called me 'Pound Shop' for the last three years. My school costs eighteen thousand pounds a year but I am on a full day fee scholarship, meaning I get everything paid for. Meanwhile, Audrey and Virginia's parents drop them off in shiny black Range Rovers every morning.

"I hope you didn't stay up too late revising Pound Shop," Virginia said loudly, squeezing hand cream into her palms and rubbing them together.

"You look like rubbish, so..." Audrey grimaced at me in mock embarrassment.

"Wait, Audrey, don't say that. She doesn't look any different than usual," Virginia said.

"You're right, Gin. She can't help it if her clothes make her look like a refugee."

They grinned as I summoned up every ounce of my courage.

"There is a special place in Hell for women who don't support other women," I managed to whisper, my hands trembling. I stuffed them in my pockets as they rolled their beautiful eyes.

"Her voice is so boring it makes me want to cut myself," Audrey said.

Virginia smirked. "Diana thinks that being clever is soooo clever."

They jumped down from the wall and moved towards me until they were close enough for me to smell their Smints. I could feel the tears swelling dangerously in the corners of my eyes.

"What is it that your Dad's always saying, Gin?"

"It's not what you know, it's who you know."

"Who do you know, Pound Shop? The woman at the food bank? Are you hoping she'll get you a job checking the use-by dates on the tins?"

"The world isn't like that anymore," I whispered.

"Oh, it's exactly like that Pound Shop. But good luck with the exam. I'm sure you'll put the rest of us to shame. *Again.*"

To be fair, we are poor. Dad hasn't worked since his first episode, when the police found him at midnight, collapsed in the snow outside the gates of Richmond Park. He'd been trying to break in, to steal a deer they said, which was ridiculous: we don't have the space for a pet. The babysitter woke me up to tell me he was in custody, and that she needed the money for her taxi home. I was 12 years old. They took him straight into surgery and put a metal rod in his back. His drinking got worse after he came out of hospital. Most nights he just sits in front of his PC, scrawling shorthand on a pad. When I ask him what he's doing he always says, "This and that." Mostly I leave his crazy alone because I love him, and he loves me, and also: where would I go without him? He's all I have.

And, to be fair again, I don't have any new clothes. I grew four inches last summer and suddenly nothing fitted me anymore. Dad disappeared in to the loft one day muttering, and I braced myself for the worst when I heard an almighty thud on the landing. It was quickly followed by another, and another. Dad threw four bursting black bin liners down from the loft. They were Lana's old things - the bags that survived the fire. T-shirts that said Adidas or Coke, and a *tonne* of checked shirts. When I pulled her skinny jeans over my thighs I felt so happy, but then I realised I can never tell her that we are the same, she and I. I have her crazy red hair too. At least I don't cry about it anymore.

6

Amy, Betty and I used to walk to Starbucks side by side every day, spread out across the pavement, nobody in front or behind, everybody the same. Even our steps were identical, like a slow march. We don't walk like that now. I stopped caring about Betty and Amy's Big Trip™ months ago (it should be trademarked, they say it so much). Now, as soon as somebody even mentions the word 'Cambodia' I look at my phone.

That day was no different. We didn't talk about the exam we'd just taken, our last exam in year eleven, or the relief or the magnitude or anything. We didn't talk about *anything* but Cambodia.

"So, we land in Cambodia at 5pm," Amy said, "and my brother says it will be raining so make sure your poncho is at the top of your rucksack."

"I read it's going to be, like, 90 percent humidity," Betty said. "I hope my hair doesn't frizz out."

"What does that even mean - 90 percent humidity?" Amy asked.

"It means the air is 90% saturated with water," I said.

They looked at me, surprised. They'd forgotten I existed.

"Dido, what are we going to do without you around to tell us all the answers?" Amy said, smiling.

Amy has always called me Dido. I used to LOVE it. It happened on my third day at St Jude's. I was sitting on my own in the corner of the canteen. Amy sat down in front of me, took a bite of her apple and said, "Look, I don't call people by their real names, so you'll need a different one." Then I became Dido at St Jude's, the best girls' school in London, and nobody knew about my crazy dad, or my dead mum, or anything else rubbish about me. From then on Amy, Betty and I came as a three, in everything. If we got split into pairs in gym, we'd take it in turns to go with the random. That was then at least. The last time I cried in front of them, about Betty and Amy's Big Trip™, they both got really embarrassed. That's when they started meeting up in secret.

"Hey, how's your Dad?" Betty asked finally.

"Yes, how is he?" Amy seized on it too.

We breathed a collective sigh of relief. It was *something* to talk about.

"He's been fine for ages, but he started being weird again last night. I'm sure it will be okay," I said, but all I was thinking was: don't cry. DON'T CRY. We sipped our Frappuccino's in silence.

"We'll send you loads of pictures and we'll miss you every day," Amy said.

I concentrated on pulling the paper away from my straw, so I didn't have to look at them.

Walking home along the river, it was crazy hot but two old women in overcoats and hats were chatting together on a bench. I couldn't remember ever feeling quite *this* shit. Dad was still out when I got home, but I was overwhelmed with the urge to sleep. I laid on my bed and closed my eyes.

The angry fist banging on our front door woke me up first. Then I heard the house phone ringing like an alarm from my childhood that I thought I'd forgotten. That phone never rings anymore. I ran downstairs and threw the door open. A woman I recognised was standing on the doorstep.

"For Christ's sake, don't open the door without checking who it is first Diana, especially at midnight. And answer that bloody phone."

She walked past me into the hall.

"Hello?" I said to the phone.

"Is that Diana Lind?"

"Yes. Who is this?"

"My name is Detective Inspector March. I'm a policeman."

"I know what a Detective Inspector is," I said. "What's going on? Where's my Dad?"

The woman was standing in the kitchen doorway holding my schoolbag.

"Is this yours?" she asked. I nodded. She put it next to the front door.

"What's going on?" I asked her and the phone at once.

"Diana, I'm afraid we have your father in police custody," the phone said.

"Oh God, has he tried to steal a deer again?"

"No, it's a little more serious than that."

The woman sat down on the bottom step of the stairs. She was wearing a long, tight, silver, sparkling evening dress, a massive man's watch, and green wellies, covered in mud. Her hair was long, and curly like mine. She was beautiful. She smiled at me but there were tears in her eyes. So I do recognise you after all, Aunt Vita, I thought.

"Diana," Detective Inspector March said, "your father has been arrested on suspicion of attempted murder."

PART II

1

"Diana? Diana? Diana?"

Detective Inspector March repeats my name three times, but I don't answer. He sounds important though. I picture him wearing a uniform with lots of medals. Maybe a special hat. I have a very traditional relationship with authority figures: I just do what they tell me. I should answer but I can't make my voice work. Aunt Vita takes the phone out of my hand.

"Hello Inspector. This is Vita Varmint, Diana's Aunt...his dead wife's sister...yes, I was visiting...yes, I understand that legally she could stay here, but given that she's not legally old enough to operate a forklift truck we'll apply some common sense, shall we?"

Aunt Vita says 'legally' like they both know it's a joke.

"I know exactly what I'm talking about Inspector, I've been a criminal barrister for fifteen years."

The voice on the end of the phone goes crazy but she just talks over him like he's not even there. She clearly doesn't give a shit about authority. Or maybe she thinks she's it?

"Diana has committed no crime, poses no risk. The accused is already in your custody. We will cooperate fully with the authorities from a distance..."

When she says 'we' I feel something unfamiliar, like someone reaching in to my chest and squeezing my heart. Aunt Vita is still talking.

"Try intentional infliction of emotional distress for starters. Are jokes your way of flirting Inspector, because it's thoroughly unprofessional?"

Aunt Vita winks at me and smiles, a broad pink grin, as the Inspector's voice reaches new levels of loud on the other end of the phone. I sit down on the bottom step and stop listening. My dad is in police custody. This is my fault. I should have done something.

The shouting on the phone stops suddenly, and Aunt Vita smiles.

"Good. We'll be in touch." She hangs up and stares at me expectantly.

"What?" I say.

"It will be much harder to escape once they get here."

"Is it true? Did my dad really try to kill someone?"

She takes my hands and pulls me to my feet. The push of her fingers through mine feels odd: I don't know her.

"Don't believe everything the police tell you, Diana. Let's go. Wait! I have to get something."

She dashes upstairs and emerges thirty seconds later. An envelope is clearly sticking out of the top of her dress. If she thinks she's hidden it she's an idiot.

"What's that?" I ask, pointing to it.

"Nothing important. Just some money for you."

"Money? What for?"

"For your holiday. With me. This was always planned Diana, your father called me yesterday. It's a staycation, of sorts, just with a bit of an unexpected twist. It will all be fine soon, I promise. Don't worry. But we do have to leave now."

Aunt Vita loads my stuff into the boot of her car, which is even older and browner than ours. I just stand there, feeling like I've jumped into one of those ice-cold plunge pools; I'm numb but it hurts. She readjusts things to make them fit and slams the boot closed. She runs past me and yanks our front door shut, glancing at her man-watch.

"By my reckoning we have about four minutes."

She ushers me on to a dirty looking pink blanket that's draped over the passenger seat, slamming the door behind me. In the terrifying silence of her car, a wet snore makes me jump. A tiny, biscuit-brown dog is asleep on the back seat. Aunt Vita throws open the driver door and jumps in.

"That's Howard," she says, nodding at the puppy. "He's new, too."

2

Aunt Vita reverses out of the driveway so fast that the wheels spin and we knock over the dustbin. A police car glides noiselessly alongside us at the traffic lights at the end of our street. I glance over at my aunt. Her jaw is clenched, and her fingers are gripping the steering wheel so tightly they are turning white, the veins in the back of her hands blue and protruding. I feel the eyes of the policemen on me. I open my mouth to speak just as the lights change to green. They turn left and Aunt Vita loosens her grip on the wheel. Sirens wail in the distance as we speed away.

3

Aunt Vita drives like it's a dare. I focus on the hazy red taillights of a lorry way ahead of us and try not to feel sick.

"Do you have a phone?" she says.

I nod. I'm not five.

"Did you bring it with you?" she says impatiently.

"It's in my schoolbag, wherever that ended up."

I look around. Her car is a mess.

"It's behind my seat," she says. "Lean over and get it."

Dragging my bag over the top of her headrest I'm showered in bits of old biscuit and other unidentifiable crumbs.

"Gross," I say, shaking my head furiously.

I pull out my phone. It's almost dead. Four messages.

"Throw it out of the window," she says.

"Ha ha." I roll my eyes. She's weird.

"I'm not joking Diana, toss it," she says, trying to grab it from my hand, but the car swerves sharply and she has to grab the wheel.

"Are you insane?" I say, stuffing my phone behind my back.

"Fine, take the SIM out. Can you do that without having a breakdown?" She raises one eyebrow. I can do that too, it's my party trick. It makes Amy and Betty laugh.

"Why?" I say.

"Because I'm asking you to, Diana."

That's the kind of thing my dad says when he's lost an argument.

We are driving at one hundred miles an hour. Who is this woman? Just because she's related to my mum, I'm trusting her, but I didn't know my mother and I don't know her.

"Just give me the SIM please, Diana. You can have it back again in a few days, when things have settled down."

"But why?" I say again.

"Well, for starters you could get hacked by the press. Is that what you want - no privacy at all?"

"Why would the press hack my phone? I'm not important. Wait, who exactly is my dad supposed to have tried to kill?"

She sighs and tuts simultaneously at the ridiculousness of it all, as it plays out in her head.

"Oh, just some off duty policeman, no one fancy, but you know what the gutter press are like, darling."

"He tried to kill a policeman?" I say, incredulous. "But why?" I'm so confused, my voice is higher than a whistle.

"Oh, Christ no! Kill is much too big a word for what he did. It's more that he was caught inside a house where he arguably shouldn't have been, in that it wasn't his house, and a shot was fired, yadda, yadda, yadda..." She rolls her eyes like it's the most boring thing she's ever heard.

"A shot? Like from a gun? But Dad hates guns!"

"You see?" She smacks the steering wheel hard, like it's the bottom of a bad child. "Exactly. The charges will be dropped really soon, I know it. But, in the meantime, better to be safe and ultimately you'll be protecting your dad as well of course..." She eyes my phone.

I sigh and press and hold the 'on' button. The screen goes gently to sleep. I have a bad feeling about this. What is it with me and authority? I pop the SIM out with my earring and hand it to her.

"Christ, it's like somebody died," she whispers, tucking it inside her dress. "You can have it back when I'm sure. I'm so hungry. Are you hungry, Diana?"

She magics a Curly Wurly out of nowhere and peels the plastic back with her teeth.

"You want?" she asks, waving the half bitten chocolate ladder at me. I shake my head and look out of the window. I see the occasional tree but it's so dark. Random houses are dotted a few hundred yards from the road. They are in fields. They could be farms I suppose? They could be empty and desolate or haunted by the ghosts of the tragic and disturbed. Or they could just be perfectly normal houses, protecting perfectly normal families from the night, as they innocently sleep, unaware of just how dark it's got outside, and the wolves creeping towards them in the forests, and the strange girl staring in wondering about them as they lie, eyes closed, defenseless in their beds. I don't know the answer. I will never know, now. Yesterday it felt like I was sure of everything. Tonight, I don't know anything at all. I turn to face my aunt.

"When you are sure of what?" I say.

She sighs.

"When I'm sure you are safe Diana."

Howard snores loudly on the back seat. I wish I was him. My eyelids feel like weights have been slyly sewn in to them. I need to stick my head out of the window and let the wind slap my face awake. Dad used to say, 'If you put your arm out of the car while I'm driving it will blow away'. I was horrified. I still half believe that. Impressionable.

She turns on the radio.

"Nina Simone," she says like someone just gave her all the drugs. I close my eyes.

4

W hen I wake, we are veering crazily down a pitch-black lane with sharp bends she clearly knows by heart because we don't see them coming. Instinctively, I look at my blank faced phone, still in my hand. I think of my dad and want to cry. I wish I knew they weren't laughing at him. I wish I was certain he hadn't done anything wrong.

"I didn't mean to fall asleep," I say, rubbing my eyes.

"De nada," Aunt Vita says. "You do Spanish at school I hope?"

I nod my head. "And German. And I'm trying to teach myself Mandarin."

"Spanish is the important one. Then no one will know what we're saying."

"Except if they're Spanish," I say.

De nada means 'it's nothing'. My mother's parents were Spanish. Everyone called them Tito Matias and Mima Rose. Tito already had cancer when Mum died. His funeral is one of the first things I remember, full of old women draped in vast black dresses and gold jewellery. One of them squeezed me so hard I coughed. Her face was full of creases and she smelt of dust and flowers. She pressed her tear-soaked cheek against mine and said, in the strongest accent I'd ever heard, "Tito with tu Mama." My dad swore and yanked me away to the swings behind the church. He pushed me on that swing for an hour, in silence, as I kicked myself higher and higher. Mima Rose died a year later. Dropping like flies.

5

"Are we nearly there?" I ask. She makes an affirmative noise. London is never this dark. I think that thing I can smell is the sea?

"Aunt Vita?"

"Yes, Diana?"

"Is my dad going to be okay?"

She rolls the car to a stop, with the ocean behind her. She takes my hand and, like a Pavlovian response, I start to cry. I know I'm an ugly crier. I don't want her to see me like this.

"What's important is what they can prove, and that you are taken care of." She squeezes my hand when she says 'you'.

"Let's talk about all of this in the morning," she says. "It's late now. Howard needs to stretch and so do I. And then we all need our beds."

"Where are we?" I say, climbing out of the car. My legs are stiff from sitting, and the ground shifts beneath my feet. I think it's sand.

"At my house," she says, scooping up Howard from the back seat of the car. "You are going to live with me for a while. It's what your dad had planned for the summer."

Howard stretches then goes dead weight in her arms. I wish I'd thought of that first. I smile but I don't believe her. Why would my dad let me get my old summer job back if he knew I wouldn't be there to do it? I smell a big fat rat.

"Here, you take him, and I'll get your stuff." She hands me the puppy and I pull him tightly into my chest like he's keeping me afloat.

Her front door is Barbie pink, but the paint is peeling so badly you can see patches of green beneath. Wind chimes hang on either side of the doorframe, banging out a tune in the breeze. She drops my stuff on the wooden boards of her old white porch.

"Found you, swine!" she says, selecting a key from a bunch of about twenty and jamming it into the door. She's weird.

"For how long?" I say.

"How long are you staying here?" she says, turning, picking up all my stuff. "For the summer." She smiles and shoves the door open with her bum. "Diana, welcome to Lattering."

BEFORE

*J*uan loiters on the beach, watching. An attractive young woman and her daughter are splashing around in the shallow water, but she stops and straightens as the man in the suit walks past her into the waves. Her brow knots with concern as she raises her hand to shield her eyes from the sun. She looks quite beautiful, and he takes a mental picture. He will sketch her later as the world sleeps.

"Are you okay?" she shouts, but the suited man doesn't turn around.

"Are you feeling okay?" She shouts again. "You'll ruin that suit."

This time he turns to face her. He is handsome like a statue, but his eyes are red and swollen. The suited man is Hugo Beltrome Jnr. As of 7.15am that morning, Hugo is Juan's employer.

"My grandfather died this morning," Hugo says to her. "He's the only person who ever cared for me.'

The child splashes around at her feet, filling a bucket with sea water, tipping it clumsily over her tiny belly.

"Is that your daughter?"

She nods.

"I have two sons," he says. "They live in America with their mothers. Different mothers. I don't see them. I give them money, they are taken care of."

"You should see them," the woman says.

"What for?" Hugo asks, as if he were a child himself.

She runs her fingers through her daughter's hair. "Her love silences the monsters in my head."

The woman is covered in freckles. The straps of her costume are pulled down from her shoulders. Her skirt is tucked in messily at the tops of her thighs.

"I'm Lana Lind," she says. "Come back out of the water."

"I don't let people tell me what to do," Hugo says.

"Okay. I'll ask instead. Please come out of the water? I think I know how you feel. You can talk to me, today. Then, if you still want to, you can come back tomorrow. The ocean isn't going anywhere."

Hugo contemplates the waves before him.

Juan watches them from a distance, as they walk back up the beach together. The child runs ahead to a windbreaker surrounded by plastic toys and towels.

"You are very trusting, Lana," Hugo says.

"Why, are you the devil?" she says, scrunching up her nose.

"No." He offers her his hand. "But I doubt the devil would admit it anyway. I'm Hugo Beltrome."

"Well, it's nice to meet you, Hugo."

"Do you live in Lattering, Lana?"

She shakes her head. "No. We are just here for the summer."

"Lucky for me," Hugo says.

Her daughter empties her bucket of water over their feet. Lana grabs her, spinning her around as they both shriek in delight.

"And this little trouble-maker," she says, tickling the child who giggles uncontrollably, "is Diana."

PART III

1

A seagull wakes me up. It's sitting on the windowsill, tapping on the glass.

Tap.

Tap.

Squawk.

Tap.

Tap.

Squawk.

Nature is unnerving. What does he even want?

I roll over and the bed creaks as if I weigh a tonne. I rub my eyes. Everything is twinkling. The walls of my room are covered in gold and silver sparkly frames. Some of them are old-fashioned and a bit broken, decorated in angels and arrows and branches and skulls. The quotes that my aunt has sent me over the years are handwritten inside. My favourite is there, as is 'Nobody can make you feel inferior without your consent' which was said by Eleanor Roosevelt, apparently. Dorothy Parker's words are there too: 'They sicken of the calm, who know the storm'. I've never understood that one.

The biggest, cheapest frame is in the middle of the wall. It says, 'Anything is possible if you believe you can fly' in gold handwriting with glitter pen swirls underneath it. A girl at my school believed she could fly when she took a pill last Christmas. She broke both her legs flying out of her bedroom window and was off school for three months. So, hospitalization is definitely possible…

I have an uninterrupted view of the ocean through the window. Rays of sunlight stretch across the flat spaces between the waves. Clumps of those fluorescent stars that they stick to kid's ceilings shine weakly above me. My dad suggested he get me some when I was little. I told him I'd be terrified if I woke up in the middle of the night and thought the roof had blown off. (The dark doesn't scare me. It's being left alone that tightens my throat.) Cheap fairy lights are strung twice around the window and across one wall, trailing off in a line, like ants marching down to the plug socket by my bed. I lean over and flick them on. They are pink and gold, and flashing. I think Tinkerbell may have been slaughtered in this room. It's nuts but then madness clearly runs in my family, and not the fun kind. It's the bad kind that butchers fairies, or shoots at off duty policemen, or walks into the ocean at midnight, and that I probably shouldn't joke about because…genetics.

A door slams downstairs.

2

Aunt Vita's house is a proper mess. A wooden dining table that could seat all the apostles occupies half of an open plan kitchen. I only know that it's wood because I can see the legs. It's covered in coffee cups, and wine glasses, and newspapers, and 5p shopping bags, and dog poo bags. There are three different half empty bottles of wine and one full bottle of gin. There are five different shoes strewn across the floor, none of which make a pair, and cardigans hanging on the backs of chairs which don't match the table, and scarves, and straw hats, and big black sunglasses, and plasters, and beach bags, and bottles of sun cream. There is no actual food, or plates, or cutlery. The cooker is spotless.

The news babbles on the radio in the corner as Aunt Vita makes coffee, and she smiles as if I've lived here forever. She flicks the radio and some old song plays instead. She doesn't know any of the lyrics, but she sings anyway. Jam jars are dotted around the edges of the room on shelves, and in a neat row along a mantlepiece over the fire, and on piles of books in the corners. Each one holds two fresh looking flowers that look like they've been picked from other people's gardens. I sit down awkwardly. Howard is asleep in a basket in the corner. A candle is burning. Aunt Vita's wellies are by the back door, covered in fresh sand.

"Good," she says. "I was about to come and rouse you."

Rouse? Really?

"Howard got me up for a bloody dawn jaunt around the garden. What on earth was I thinking, getting a puppy?"

Jaunt?

"A seagull *roused* me," I say, "and all the twinkling."

She turns and smiles, leaning back against the kitchen counter, cradling her cup of coffee. She is wearing tight navy jodhpurs and a huge, old, grey T-shirt with noticeable holes, and the words 'Oxford Law' written in the middle in faded white letters. Her hair is twisted on the top of her head and appears to be held in place with a biro. I don't understand how that's even possible. She looks younger than she did last night.

"How do you take your coffee - black? Like your mum did?" she asks, holding up the coffee pot.

"Sure," I say. I've never had a black coffee in my life, of course.

She passes me a steaming hot mug with a picture of Hilary Clinton on it. I force myself to take a sip and it burns everything within a 10cm radius of my mouth. It tastes like a melted tyre. My tummy rumbles so loudly that we both jump, and she yanks open a drawer. Inside there is a syringe, and a scalpel, and a small cereal bar that's stuck to a flyer. She hands me the cereal bar proudly.

"Here," she says, beaming.

"What are you having?" I ask.

"Oh, I don't eat breakfast. It's a total myth that it's the most important meal of the day, invented by the bloody cornflake pushers. The world is full of liars, Diana, even about muesli. Also, I clearly love food," she smacks her own bum for emphasis and it makes me jump, "but I find cooking disruptive. Mostly, I hope people will bring me things I can eat at regular intervals throughout the day."

She takes the almost full mug of coffee from my hand.

"I'll make you a cup of tea instead."

She's filling up the kettle before I can even answer.

"Let's go outside and sit on my bench, Diana. There's something I need to tell you."

42

3

We sit facing the ocean in Aunt Vita's garden. 'Shalimar' is painted in white letters on a large piece of driftwood by the gate. On the other side of the gate is a path. On the other side of the path is the beach. Some people would love a house by the sea, but I'm no fan of sand. I don't know what Shalimar means. Aunt Vita places her mug on the grass by her feet. There is a hole in her sock and one expertly polished, dark red toenail pokes through.

"Diana, your father called me a few days ago. It was the first time we'd spoken in years. He told me something important."

I nod and smile for her to go on. I know all his crazy. Nothing can surprise me here.

"He believes your mother's death was more complicated than we first believed."

I take another sip of my tea. That was unexpected, actually. "She walked out into the ocean at midnight Aunt Vita, I think it was pretty clear what she meant to do."

She takes the biggest breath. "Diana, your dad believes Lana was being threatened…'

I'm already shaking my head and she stops when I talk over her. "Nope. No. He just can't admit she didn't want us, that's all." I shrug and it's like I've shot her. "She had post-natal depression," I say. "I know it wasn't my fault. I've had the counselling, I'm not on suicide watch."

An old woman cycles past, with a dog in a basket. Aunt Vita still looks like she's in shock but she smiles and nods, and the woman smiles back and gives a little wave. The dog barks. Everybody knows everybody here, then.

"You do know that my dad struggles sometimes Aunt Vita? With life."

She nods and bites her lip but doesn't say anything else. We stare at the ocean as a seagull screams above us, and her eyebrows move as if she's talking to someone. She turns back to me.

"Well, you can stay here until your dad is released. Nobody was even hurt so…it could be much worse."

She attempts a smile but I don't return it. It couldn't *feel* much worse. We sit in silence for ages.

"It will be nice having you here, Diana. I should have asked you to stay a long time ago. I miss your mother so much, even now." There are tears in her eyes but my fists ball up in rage.

"Well, I don't miss her because I didn't even know her. She made sure of that," I say, throwing cold tea on the grass.

4

There are bodies floating in the sea.

"Those are the surfers," Aunt Vita says, after what feels like forever. "You loved them when you were little. You called them fishy men."

Wait, what?

"I was here before?"

She nods and pinches the skin at the bottom of her neck.

"We hired a huge, old house on the beach. It's being renovated now of course."

"Aunt Vita, is this the beach where my mother...?" I can't finish the sentence.

She nods sadly. I've stopped breathing. I gasp for air before it's too late.

"Why do you LIVE here?" I shout, incredulous.

"Well, at first I just wanted to stay close to her. I still talk to her every day," she says, nodding towards the ocean, as if that's not just fucking crazy and mixed up and awful. She tugs the biro out from the back of her head and grips it between her teeth, shaking out her hair, pulling it into a ponytail at the nape of her neck and twisting, winding it into a thick, dark rope that she pulls to the top

45

of her head. She grabs the biro from her teeth and pushes it into her hair, and the rope stays put.

"I'm sorry. I know it's not ideal, but now it's my home," she says.

Not ideal.

I take a deep breath and force myself to look back out at the ocean. I picture Aunt Vita sitting here on her own for all these years, chatting away to the sea like a crazy person, but I can't picture my mum at all. All I can think about is my dad, and what he used to say whenever he was teaching me something new like riding my bike, or swimming without armbands, or rolling on my skates alone. I'd be looking around at some random noise - a car horn or a dog barking - or just to check that he was still there, and he'd shout, "Diana, you have to face the way you are going!"

"What does Shalimar mean?" I ask.

"I'm not actually sure," she says, blowing out the breath she's been storing in her cheeks, looking up at the sky. "Houses with names, and surfers, and no rain yet this summer. That's Lattering in a nutshell, really. You won't find any big city shenanigans here."

Shenanigans? Really?

She looks up at the sky again, closes her eyes and whispers,

"Christ, we need a storm."

5

"So, what now?" I ask. I've been sitting at a kitchen table in Lattering for twenty minutes without my phone. I'm sad and bored. Aunt Vita checks her massive man watch.

"You're going to be late."

"For what?"

"Seagulls," she says, beaming.

Like, the birds?

"Oh, Aunt Vita, I'm *bookish*. I don't enjoy nature…"

"Don't be absurd, Diana. It's a bloody café *called* Seagulls. In the village. You have a job. I can't keep you in lattes and leggings all summer, and you're already bored, so I spoke to my friend Felix and…"

I'm shaking my head but she's ignoring me. "Oh, I've never been a barista Aunt Vita, I won't be good at that…"

"Not bloody Starbucks Diana, a proper café. You'll be a waitress. I thought you'd find it exciting, meeting new people…"

I shake my head so violently my glasses fall off.

"But my hair won't fit into a hairnet."

"They aren't a hairnet kind of place," she says, heading towards the stairs.

"But where are you going to be?' I say. My voice is so high it's like I'm pretending.

"I have things to do in the mornings, but I'll see you in the afternoons when you come and help me at the Women's Refuge Charity Shop."

"But if I can't even have a phone, why is it safe for me to go out? What if the press finds me?"

"You still have to live, Diana. You can't mope around here all day. And you'll be fine in Lattering, it's a small town. We are officially *sleepy*. Nobody knows you are here. We'll just have a peaceful summer, no more dramas. Okay?"

"So that means I can have my phone back then? If everything is fine?"

"Yes, Diana. Jesus! You can have your phone back in a couple of days. You might actually enjoy life more without it, have you thought about that?"

I make a strange noise in reply. I don't know what it's supposed to be, but we both know it means I don't agree with her.

I stare at my reflection in the mirror as I brush my teeth. Betty and Amy are on their way to Cambodia for the best summer of their lives, and I'm working in a café and a charity shop in boring-on-sea with no friends for the foreseeable.

"So, Snoopy is outside," Aunt Vita says when I come back downstairs.

"Who?" I ask.

I'm so exhausted. New is exhausting.

"Snoopy is my bike. I haven't ridden him for a while, and he's not in great shape, but he will get you from A to B. Follow the path along the beach until you reach the fish stand, then turn left. Seagulls is on Beach Road, about half way down. If it takes you more than ten minutes you've gone wrong. And take my scrunchie."

She passes me a huge, red, flowery piece of material and grubby elastic from the olden days. It's not the cool kind. There is no irony in Lattering, it seems.

"Do I really have to wear it?" I ask, trying to give it back, but she just rolls her eyes.

"Yes, Diana, you're working with food. We are sleepy, we aren't animals."

I catch sight of myself in the full length mirror by the door. I'm wearing Aunt Vita's orange vest, and her size large knee length brown shorts that make me look like a scout leader. My hair is crammed in to her scrunchie. She actually grimaces when she sees me.

"Yeah, those shorts are a bit big on you. Sorry, darling, but I don't let anybody tell me what to do, least of all bloody Slimming World. And I love my big fat ass!" she slaps her bum as she says it. She's so fucking weird I could scream. She points to a pair of old trainers kicked off by the table. "You can't wear your flip flops on the bike. Those are too big for me, use them."

Yesterday, I thought my summer couldn't get any worse… That told me.

6

Snoopy is silver and older than me, with purple stripes on the side, and patches of rust. It's heavy, basic, and broken. The seat is too high, and stuck. I'll have to actually ride it in to something to stop, or throw myself off while it's still moving. Either way, it's going to hurt. The handlebars are covered in stickers. One says 'You're my best friend Charlie Brown' with a pink heart around it.

Amy and Betty will have boarded their plane by now.

The sea is directly to my right, just beyond a vast stretch of clean sand. The water is glistening, the way they always say it does, the people who love water. There is a massive cruise ship parked a long way out, directly in the middle of two cliffs that hug the bay at each end. Low sand dunes shield the path, like golden snow drifts. I could just throw myself into them and disappear. Groups of surfers laugh in the gardens of every other house that I pass. The noise of them comes and goes as I ride by, like somebody turning the volume up and down. What's the collective noun for a group of surfers anyway - a swell, maybe, or a shoal? If I had my phone I'd know.

The scrunchie puts up a good fight but finally liberates itself and strands of my hair are streaming out behind me in the wind when I hear it. Someone is running behind me, fast. If I turn to look,

I'll fall. I pedal faster but the breathing is getting closer. I can hear him panting, excited. My heart is banging in my chest. It's a paedophile or a kidnapper.

"I've got no money!" I scream in to the wind, praying he'll hear me and give up, but the panting keeps coming, louder and faster and more agitated. "I know karate! We do self-defense at school you fucking weirdo!"

The houses to my left have given way to lonely looking apartment blocks. His breath is right behind me now, loud and quick and hard with excitement. My heart is punching my ribcage. Sweat drips in my eyes and it stings. Something brushes my thigh. I look down and start to scream...

7

I'm still screaming, but it's not a kidnapper or a pedophile. It's worse. It's a wild animal.

A huge, black dog jumps up at my leg, bloody drool dripping from his mouth. His eyes are glazed. He misses me and stumbles. I scream again. He jumps and his claws scrape my thigh. I cry and kick out, but he swerves it. His teeth are clenched together as he launches himself at my front wheel again.

Wait.

That's not blood and drool hanging from his mouth - it's my bloody scrunchie!

I reach out with one hand and try and snatch it from his teeth. The bike hits a bump and I pull at the brakes but nothing happens. The dog jumps again, leaving three long, bloody scratches down my arm. Does he think it's a game? Tears are streaming down my face. He jumps at my front wheel, throwing his full weight behind it. I scream one last time as the bike veers towards the sand. The handlebars lock. I pull on the breaks, as hard as I can. Then I'm flying, soaring over the handlebars, somersaulting in mid-air, the sea in front of me, the sand beneath me, before everything goes black.

8

"Can you hear me?"

I open my eyes and stare up at him. I must be dreaming or watching a film. He cannot be real.

"Go back to sleep," I say to myself, closing my eyes.

"Hey, no, wake up!" he says, holding my head up off the sand. I open one eye. He's still there.

"Good. You're alive. Why was that beautiful dog trying to kill you?"

I push myself up on to my elbows and he sits back on the sand, relaxed.

"He wasn't trying to kill me," I say.

"He really was! We saw him chasing you."

"He was just trying to give me my scrunchie back, that's all. Dogs don't hate me."

I look around. The dog is sitting patiently about ten feet away, his tongue lolling, the picture of innocence, the scrunchie at his feet.

"That dog's an arsehole, though," I say.

The Dream Boy smiles, a dentist's advert of teeth, and I want to laugh out loud at how beautiful he is. The dog barks happily, and I remember where I was going: job, waitress, Seagulls.

A guy shouts loudly on the beach behind us, and I turn and

shield my eyes to see. He is dressed in the same navy T-shirt and shorts as Dream Boy.

"Is he shouting at you?" I ask.

"Probably. Are you going to be okay?"

I stand up, dusting the sand off my shorts and legs.

"I have to get to Seagulls," I say.

The boy on the beach is shouting 'jam' over and over like a maniac.

"That awful old man's café you mean? You must be concussed!" He laughs and I wonder if anything ever makes him angry, or if his life is perfect because his face is perfect, and everything is simple. The world treats some people differently.

The arsehole dog is sitting on the path next to my bike, panting happily, no owner in sight. Irresponsible. I hold my breath and snatch up the scrunchie. It feels wet in my hands. I shove it in my pocket and gag.

"Look, if you need coffee go to Breakers," Dream Boy says.

"I can't."

"Why not?"

I take a deep breath,

"Because I work at Seagulls, okay?"

"Why?" he says, alarmed, but there is no point explaining because he won't understand, so I just shrug. Nobody will ever force him to do anything he doesn't want to. He reaches down and lifts Snoopy up with one hand, presenting it to me.

"Will you still be able to ride it?" he says, grimacing.

"It looked like that before." I'm too tired to be ashamed.

"Oh God, your elbow is bleeding," he says, nodding at my arm.

"I'll get a plaster at the café."

"Are you sure your head is okay? You passed out for a few seconds, you shouldn't just be riding off. Do you live in Lattering? I haven't seen you here before."

The guy behind us on the beach is screaming 'jam' like a fucking crazy person.

"Just temporarily," I say.

"On holiday?"

"More of a forced summer retreat."

"That sounds intriguing."

"It's not. Are you on holiday?"

He shakes his head and smiles.

"I'm Thetis." He taps a small Greek symbol on his T-shirt and looks down. His embarrassed face is the most beautiful version of him so far.

"What's Thetis?"

"It's the school," he says, pointing to an old castle surrounded by glass, violently reflecting the morning sun on the cliffs behind us.

"That's a school?"

"You really don't live around here, do you?" he says quietly.

"Who's that?" I ask, nodding towards the angry shouting guy.

"My brother." He grimaces but doesn't move.

"Is he Thetis too?" I say, like I knew what it was all along, and he nods.

"JAMIE!" the guy screams.

"Is he normally this chill?"

"I'm Jamie Beltrome by the way, in case you didn't get that," he says smiling, walking backwards. He stops, staring at me.

"What?" I say.

"What's *your* name?"

"Oh. It's Diana."

He puts both his hands on his heart, as if I've just shot him with an arrow.

"Like the princess. It was nice to meet you, Diana. You've got great hair."

Wait…what?

But he's already turned and jogged off. I jump on Snoopy and ride like hell.

9

Seagulls is like somebody old's rubbish house, with a wooden front door and net curtains. A piece of paper stuck in the window advertises 'Full English with black pudding and fried bread'. I literally start gagging. I knock but nobody answers, so I push the door and it opens as a tiny bell rings above my head.

The floor is pale and sticky. There are about twenty tables, square and plastic, and a counter at the end of the room. One of those multi-coloured beaded curtains hangs across a doorway behind the counter. A big poster of a lemon is stuck on the main wall, with Sellotape.

"Hello?" I say.

"Diana?" a voice shouts from behind the curtain.

I hear a huge thud, alarming grunts, and wheezing. If I was a kid I'd run and hide. A man pushes through the curtain, sideways. He is vast, and round, and solid, and old. His white, spiky hair stands to attention. Black reading glasses hang on the end of a gold chain, against a mahogany chest infested with silver hair like glow worms. His Hawaiian shirt is the size of a boat sail, patterned with rows of dancing hula girls, unbuttoned to the swell of his stomach.

"Right, okay. I know Vita says it's fine but don't put ya' earphones in when it's early, alright Diana, for me?"

"Why?" I ask. Who is this guy? Why should I do things for *him*?

"Julie Peters, the girl that went missing. It was before Christmas, so it was darker in the mornings, but she was your age. Vita didn't say?"

"No, she *didn't* say."

"Oh, no dramas, Diana. The police 'fink she moved anyway but I 'fink just be careful. I'm Felix by the way, the cook. Have ya' done much waitressing before, Diana?"

"Never. I won't be very good at it, I'm afraid, but I can work a till."

"We don't 'ave a till unfortunately, Diana. We 'ave Elvis."

He presents a tray as evidence, with a picture of the old, dead, singer Elvis Presley on it, littered in pound coins and twenty pence pieces. Dad likes Elvis.

"Okay…" I say, and blink three times. He passes me a tiny note pad and a biro with actual bite marks at the end. I look around.

"When do the rest of the staff get here?" I ask nervously.

He stares at me blankly. I blink five times. FIVE.

"You mean…I'm on my own?"

He laughs so loudly I think my ears may have started bleeding.

'I'm joking. Of course there's 'anofa waitress."

The door flies open and the tiny bell rings.

10

A tall, black girl walks in wearing red Ray-Bans and singing. Her voice is like the best audition I've ever heard. She walks straight past us and disappears through the curtain.

"That's Gloria," Felix says.

She comes back out and starts counting the change on the tray. Felix waddles to the front of the shop and flips the sign, whistling along.

"Hi," I say to her.

Nothing.

"I'm Diana."

Nothing. I wave at her, a low timid hand flap. She walks off, back through the curtain. Felix waddles past me to the kitchen. I stand on my own on the sticky floor, looking at the lemon on the wall.

I know how it feels.

11

"Can I help you?" I say, standing in front of a table.

"The usual," he says without looking up. He licks his finger and turns the page of his newspaper. I walk away, turn around and walk back.

"Sorry, I'm new, can you tell me what that is?" I say, standing in front of him again.

"Ask Gloria," he says.

Gloria is sitting on a stool, flicking through her phone with a long, dismissive finger.

"There's a man here and he says I should ask you what his usual is." I laugh awkwardly.

She doesn't look up. Her hair is dark brown with pink ends, piled on the top of her head like an old film star, except there's an undercut on one side. Her T-shirt strains 'NO' in small, white letters across the middle of her chest. She's wearing ripped jeans, and army boots that could be used for weight training. She's got tiny diamonds all the way up one ear, and eyeliner ticks point up at her immaculate eyebrows. Her lipstick looks like it stains. Her cheeks are flushed pink, but her skin is dark golden brown.

I cough – I'm so intimidated I think I might actually be shaking, but she still doesn't look up. I go back through the curtain as three men walk in holding hard hats.

"Three cups of tea and three bacon sandwiches," one shouts, as they sit down at a table in the corner. "And turn the TV on, love, will you?"

A battered old TV set pokes out on an arm in the corner, about a foot above my head, but there is no remote. Gloria appears with a plate full of toast, and bacon, and fried eggs, dripping in grease.

"Here you go, Arthur." She drops it in front of *usual* guy, as the builders look up.

"Gloria, turn the TV on will you please? New girl doesn't have a clue."

"Summer rubbish," she says, winking at him. She grabs a remote from her back pocket and points. Good Morning Britain comes on but she mutes it. An old tape cassette player sits on the counter and she presses play on that instead.

After ten minutes, I realise it's pointless asking people anything. Everybody just wants their five seconds of Gloria. And NOBODY calls her *love*.

At 11am I lean forwards on the counter and rest my face on the cool plastic surface of the top. My vest is stuck to my skin. Felix emerges from the beads and surveys the Elvis money tray, nodding his head. He slaps me on the back and I fly forwards like I've been shot. Gloria emerges through the curtain, red Ray-Bans back on, earbuds poised.

"Nice one," Felix says to no one, and thuds back in to the kitchen.

"Not good at *everything*, then?" Gloria says evenly, ejecting her tape from the cassette player, shoving it in her bag, and striding out.

12

Aunt Vita is leaning against a giant plastic ice-cream, talking on her phone. When she sees me, she points to the bench in front of Two Scoops. The bench is painted in the same cream, pink and brown stripes as the sign above the window. In the middle is a picture of two scoops of ice-cream with cherries sticking out that deliberately resemble a woman's breasts. The old man inside is wearing an apron in the same colours, with the ice-cream breasts on it too. Branding.

We studied Coke and Apple and NIKE and Volkswagen and British Airways for a week in my 20th Century History class. Mostly they want you to *trust* them. Trust the apple, trust the swooshy Nike tick-thing, trust that people will like you more if you wear them or carry them around, because then they'll know you are just like them.

My dad only trusts a clear plastic bag with a carrot in it. I miss him. He's been gone for 24 hours already, the longest we've ever been apart. What the hell did he do, and why the hell did he do it?

An old bell above the clock on the town hall announces midday with a clang that makes me jump as a huge, black, shiny car moves slowly down the road like an oil slick creeping through town. Everybody turns to look. The windows are so dark it's as if no one is at the wheel, and it's being driven by computers or ghosts. It disappears around the corner at the end of the road.

Aunt Vita hangs up the phone and turns to me, oblivious to the ghost car.

"Come on," she says, "we're late again."

13

The Lattering Women's Refuge Charity Shop smells of old. There are racks of clothes everywhere, and tables full of books and CDs and DVDs. Toys are jammed in the corners.

"Do you wash the clothes, Aunt Vita?" I ask, trying not to gag.

"Some of them," she says, cheerfully.

"Which ones?" I say.

She sighs and rolls her eyes, pulling on a pair of rubber gloves.

"The ones that don't smell clean, Diana."

"Whose job is it to smell them?" I ask. I cover my mouth with my hand.

"Diana, for Christ's sake, you can just tell, okay? I'm not asking you to peel them off dead pensioners' bodies. Most of them are washed. Come through to the back, I want you to meet someone."

A nerdy guy in glasses is standing in the middle of a mound of clothes, wearing washing up gloves. His T-shirt has the dog from Family Guy on it. He's average *everything*. He should rob banks because you'd never pick him out of a line up.

"Diana, this is Richard. Richard is our champion box lifter, when he's not at college." She disappears back through the door.

"Is it gross?" I say.

"Only the underwear," he says, pushing up his glasses on his nose. Two violent red circles appear in the middle of his cheeks, and his neck rashes up like he's allergic to something.

"Do you live here?" I ask, embarrassed.

He nods, without looking up. "With my grandad."

"Where are your mum and dad?"

"They moved last year, for my mum's job."

"Where to?"

"San Francisco," he says, and coughs nervously.

"And they left you *here*?"

"I wanted to stay," he says quietly. He's not ugly but it's like he's never even thought about kissing someone, or sex, or anything like that.

"I'll see you later," I say, and go back out to the front of the shop.

"Let me show you the till," Vita says, "then pick a book and sit. I need to go out again. Oh, and take this, I forgot to give it to you this morning."

She passes me a key on a keyring with an 'S' on it. I accept it reluctantly.

"What does the S stand for?" I say, as she's already walking away. She stops walking, turns, sighs, and smiles.

"Spare," she says, and walks away again. Sounds about right.

A young Indian guy walks in an hour later carrying a skateboard, and it makes me jump. I genuinely forgot we were open. Richard comes through the door at that exact moment, and the guy glares at him.

"This is Diana, she's Vita's niece, she's working here for the summer," Richard says, like he's talking him down from a ledge. "This is Ralph."

"Hi," I say, but Ralph doesn't reply. He walks up to Richard and starts whispering.

"You should go," Richard says to him. Ralph nods and leaves. "He's just shy," Richard says, not looking at me.

I shrug, like I don't care, but FOR FUCK'S SAKE!

Aunt Vita goes to buy us dinner and I ride Snoopy home along the beach path. People are sunbathing and eating ice-creams, kids are running into the water and screaming, and burying their dads in the sand. A few young guys walk down the path towards me in pairs, sharing cigarettes, T-shirts hanging out of the back pockets of their oversized jeans, gold chains swinging against their skinny chests.

In Aunt Vita's garden, I let Snoopy fall and lie down on the grass.

I wake up to the sound of music. Parties have sprung up all over the beach. I start crying, and I don't even know why. Except everything.

14

I'm trying to teach Howard to hold out his paw for a biscuit when Aunt Vita gets back carrying fish and chips wrapped in newspaper.

"Come on," she says, "let's sit in the sun."

Eventually, she wraps up what's left of her fish and turns to face me seriously.

"Diana, would you mind if I rolled a joint? It's been a really long day."

"I don't mind," I say, but WHAT THE HELL?

She pulls a small, plastic bag out of her pocket, and her long fingers start twiddling tobacco on a tiny piece of white paper, on top of a crate. Finally, she sits back, lights the white stick hanging from her lips, inhales, and sighs happily. "I don't do it that often," she says.

I shrug. They aren't my lungs. She takes another long puff.

"So, I went to the police station," she says. Irony. "I've told them this will be your address for the foreseeable and they are happy with that. They'll want to interview you soon, but it sounds like your dad is cooperating."

"Can I talk to him?" I say.

"Yes, I'm sure you can. Leave it with me but, honestly, I promise this will all be over soon."

"Can I sleep with my windows open tonight?"

"Of course, you're not in a cage."

"Okay, I'm going to go and read."

"Well, goodnight darling," she says, and blows me a kiss.

I turn off my lamp, but the sun is still visible through my window. I can hear the waves crashing on the beach, and I watch the room sparkle as the light fades. I close my eyes and picture myself walking into the ocean. I dream my mum comes into my room. She lays down next to me and strokes my hair, but when I turn to face her it's not my mum anymore, it's Aunt Vita. I turn away, but when I look back it's my dad. He's holding a gun and pointing it at my head. He pulls the trigger and I wake up.

BEFORE

J uan sits in shadow, where he always sits, with the moon behind him, leaning against the pillar at the end of the wall. He watches her gently close the door, and tip-toe down the path. She squeezes through a narrow gap in the gate rather than risk the hinges creaking. She turns left, walking towards town. He smiles. Where are you going, beauty?

She's looking up at the sky as if it's important. She walks quickly. He checks his watch. It's 1am. The waves are noisy and strong; the storm hasn't passed yet. She stops suddenly and pulls off her shoes. With a trainer in each hand she clambers over the dunes, towards the sea. Halfway down the beach, before the sand turns dark and wet, she peels off her T-shirt. She removes her shorts and folds them neatly. She stands naked, shivering, staring at the raging ocean. His smile fades as he kicks off his boots.

He covers the distance between the dunes and the sea in seconds. He's always preferred running barefoot. His toes barely graze the sand. Her head is still visible as he reaches the water. The storm has churned up the ocean bed. The waves come in sets, and he dives early. He surfaces for air and spots her. The water is too powerful for her already. He picks his line, fills his lungs, and dives again.

She is unconscious but alive. She weighs practically nothing, and it is *easy for him to ride the waves with her on his back. Laying her on the sand he checks her breathing and pulse. He presses his flat palms on her chest and she coughs violently, her back arching as sea-water explodes from her mouth like vomit. She is shaking violently. Her lips are blue.*

Juan carries her past the pile of clothes she left as a goodbye. He places her on a sand dune and fishes out the tiny earring from his boots, pushing it back in to the self-made hole in his earlobe. She coughs again, but now he meets her mouth with the handkerchief from his other boot. Her head rolls as the drugs take effect. He lifts her, deadweight, retracing their steps back along the path.

On the back seat of his car is a blanket and he rolls her in it. As a rule, he puts bodies in the trunk, but it's dark, and it's quiet, and it's a short drive to the cliffs. He whistles a tune as the first signs of rain pester his windscreen. Their footprints will be gone by morning. As he suspected, the short drive to the house is uneventful. The new security gates open smoothly. Scaffolding frames Poseidon's huge front door.

Juan carries her up the grand stairs, his heels clicking the marble like a dancer. He stops in the hallway, straightening the blanket around her shoulders. The colour has returned to her lips and cheeks. She groans faintly as he knocks on the bedroom door.

'She tried to kill herself?'

He nods, lowers her on to the bed, and steps away. Hugo Beltrome covers her with his sheets, stroking her hair, muttering, "Oh, Lana. Not like this, that's cheating."

Juan walks quickly, back downstairs and into the study, but instead of picking up the phone he unlocks the large, black, lacquered cabinet in the corner. He removes an elaborate blue-tinged bottle and pours a long shot into a crystal tumbler. Raising the glass, he pushes a strand of wet hair from his face. "Arriba, abajo, al centro, y pa dentro."

He downs the tequila in one gulp, and whispers, "For the almost dead."

PART IV

1

Lattering sucks. Gloria shouts at me every morning. I mess up everything. She tells the customers, "Don't worry, she'll be gone soon." (With her awful wink and her stupid, massive smile.) My arms are striped with toaster burns, and I *still* can't look at a slice of fried bread without gagging.

Gloria reads Felix his horoscope every day. He's a Sagittarius. Gloria is a Scorpio, with Scorpio rising. That matters, apparently. She hasn't asked me what sign I am.

None of the regulars come in early on Saturdays. A couple of old guys nurse cups of tea, but at 7.30am it's dead. I stand behind the counter, watching muted kids cartoons on the TV. A guy walks in while Gloria is in the kitchen and sits by the window. He's good looking, in a teacher sort of way.

"What can I get you?" I ask, my pen poised above my pad.

"How are you?" he says.

"I'm okay, thanks. What can I get you?"

"That's better. Do you have a menu?"

"It's on the board," I say, pointing behind the counter.

"What do you recommend?" He's smiling at me like a crazy person.

I shrug.

"Literally nothing is worth having here?" He winks. This is weird.

"Some people like the bacon sandwich," I say.

"What do you like?"

"I work here," I say.

He rolls his eyes. "I can see that, but if you *didn't* work here, what would you have?"

I shrug again.

He scans the board, looks back at me, scans the board, looks back at me, like it's a game. "Okay, I'll have the bacon sandwich and a smile please…what's your name?"

"Diana."

"So, I'll have a bacon sandwich, a cup of tea - skimmed no sugar - and a smile from the beautiful Diana."

I walk away. Gloria races out from the kitchen, spots him, turns on her tangerine smile. "Sorry for the wait, what can I get you?"

"It's okay, Diana took my order." He winks at me.

I wish I felt happy, but I don't. I stand behind the counter and pretend to check the change on Elvis. Every time I look up, he's staring at me.

Five minutes later Felix shouts, "Bacon sandwich!" I look over at Gloria.

"What? I'm not your slave," she says, and walks off.

"Here you go," I say to the man, but his newspaper covers the whole table. He doesn't move it. I don't know where to put the plate.

"Thanks Diana," he says. I feel his fingers on the back of my leg. His thumb slips under the material of my shorts, pressing hard into the flesh of my thigh. His fingers fan out like a spider, creeping up my shorts. He strokes the skin beneath my bum, digging his thumb in harder.

When the plate smashes on the floor the old guys turn to look.

"What is wrong with you?" Gloria whispers through gritted teeth, as I stand and stare at him.

"Don't worry, I'll get you another one on the house," she says.

He smiles gratefully, as if nothing happened.

74

"Clear that up," she snaps, but I follow her into the kitchen.

"We need another bacon sandwich because Brain of Britain just dropped the last one on the floor," Gloria shouts at Felix.

"I'm sorry," I say.

"This," she looks at Felix but points at me, up and down, like I'm an exhibit, "is pathetic. I'd be better on my own and you could pay me her salary!"

She storms out, and Felix looks at me sadly.

"I'm sorry," I say again, as she storms back in.

"And no, she can't share my damn tips!"

The afternoons are barely any better. The four hours I spend in the Lattering Women's Refuge Charity Shop each day are the most boring of my life. Richard barely talks, but his neck gets redder every time I see him. His friend Ralph won't even come into the shop if I'm there, like he'll catch something, so he literally makes dove noises by the window and Richard scampers out to meet him. I use the till so rarely that I keep forgetting how and Aunt Vita is always 'just popping out'. She forces a smile when she sees me, but I already know I'm a bind. It's been ten days and I still haven't spoken to my dad. Aunt Vita's "Yes, definitely" and "I'm sure it will be tomorrow" are getting on my nerves. And I haven't seen Jamie Beltrome again.

Aunt Vita doesn't actually eat meals. She sits at the kitchen table shelling handfuls of pistachios, drinking huge glasses of wine, or throwing olives in the air and catching them in her mouth. Sometimes she misses and laughs. She listens to the radio and pores over her newspapers. I suggested Spotify but she said, "The internet makes me feel like I'm drifting off into space." Her Wi-Fi is non-existent. I hear her talking downstairs on the phone at the same time every night, but not what she's saying. I don't care enough to sit somewhere I could hear.

2

A single drop of sweat is rolling down the back of my leg, trickling its way from the back of my knee propped up on the counter in front of me, and I watch it disappear into my shorts. I've read the same paragraph three times. The sore spot on the back of my thigh has turned black overnight. Every time his creepy smile slithers in to my head I physically shake it away, only for it to snake back in, minutes later, leaving its dirty, slimy residue all over my mind.

I walk over and stick my head out the front door. Teenagers swarm around Breakers, the milkshake bar across the road from Seagulls, like they are giving away puppies. Gangs of girls huddle together, shrieking and laughing, sitting on each other's laps. That would never be me anyway.

Richard comes through from the back with an armful of shirts and starts hanging them on a rail.

"Richard, what are you doing tonight?" I ask.

His neck goes red, of course.

"I'm meeting Ralph at the beach."

He shakes his head and carries on hanging shirts. Even Richard has more friends than me.

"What are you *doing* at the beach?" I say.

He pushes his glasses up his nose with his arm.

"There was a mock invasion on East Lattering Beach, in 1943. During World War Two."

"So?"

"I got a metal detector for Christmas."

"And?"

"We look for bullets."

"Oh. Have you ever found any?"

"Ralph found one once."

He picks up a purple sweatshirt with Mickey Mouse on it and sniffs it.

"Can I come with you tonight, Richard?" I smile weakly. I just want to do something, with someone.

"Ummm..." His neck is the reddest I've ever seen it, and the tomatoes in his cheeks look like they are going to explode.

"Don't worry about it, I don't even know why I asked," I say. I go back to the counter and pretend to read my book.

An hour later Ralph darts across the doorway making his dove noise.

"Ralph's outside pretending to be a bird again," I shout.

Richard scurries out, head down, muttering thanks. I hear them arguing on the street. I hear Ralph say, "No way!" and "But why?"

"Do you still want to come with us tonight?" Richard says when he comes back in.

"I don't want to cause problems," I say.

"It's not a problem," he says. "Ralph wants you to come."

"Richard, he doesn't, it's okay." I pretend to read my book again.

"Okay," he puts his hands up like he's guilty, "I want you to come." His neck flushes.

"Okay, I will," I say, nodding. "If you're sure?"

When he smiles he looks different. Older.

3

R ichard and Ralph are shuffling around on the beach. They
both have one extra-long, metal arm. They wave them
slowly in front of their feet.

"Sorry I'm late," I say, as I catch them up.

"Hi," Ralph says, like we've always been friends.

"Hi," I say. He's 17 but he's the height of the average 12 year
old. His Yoda T-shirt is three sizes too big for him. It hangs off his
matchstick arms and stops half-way down his baggy jeans. His
face, hiding under a floppy fringe and metal rimmed glasses, is like
a tiny Indian doll.

"Hi Diana," Richard says, and gives me an awkward one
handed salute.

The waves are bigger tonight, crashing on the sand and
dragging it back out. About a dozen surfers are still out there, and a
few final families are packing up their windbreakers, trying to get
dressed under beach towels.

"So, tell me about this invasion," I say.

"Mock invasion," Ralph corrects me.

"Sorry, *mock* invasion."

Richard clears his throat. "Well, it was top secret, at the time. It was just supposed to be a practice for D-Day, but it went horribly wrong. The troops that landed on Lattering beach were mostly Americans. They were only supposed to be shot at with dummy bullets but nobody on the British side actually thought to change their ammunition. They netted up the bodies like tuna, and the coffins were gone before sunrise. Nobody talked about it until after the war, in case the Germans found out what was being planned. Now there are bullets all over the beach."

"Okay, that is cool," I say.

Richard smiles, embarrassed at the success of his own storytelling.

"I'm thirsty," Ralph says. He drops down on the sand and pulls out a can of coke from his bag. Richard reaches into his backpack, pulling out two cans, passing one to me.

"So, is this what you normally do on a Saturday night? Search for bullets?" I say, gulping, trying not to burp back coke bubbles.

"And bodies," Ralph says.

Richard glares at him.

"What are you talking about?" I say to Ralph.

"We're looking for a dead body, too," Ralph says.

"Ralph, shut up," Richard says.

"What body?" I say.

"Julie Peters. The girl that went missing," Ralph says.

"But Felix said she moved away?"

"We know what really happened," Ralph says, considering a Twix before biting it.

I look at Richard for confirmation.

"We don't know anything," Richard says. He looks visibly upset with Ralph, who jumps up on to his knees.

"You know why the police said she moved! Because of who took her!" He turns so he is only facing Richard, but pointing at me. "Tell your girlfriend to shut up, she's the one who keeps asking questions."

"Someone took her?" I look from one to the other.

Richard's face is red. He says something to Ralph under his

breath and Ralph storms off, jumping on his skateboard and disappearing down Beach Road, with his metal detector strapped across his back like a sword.

"I'll walk you home," Richard says.

~

Bonfire parties are everywhere now. Dance music plays from portable speakers, interspersed with the shouts of kids getting drunk.

"So, Ralph's odd," I say.

"Not really. He's just ridiculously smart, and small. That's not a great combination. Plus, he's had a load of other stuff going on," Richard says.

"Like what?" I say. We *all* have our stuff.

"His dad just got out of prison."

"Jesus. What for?"

"Fraud, but somebody at college started a rumour, and…"

"A rumour about what?"

Richard sighs. "Ralph's dad teaches piano and some idiot said he messes with the kids, which is why he was in prison."

"Oh, shit. Did he?"

"No!" Richard glares at me. "Mr. Srao is lovely. They just got in some financial trouble and he made a mistake, but Ralph keeps sticking up for him, and starting fights."

We've reached Shalimar.

"Have you been getting into fights, too?"

I point to the plasters on his arms, hiding under the sleeves of his T-shirt. He never takes them off. His neck goes red and a twig cracks in the bushes behind us. I jump and grab Richard instinctively.

"It's probably just a cat," he says, looking embarrassed. I am still holding on to him.

"Sorry," I say. He is actually taller than I thought, he must be six feet. I step away and scan the darkness. I can't see anything but leaves and shadows. A drop of rain lands on my nose, and I look up. The sky is a blanket of black clouds and it's suddenly very dark.

"I have to go," Richard says, dropping his board and skating off without saying goodbye.

Aunt Vita is sitting at the kitchen table with a vat of red wine. Her glasses are falling off her nose, and her eyes are wine glazed. Every adult I know drinks soooo much. How bad must life be?

"Aunt Vita, do I have to go back to Seagulls?"

She puts her paper down and rubs her eyes as she speaks.

"Why don't you want to go back, Diana?"

"It's horrible. Gloria, the other waitress, hates me."

"Can't you try to win her over?"

"But it's her problem, not mine. I've been really nice! What else am I supposed to say to her when she's being so mean? She says I'm pathetic!" I say, crossing my arms.

"Well, do you stand up for yourself? Do you tell her she's wrong?"

"But it's true! I am a pathetic waitress. I didn't even want to work there - you made me."

I stare at the table. After five minutes, she picks up her glasses again and sighs.

"If it's no better by next weekend, you can quit," she says sadly.

"I'm going to bed," I say.

The rain hammers at my window as I look at myself in the mirror. Do I really look like my mother, is that why Aunt Vita thinks I'm stronger than I am? But I'm not Lana. I'm not some prize that everybody wants. I'm just the girl creepy men touch when nobody else is looking.

"Gloria, what the hell?" I whisper to the mirror, angrily. "What the hell? Gloria. Gloria!" I say, louder. "Gloria. What the hell? You're so fucking weird!"

There's a knock on my door.

"Come in."

I watch it open in the mirror.

"Is everything okay?" Aunt Vita asks, hovering in the doorway.

"I was singing," I say.

It's obvious she doesn't believe me.

"Okay, darling," she says, smiling unconvincingly, and leaves.

4

I don't spill a drop of tea, or smash a single plate, now that I know I'm quitting. Irony. I've prepared a speech for the next time Gloria shouts at me, but today she's pretending I don't even exist. Her hair is bigger, with pink ends. Her lips are blood red.

A small gang of builders in hard hats and hi-vis jackets take the table by the window.

"Hello, what can I get you?" I say, smiling. It genuinely doesn't matter what they think now.

"You've cheered up," the little one says, with a laugh.

"Three bacon sandwiches and three cups of tea, with milk and three sugars in each," the leader says.

"You're like the musketeers," I say, trying for a wink and failing epically, but who cares? I'm quitting in four day's time.

I shove a fresh tomato ketchup under my neck, and three sachets of brown sauce in my pockets. I bang the door open with my bum, head up, balancing the plates across both hands. I might actually look like a professional waitress.

Nobody even looks up when I trip over the stool in the middle of the room, and three bacon sandwiches soar across the room like soggy meat Frisbees. The thud of me hitting the floor doesn't surprise them these days; they are used to it. Strips of bacon lay sadly on the lino. There's a graze on my knee, and a trickle of blood running down my shin. A brown mess seeps through my shorts: the sachets of sauce burst on impact.

"Sorry guys," Gloria says, racing over. "I'll sort it. You can't get the staff." She rolls her eyes and tuts at me. I get up and follow her to the kitchen, but Felix has disappeared.

"Why was that stool there?" I say, to her back.

"Oh, go away," she says, laying slices of bread out on the counter.

"You put it there on purpose, so I'd trip."

"You're high," she says, peeling out strips of cooked bacon from a simmering pan.

"You couldn't stand that I was actually doing it right."

"God, ego much? Get over yourself Diana."

She swipes butter on to the bread like it's a martial art, and I feel the lump swell in my throat, again. This isn't fair.

"There's a special place in hell for women who don't help other women," I say to the back of her head, but my voice breaks half-way through. She places the knife down carefully on the counter and turns, slowly, to face me.

"Do you think you're helping *me*, Diana? When you constantly drop things, and muck up the orders, and make my job twice as hard? You do know that all your mistakes are costing Felix money, don't you? If he goes bust, I'm out of a job, and there isn't any other work around here for girls like me, but then you go back to London like nothing happened, oblivious to the mess you've made and the harm you've done. Are *you* helping *me*, Diana, or is it only supposed to work the other way around? Are you the only one that's got it bad?"

She steps forwards. I see the expert flicks of her eyeliner. I see her dark scalp under her undercut. I see the time that goes into Gloria each morning.

"Poor little Diana sent to live in the boring town for a boring summer. Are you helping any of the other *local* girls who have been asking Felix for a job, every day, for the last six months? Look around, for fuck's sake."

She turns her back to me, plating up the sandwiches, and sighs.

"I didn't know," I say quietly.

"Yeah, well, why don't you stop thinking about yourself for one fucking minute?"

The first tear hits my cheek, but she pushes past me shaking her head.

"You see, that's the difference between us, Diana. I don't spend all my time feeling sorry for myself, turning on the tears."

She strides out, just as Felix storms in from the storeroom, holding a lightbulb.

"Got the right one this time," he says, waving it at me, following Gloria out. "Can you come and 'old me stool Diana? It was shaking like an earthquake just now. I must 'ave put on a few pounds."

5

A make-shift stage has been erected on one side of the square, outside the old library, and I've been watching people gather in front of it for the last fifteen minutes. Thirty OAPs bleat like obedient sheep as a man climbs the steps at the side of the stage and everyone stops talking, angling their faces towards to him expectantly, like he's God.

"Richard, I'll be back in a minute," I shout.

The big, black, shiny, ghost car from my first day in Lattering is parked in front of the library. A small man, older than Aunt Vita, leans casually against the bonnet with his arms crossed. His shirt and trousers are tight and black, like a ballroom dancer, but his cowboy boots are bright red. He is wearing thick, black sunglasses, and his shoulder length, shiny, grey-black hair is really neat, like it's just been brushed for a photo. He lifts his head slowly and lowers his sunglasses as I cross Beach Road. His eyes are yellow, and his neck is crumpled with scars. He kisses the palm of his hand and blows me an exaggerated kiss. I shudder, like somebody just ran a finger down my spine. I look away and practically run towards the crowd of people. What a freak.

The man on the stage is making a speech. His voice drips with money, like he's the Prime Minister *after* he's won the election.

Everybody here would vote for him. He's talking about building a new Lattering library, and the importance of good schools, and then I hear Aunt Vita calling my name. I turn to see her striding furiously across Beach Road, a picture of confusion and anger, but as she glances at the stage her face drains of colour. She walks straight past me to the front of the crowd.

On the stage, Lattering's Prime Minister looks down and smiles, as if he's been expecting her. "Hello Vita, how wonderful to see you again after all these years."

He is bathed in sunlight. Instinctively, I look around for the freak with the pony-tail. I spot him in the crowd, his shiny hair moving slowly towards Aunt Vita, but the man on the stage sees him too and shakes his head softly. The pony-tail stops moving. A hush spreads like a blanket has dropped over everyone there.

The man on stage says, "You look beautiful, Vita. You've barely aged."

I can see her chest rising and falling from twenty feet away. She looks terrified.

"But you, you haven't been here, since…" Her voice is shaking. I want to protect her, but I don't know how. She looks around, and she's scared. Her eyes meet mine across the crowd. She actually sobs. She turns back to the stage.

"What did she say?" an old woman says from the back of the crowd.

"She said 'I know it was you' a man in front of her replies.

The old woman tuts and says, "Eh, what does that mean?"

"I don't know what you are talking about, Vita," the man says, smiling, but his eyes flash like lightning just went off in the sky behind us. I actually turn to check but the sky is still blue. Aunt Vita turns and storms away.

"Where was I?" he says, rolling his eyes, and the crowd laugh.

Her fingers tremble as she takes my hand. "We have to go," she says, pulling my arm. I look back over my shoulder for the freak, but he's disappeared.

6

Aunt Vita paces back and forth at the back of the shop.

"Who *was* that?" I ask.

"Somebody I haven't seen for a very long time," she says, without looking up, back and forth, wringing her hands.

"I think I recognise him," I say.

She freezes. "Do you? Why?"

"I don't know, from TV or something."

She sighs and starts pacing again. "He's nobody," she says, clicking her fingers, muttering, "think, think, think."

"He doesn't seem like nobody," I say, picking up a Pepsi T-shirt that has come in that morning. "You've gone crazy." I hold the material gingerly between two of my fingers, sniff, and drop it immediately.

"He's the devil," Richard says, emerging from a rack of clothes in the corner. I didn't even know he was there.

"I don't understand." I look from Richard to Aunt Vita and back again, like they are playing tennis, but neither of them will meet my eye. "He's doing a good thing; he's building a new library. Nobody else is doing anything for free around here." And there was something about his voice. He was so charming, like a king or a famous actor. I can tell why the crowd loved him. I sort of did, too. Authority.

"We all work here for free," Aunt Vita says indignantly, throwing up her hands, "and not because anybody is putting our name on a building. If you want applause join a bloody circus."

"How do you even know him?" I ask Richard as he grabs a handful of clothes, still refusing to look at me.

"He owns the school on the cliffs," he says quietly, "and everything else in Lattering."

"Oh, Thetis? Yeah, I know it," I say casually.

Richard looks surprised, but Aunt Vita turns on me like an attack dog. "Why were you even out of the shop, Diana, when I explicitly asked you to stay inside?"

"It was too hot in here, okay?"

"So? We're all hot. I'm hot! You have a fan beside the till for Christ's sake!"

She throws her hands up in the air again, like she gives up. I don't know what her problem is. I really want to say, "Calm down," but I don't. "What is wrong with you today?" I say instead.

She stops walking. "Nothing. I just have to think." Then she walks out.

"What's his name Richard?"

He pretends not to hear, but I stand directly in front of him so he can't ignore me.

"The guy on the stage, what was his name?"

"Hugo Beltrome," he says, practically whispering.

"Beltrome?"

"Yeah, so what?" Richard looks at me like he's trying to read my mind, and for a second I think it might be working.

"I just didn't hear you properly, alright? God, why is everyone so touchy today?"

I storm off so he can't see that my mind is actually screaming 'That's Jamie's dad!'

7

Aunt Vita comes bursting back in an hour later. Her eyes are red from crying, but she's not shaking anymore. I ask her if she's okay, but she just says, "I'm fine, Diana," so I don't ask again. We walk all the way home without mentioning it.

Just before 9.45pm I creep to the top of the stairs. Howard is curled up on my aunt's lap, and her bare feet are resting in front of her on a chair at the kitchen table. Her phone rings bang on schedule. She gulps down a slug of wine before she answers.

"Hey. Yes, he got here this evening, and he's already started. No, I talked about that with him but we agreed that we can't protect her anywhere else, not if we want her to have a life. We can keep her safe here, I know it. With him and me. You know everyone else will help, and I trust them."

Aunt Vita listens to the phone, and in the silence I hear my own breathing.

"Yes, I've thought of that too," she says. "It could just be a coincidence, an awful one, but a coincidence nonetheless. We are going to see what happens in the next few days. We are on red alert at least." Aunt Vita downs the rest of her glass and immediately refills it, her phone cradled in her shoulder. I can't see her face. She listens to the phone, and her shoulders sag.

"Christ, I wish you were here. I miss you so much. Maybe we made a mistake, but I can't risk it. Not yet. I'm so sorry. But that's another thing - I can't move further away from you, it's killing me. Okay, okay, enough about me!" She takes another huge swig of wine. "Christ will you please tell me about *your* day? Talk to me about normal things. Talk to me about life before Diana."

I tiptoe back to my room. 'Life before Diana' she said. Well, I don't have to be here. Yes, my dad freaked out, but he's freaked out before. Everybody is being weirdly paranoid, but I know how that feels because this has happened to me before. Once my dad calms down everything just goes back to normal, no matter how much you worry in the meantime. Life just stays the same. So, the police will call soon to say it's fine, and Aunt Vita's boyfriend can come back, and my life will go back to how it was. Also, I'm sixteen. Some people have babies at sixteen, and full time jobs. I'm allowed to live on my own. I'm allowed to leave.

8

Aunt Vita knocks on my bedroom door.

"Just a minute," I say, for no reason. I'm reading on my bed. I'm not naked, or smoking crack, or anything that needs to be hidden. My dad would call this behavior *petty*.

"Can I come in?" she asks, after an unreasonable amount of time has passed.

"Sure," I say breezily, like I'd forgotten she was there.

She drops on to the bed next to me and folds her legs. Her toenails are now painted bright pink.

"Diana, I know I was odd today and I'm really sorry. I'm still getting used to having a teenager around, and I think it's making me a bit anxious. But I promise to try harder."

"Who is that guy, Hugo Beltrome? Why did you freak out so much?"

"Well, he is a man from my past. And unfortunately, I don't really trust him." she says.

"From your past. Like, an ex-boyfriend you mean?"

"Kind of, not really. I knew him a long time ago, for a very short period of time, and while I know he owns the school he actually hasn't been in Lattering for many years. He's literally never here. I was just surprised to see him, that's all. And I don't like him."

"Who was on the phone just now?" I say.

She coughs and touches her neck. "Oh, no one really, just a guy from work." She scratches her cheek and rubs her eyes. These are all classic CIA *tells*. I saw it on a documentary with my dad. I know you're lying Aunt Vita, but why? "Well, sleep well, darling," she says, standing up.

"Shut the door on your way out," I say.

She looks at me really weirdly, just before it closes behind her.

9

I wake up breathless and sweating, like I've been running. My heart is bouncing in my chest like one of those kid's balls that won't stop moving. I turn the lamp on by my bed. It's 3.30am, but I already knew that. I've had the same dream every night this week. She's walking out into the sea and I'm shouting at her, but she can't hear me. If she could hear she'd turn around and see me waving. I try to run, but my feet are sinking in the sand. If she could hear me, she'd turn around, but I can't shout loud enough. I watch her disappear into the waves.

I hate Lattering. I want to stop dreaming about Lana, and I want to go back to my normal life. The buildings are too small here, and there's too much sky. I'm too visible. In London the traffic, and the shouts, and the sirens drown out the noises in my head. Everything feels too important here. It feels like everybody is watching.

And I don't want to be a waitress anymore. I want to feel like I'm good at things again. I don't want to meet anybody else that's new and make small talk. I want to talk to Amy and Betty. I just want to know the people I already know. I want my dad back. I check the clock. It's 3.53am. It makes no sense to go tonight; there won't be any trains anyway.

I'll leave tomorrow.

10

I wake to the sound of seagulls fighting, and rain tapping against the window. I have a shower and wash my hair, pack my bag, and stuff it under the bed. Howard is still asleep at the end of my duvet, and I stroke him sadly. He wriggles on to his back, trying to cover his eyes from the light.

Aunt Vita is standing by the cooker with her back to me, talking quietly. I cough. She turns, smiles, and holds out the phone. I shake my head, because I don't understand. She puts it in my hand anyway.

"Who is it?" I ask.

"It's your dad."

I put the phone to my ear carefully, like I don't trust it not to explode or disappear.

"Daddy?" I say, quietly.

"Hello, Sausage," my Dad says, and I burst into tears.

"Oh no, Sausage! No tears for me, Diana. Everything is fine, no crying." He sounds different. He sounds really calm.

"What did you do?" I say, sinking into an armchair in the corner of the room.

"I didn't do anything, I promise you," he says.

"So why have they arrested you for attempted murder?"

'To scare me, Sausage, just to scare me. But they have no evidence, so they can't hold me for much longer. They'll have to charge me or release me soon, and in the meantime you are having a lovely time with Vita. Can you please just try and forget about me? Pretend I'm on a course or something, and enjoy your holiday.'

"But you're in prison, and I'm here, and it's not a bloody holiday, and I miss you." I'm crying again. A box of tissues appears next to me on the arm of the chair, and I rip a handful out.

"Diana, I promise you, everything will be okay. Hey, how is Vita? She's crazier than me, right?"

"Are you on different pills?" I say. "Why are you so calm? Why aren't you freaking out? You're in prison!"

"Oh, it's not so bad, Sausage. And I haven't shaved, which helps of course."

"What's that got to do with anything?"

"Well, they say that having a pet relaxes you, and having a beard is like having a pet that lives on your face. I can't believe it's taken me this long to realise that. I just stroke my face and it calms me down. I may never shave again."

Standard Dad, making stupid dad jokes. I feel better for about two seconds. "So, you definitely aren't staying in prison?" I say.

Aunt Vita is leaning against a kitchen cupboard, cradling a cup of coffee. She shakes her head when I say prison, like it's preposterous, but then she shrugs. Maybe.

"Oh, they might trump something up and I'll get three months for threatening behaviour, but I'll be out soon enough and then we'll go away, you and me.'

"Three months?" I say, desolate. My face crumbles.

"Let's just wait and see, Sausage. Please, tell me how you are."

"I'm fine. I mean, it's weird here, but I'm okay."

"It won't be forever. Just as long as I know you are with Vita, that's all that matters. I need to know someone is looking after you."

"Dad, I'm sixteen, I can look after myself," I say.

"Promise me, Diana. Promise you'll stay with Vita until I'm released."

My heart sinks. "I promise," I say weakly. The phone starts bleeping, like a detonator.

"Ah, time's up," he says sadly.

"Please don't go," I say, starting to cry again.

"Stay safe, Sausage. Don't talk to any strangers. And stay with Vita, no matter what."

I picture my bag, stuffed under my bed. The bleeps are getting closer together.

"I love you so much, Sausage," he says.

The phone goes dead. I cover my face with my hands and cry.

Aunt Vita is still there when I look up, five minutes later.

"What did your dad make you promise, if you don't mind me asking?"

"That I wouldn't talk to strangers," I reply, without hesitation.

"Good advice," she says, nodding.

It wasn't a lie. It's just half of the truth.

11

The pink has disappeared from Gloria's hair overnight. It's mid-brown. It might even be her natural colour. She strolls in, singing, wearing a yellow spotty dress, DMs, and her Ray-Bans. Curls tumble down one side of her head like flowers from a hanging basket. She stops as soon as she sees me and yanks out her earphones, muttering.

"Gloria," I say, a while later.

She is sitting on her stool, looking at her phone. God, I miss my phone! Her earphones are on the counter. I know she heard me, but she doesn't respond.

'Gloria!' I shout, surprising myself.

'What?' she says, not looking up.

"This isn't fair," I say. I'll be reasonable. She can't argue with reasonable.

"So, leave then," she says, swiping her screen. That's *totally* unreasonable. I step forwards nervously.

"You know I didn't ask to work here, Gloria. My aunt is making me do it. I'm really sorry none of your friends got the job, but that's not my fault."

She looks up. "Who said they were my friends?" she says, shaking her head.

"Then why do you care so much?"

She narrows her eyes. "Because you jumped the queue. And I don't like you."

It's like a slap across the face, but I'm not going to cry. She *hates* it when I cry. "But you don't even know me, you've barely spoken to me," I say.

"Oh please, I meet you fifty times every summer." She mimics the confused look on my face. Childish.

"But I've never even been to Lattering before,' I say.

She rolls her eyes and puts her phone down. "Look. Just say all your shit then leave me alone, okay?"

"What shit?" I say. I've just said everything I had planned.

She yawns. "The shit, the names. This is so boring. Just say it, and we can go back to hating each other."

"What names?" I say.

Gloria stares at me evenly.

"What names, Gloria?" I say again.

"Whatever you've been calling me behind my back, have the balls to say it to my face." She folds her arms, waiting. "Hurry up," she says, reaching for her apron.

"Umm, okay, I've called you mean, to Aunt Vita. I said you are horrible to me, because you are, and you know you are. You mean stuff like that?"

"Bullshit!" She laughs loudly, shaking her head.

"What's so funny?"

"So you haven't called me a black bitch?"

I feel like I've being slapped. She thinks I'm *that?*

"Or a slut, or a whore?" she says, staring at me, trying to read my mind.

"I don't use those words, they are anti-women," I say quietly. "And I'm not racist."

Her eyes narrow with suspicion. She steps off the stool and bends down so we are face to face. She smells like oranges and baby powder. It makes me want to sneeze.

"What else do you want me to say, Gloria? My dad is in prison, okay? I don't know anybody in this stupid town. I'm living with my aunt who is basically weird...' My voice trails off, but I don't cry.

She looks me up and down. "Are you quitting?" she says finally.

I shake my head.

She bites her lip. "Okay, fine," she says suddenly, cocking her chin. "We can start again, Lady Di, but I'm telling you right now - I don't like mean white girls."

Head rush. I literally have to hold on to the counter. "Believe me, neither do I."

"Okay. You have to prove it though," she says, with a twinkle in her eye.

"Prove what?"

"Prove that you genuinely want to be my friend."

"How would I even do that?'"

"I don't know yet," she says, winking as the bell above the door rings.

12

G loria has barked a couple of orders at me, but she hasn't sighed, or tutted, or rolled her eyes.

I'm scraping bacon rinds into the bin and trying not to gag when she comes out of the kitchen, smiling, carrying a plate high up in front of her like a French waiter in a fancy restaurant. It's not the way we normally carry things at Seagulls.

She coughs and the builders in front of the lemon look up.

Gloria presents the plate to me, on the counter. Swimming in the middle is the thickest, fattest wedge of fried bread I've ever seen, glistening in its own pool of oil.

I gag. Then I gag again. I cover my mouth with my hand.

"Wait," she says. She reaches into her apron pocket and pulls something out. It's an egg. She cracks it daintily on the side of the plate, and it splits perfectly in two. She holds it above the fried bread and the yolk drops, fat and round and yellow, into the middle, the white slime stretching out to the sides and slipping off into the oil.

"Eat it," she says to me.

I stare down at the lump of congealed bread oil, at the big yellow egg head itching to be popped.

"You're not serious," I say.

"As cancer," she says.

"But what will it prove?"

She shrugs. "Nothing. Everything. It's totally up to you."

13

Grease soaks my tongue. The white slime of the egg coats my teeth. I bite down and the yellow ball explodes. I gag but I stuff more in. The cold, wet mess pushes against my cheeks. I could just spit it all out, but I don't. I gag again but I put both my hands over my mouth to stop the food falling out.

Gloria's eyes are wide.

I swallow. There is oil and egg slime on my teeth, and I wipe my lips with the back of my hand. I gag one final time. I look over at the table of builders for applause, but they have turned back to their newspapers.

"I mean, it was only a slice of fried bread and an egg for fuck's sake," Gloria says.

The anger rises up in me like a wave, but she grabs my shoulders and shakes me. "I'm joking," she says. Then I get my first real Gloria smile. "But you know you didn't really have to eat it, right? I just wanted to see if you would. I was going to stop you before you put it in your mouth, but," and she starts laughing, a low dirty laugh, "you just shoved it in so quick, I didn't get a chance!"

"Brilliant," I say, rolling my eyes, but I'm happy. "I'm just going outside for a minute."

I make it into the alley and throw it all back up behind the bins.

"Sick?" she asks when I come back in five minutes later.

"Yep." I'm not ashamed. Gloria flashes her huge red lipstick smile at me again, as Felix shouts, "Two little pigs!"

She is half way through the curtain when she turns.

"What?" I say.

"At some point, you are going to tell me *exactly* what your dad did."

I don't even know.

14

"Here," Gloria says, walking out from the back room with her Ray-Bans already on, handing me a bunch of notes and coins.

"What's this?"

"Half of this morning's tips," she says, fiddling with her phone.

"No way," I say. There is at least thirty pounds in the palm of my hand.

"Yes way, Lady Di, that's why I work here. Don't spend it all at once."

When I look back up from the money, she is still standing in front of me, clearly mulling something over.

"Look, what are you doing now?" she asks, removing her glasses.

I shrug. "I normally just read my book in the square until I have to go to the charity shop."

She grabs my arm. "Okay, today, I'm going to show you the real Lattering."

∼

"That's where all the surfers score their hash, and your aunt too, so I hear."

We are walking past the alley between Tesco's and Breakers, licking our ice-creams. I normally get vanilla or chocolate, but Gloria insisted we both get one scoop of strawberry and one scoop of salted chocolate caramel each, with crushed Dime sprinkles. I tell her that it's literally the best ice-cream I've ever had.

She nods and says, "I know."

"And that's where you go if you don't want to be ID'd," she says, pointing at an off license on a side street that I've never even seen before. "The dude doesn't care, and his wife is basically blind."

We sit on the wall and watch Hugo Beltrome's builders quietly demolishing the old library. A digger claws up the ground in the spot where they are building the new wing - an auditorium apparently - because *that's* what this town is really missing. Two big men walk back and forth from a van carrying long white body bags of stuff, dumping them in with the churned-up earth. The builders throw Gloria admiring glances, but she either doesn't notice or doesn't care.

"So, what's your deal Lady Di?" she says, coating her tongue in ice-cream. I shrug. I don't have a deal.

"I mean," she wraps her tongue around the top of the ice-cream and half of it disappears into her mouth, "why aren't you a total bitch like all the others?"

"What others?" I say.

"All the other rich bitches who come down from London every summer."

I pick at a chunk of Dime stuck in my teeth. "Because I'm not rich?" I say. I try and adjust the straps on my top, to mitigate the white lines that keep appearing across the pink of my shoulders.

Gloria hikes up her dress to the top of her thighs, laying her long, brown legs out in the sun. She doesn't take off her boots. "But Felix said you go to some fancy school?"

"I get a full academic scholarship from some women's association," I say, through a final mouthful of ice-cream and cone.

She whistles.

"I couldn't afford a bag of crisps in the canteen without it."

"That'll be it, then. So, you are super clever though?"

"Yeah." It's the first time I've said it like that, without embarrassment. Without using the word 'quite' or 'pretty' or some other qualifier that makes it less. That makes *me* less.

"Good for you, Diana," she says, nodding, and I think she means it.

The bell on the clock announces midday loudly.

"I have to get to the charity shop," I say. I want to sit here with her all afternoon. I want people to *see* me sitting with her.

She jumps down from the wall and offers me her hand. "Come on, I'll walk you," she says.

At the crossing, a gleaming black Land Rover slams on its brakes at the last minute. The top is down, and rap music blares out of the speakers.

Gloria rolls her eyes. "The two whitest dudes in town listening to Killer Mike?" she says loudly, in their direction.

The angry kid from the beach is driving. Next to him, in the passenger seat, staring at his phone, is Jamie Beltrome. It feels like my feet are glued to the pavement and my chest is going to collapse. Angry guy leans out of the window. "We don't have all day, ladies!"

Gloria is standing half way across the road, staring at me curiously, but still I can't move. Angry guy toots his horn, and Jamie looks up. He stares at me blankly for a second, but then he smiles his beautiful smile and mouths 'hello' to me. Acrobats flip around my stomach as Gloria grabs my arm and drags me across the road. Angry guy wolf whistles and she holds the middle finger of her other hand up. He laughs and toots his horn again, and they drive off.

"Diana, breathe," Gloria demands, and I inhale sharply.

"What was that?" she says evenly, stepping back and crossing her arms.

"What?" I say.

"You like Jamie Beltrome?" she says, like I'm insane.

"No. I mean, I've only met him once, weeks ago, at the beach, and he was nice. I'd fallen off my bike. I haven't even seen him since. That's the first time, that's all. I thought I'd dreamt him."

She shakes her head, whistling. "Well, you certainly know how to pick them. But yeah, I mean, Jamie is actually quite sweet."

"Who is the other one?"

"That's Josh, his older brother. Arguably, he's a real dick."

"They are so…"

Their car turns at the end of the street, and their music finally fades.

"Ridiculously hot, right?" Gloria says. "Yeah, I know. Even their dad is hot, for an old, white guy, but Diana *be careful.*"

She takes my hands and twists her fingers through mine. I stare at them. We weren't even friends yesterday, and now this? Gloria is what my dad calls 'all or nothing.' He says they are the best kind of people.

"The Beltromes are, like, insanely rich. Like, mega rich. Mega, *mega* rich. And the mega rich live by different rules to you and me."

"I know, my school is full of them," I say, picturing The Debs on their wall.

She shakes her head. "Not like this. They have their own schools, their own bodyguards, they have their own laws for fuck's sake. They do whatever they want, and it just doesn't matter."

I snap out of my trance. "They can't just do *anything*," I say, incredulous. "They can't like…" I think of the worst crime there is, "kill someone."

"They really can," she says softly, squeezing my hands. "That much money protects you from everything. It's like a giant cushion stuffed with power, and you can't fall off. Just promise me you'll be careful. I'm not telling you not to do it, if you like him, but you have to have your wits about you, okay? It's a totally different game with a Beltrome. Right, I gotta go. Hasta manana, princess." Gloria waves goodbye to me over her shoulder as she walks away.

It doesn't matter. He won't like me anyway.

15

I'm scrambling around in the dust behind the counter, picking up a bunch of CDs. My new book is all dragons and sex and swearing, and it's so amazing that I put my feet up without looking and knocked everything over. I hear someone walk in the shop and I shout, "I'll only be a minute, just look around."

"Bitch, I knew it," a familiar voice says, peering over the counter. "What are you doing here, Pound Shop?'

Virginia and Audrey stalk around the shop with their long, tanned legs, and their tiny surf T-shirts, their board flat stomachs, and their bum-cheeks falling out of their shorts. They keep glancing at me, flashing their crocodile smiles as they pick up clothes with their fingertips and hold them at arm's length. I was so stupid to think things might get better. Nothing is different, nothing will change. I'm still me.

"Please tell me you aren't here all summer, Pound Shop. You're such a fucking downer." Audrey sighs, dramatically.

"How much is this?" Virginia asks, pointing at a thick, brown, fisherman's jumper.

"It says the price on the tag," I say.

"Oh, but can you come and read it for me please?" she scrunches up her nose. "I don't want to touch it."

I walk over and check. "It's two pounds."

"Wow," she says, pretend impressed. "Things are very reasonably priced in Pound Shop's shop, Audrey."

"Do you want to buy it?" I say.

"Fuck no." Her smile is so false I wonder if her lips are actually stuck on, and there's just a gaping hole of shit behind, literally the opening to Hell.

"It smells like urine," Audrey says, smiling. "In fact, this whole place smells like piss, doesn't it, Gin? Maybe you just don't realise, Pound Shop, because you smell like that too. You know, like something died in your mountain of raggedy hair?" Her eyes sparkle as she says it.

"Just get out," I say, so loudly I surprise myself.

"Bitch, gladly," Audrey says, deliberately bumping into the stand holding last year's charity Christmas cards, knocking them all over. They crash to the floor as they leave.

"Nice girls," Richard says sarcastically, appearing from the back room in rubber gloves. "The blonde one comes here with her family every summer. She's always been vile."

"Vile," I repeat. That's an Aunt Vita word but it fits Audrey perfectly. I swipe at the tears that have formed in the corners of my eyes. I don't want to cry but it feels like I'm suffocating. Why do they have to ruin this, too?

"They have so much..." I say, confused, defeated, more to myself than Richard, but he shrugs.

"Money is just stuff. Stuff won't make them happy."

"But they are both so beautiful as well. Why do they have to be so fucking mean?"

"They aren't beautiful, Diana."

"Erm, did you *see* them, Richard?"

"Yeah, I mean, they look good from a distance, but you can't be beautiful if you act like that. It's so ugly."

I roll my eyes. He wouldn't understand. "I just don't know why they hate me so much. I haven't done anything to them."

"Are you serious?" Richard says, looking surprised, like it's obvious.

"Like you know?" I say.

He smiles at me and nods. "I do, actually. They're just scared, and fear makes people angry. It's classic Star Wars - you should watch it. They aren't as clever as you, and they're Insta-high all the time, so they think that being beautiful is all that matters for girls, but that scares them too because they think they *have* to do all that stuff to their hair every morning, and put on a shit tonne of make-up, and wear those stupid clothes that they can barely move in, and then they still only like themselves after fifty photos with a filter." Richard pauses and takes a deep breath. "But you don't do any of that. You're just you, and you're beautiful anyway."

The tomatoes burst on his cheeks, but he doesn't look away.

I want to die. I don't know what's happening. I mutter something about tidying up the CDs before Aunt Vita gets back, and drop down behind the counter.

He walks through to the back of the shop without another word.

16

Half-way home, I jump off Snoopy and lean it against the beach wall. I walk down the sand and sit where it's still dry. The waves are big this evening, the foam on the top spilling rhythmically forwards every few seconds. It's relentless. I think about Audrey and Virginia in the shop. I think about my mum, staring out at this ocean, just like I'm doing now. I take off Aunt Vita's trainers.

The waves wash over my feet, and my toes sink into black sand. I wade in. There are people dotted around, but nobody notices me, fully clothed, up to my knees in the water. I keep walking. Is this how it felt? My shorts stick to my thighs and start to feel heavy. I run my hands through the ocean as I walk. I can feel stones under my feet, but I keep going. My top clings to my body as the water covers my shoulders. It's up to my chin. I'm standing on the tips of my big toes. A wave carries me up, and the water floods into my mouth. I cough it out and try to jump the next wave, but it comes too quickly. The sand beneath my feet has disappeared, which is important because I can't swim.

BEFORE

Lana swims *fifty lengths in the pool each morning. Before lunch she wanders around the grounds, down to the pond and back. She sits in the library most afternoons, looking out over the lake to the mountains. Sometimes she moves over to the piano, and stares at the keys, but she never plays. Her stomach is swollen now. She whispers to it when she thinks nobody is listening, but Juan hears everything in this house.*

"You have a beautiful sister," she says, stroking her belly slowly. "She's funny, and silly, and so clever. You have a sister, little one."

He takes her lunch sometimes, when he is at the Geneva house. He likes being near her. She only ever says two words to him, if he brings her something or drives her to the clinic.

"Thank you." No more. She never smiles. He would like to see her really smile again, like she did on that first day, with her daughter in her arms.

"Your sister lives in Lattering now," Juan says to her one afternoon. He stands behind her in the doorway as she stares out at the mountains. She doesn't respond.

"She has an ugly cottage. She talks to the sea like a crazy woman."

Still she doesn't reply.

"Half of her fence blew away in a storm. I put a new one in and she did not even notice."

"Why do you work for him, Juan?" Lana says quietly, and he is surprised by the sound of her. Hearing her speak feels like being in the ocean, coming back up to the surface after minutes under water, filling his lungs with oxygen. Embracing life.

"His grandfather found me after my wife and child died. I was picking his pocket, drunk, angry, homeless. He took me in, he gave me a job. He saved me, as I saved you from the ocean, Lana."

"I didn't need to be saved, until I met him." She doesn't turn around. He wishes she would turn and face him.

"But is this life so terrible? You have everything you could possibly want here."

She turns to face him, and there is cold defiance in her eyes. After the baby comes, he will give her something gentle to calm her. A tea to help her forget.

"Except my daughter," she says.

"This is true, now. But maybe not forever."

She bangs her hand on the table and an antique vase jumps but doesn't shatter.

"No. I don't want her anywhere near him, Juan. He does terrible things, and you do terrible things for him. Hugo is a monster, and he's made you a monster, too."

"But where do monsters come from Lana? They are just people, who transform for a time, and then back again. Dracula was also just a man. The werewolf needs a full moon. Monsters are never just monsters. There is good in them, too. He loves you, and he will love your child more than any of the others."

"And yet he knows I don't love him. I am only here to protect my daughter, and my husband. He is holding me hostage. Do you call that love?"

He doesn't answer. Instead he walks over and drops the photos on the piano in front of her. A tear runs silently down her cheek, and then another.

"It is too early for her birthday I know, but it has been a few months, and I thought you would like to see."

Her daughter's face stares up at her, running across a snow-covered field, waving a stick joyfully. She stops on the photo Juan likes the best.

Diana is wearing a woolly hat, her orange bunches poking out. She is sitting on a bench thoughtfully eating a sandwich.

"That's the field behind our house," she says, stroking her daughter's face on the photo.

"I protect her, Lana," he says. "I will always keep her safe, I give you my word. As long as you and the baby live, so will she."

Lana stares at the small, silver plaque in the middle of the bench.

In loving memory of Lana Cadence Lind.
Mother, Wife, Sister, Daughter.
We miss you, Mummy.

PART V

1

Panic comes as stiffness. A bigger wave throws me backwards and my head goes under. The salt stings my eyes. I flap my arms and try to get my head back above the water, but the next wave hits, pulling me beneath. I am being dragged along the bottom of the ocean. I can't breathe. Stones in the sand cut my legs. I CAN'T BREATHE. Is this how it felt?

Something grabs my leg. I'm being pulled by a powerful force, back towards the beach. Suddenly I'm pushed upwards, my head exploding out of the water. The force recedes as quickly as it came, and a wave dumps me on my arse on the sand.

I drag myself out of the water and collapse, coughing, spitting out water, exhausted. I look around. There are people everywhere - a surfer carrying his board past me up the beach, a dad with his kids splashing in the shallows, and heads bobbing in front of me, swimming casually in the ocean, beyond the waves.

Did somebody save me? Or did the ocean just give me back?

2

Aunt Vita is painting in the living room. There are no walls downstairs at Shalimar, so everything is everything. An old, naked woman is standing on a crate in front of the sofa, holding a tennis racket. My aunt turns as I walk in.

"Why are you wet?" she says, raising an eyebrow.

"I went for a swim."

"Fully dressed?"

"I was hot." It's not a lie. I *was* hot, too. She turns back to her painting.

"I got you some bread. This is Eileen," she says. The old, naked woman waves her tennis racket at me.

"Hello, dear," she says, droopy breasts swinging.

"I'm getting changed," I say, and go straight up to my room.

Aunt Vita is packing up her paints when I come back downstairs. The old woman pulls on a pair of knickers bigger than a pillowcase.

"I'm going to read my book outside," I say.

I lay down in the garden, facing the early evening sun, staring at the page of my book, but the words won't go in. Music is playing somewhere along the beach.

I shut the gate and walk towards the noise. A party is in full swing at the big surf house. The sign on the white gate says 'Mandalay' in blue letters.

I stop, twenty feet away, and watch surfers come and go. The big, white, wooden deck is packed with kids, swigging beer and laughing. Others lay on the grass, dotted around like the Henry Moore statues I saw on a school trip, folding their bodies into each other. Surf boards patrol the side of the house.

One guy is behind a BBQ, naked from the waist up bar a chef's hat. He shouts, "Chook, reef & beef!" People flock towards him, grabbing buns from a table, and he loads them up with meat.

I could just walk through that gate too; nobody would even notice. I could hold my bun and stand in line. I could ask for chook, or reef, or beef, or all three. There is nothing to stop me, but me. I picture Gloria, and then I remember this afternoon, in the shop.

I walk back to Shalimar and go straight to bed.

3

G loria is singing Diana Ross at the top of her voice today. She bumps me with her hips every time she walks by.

I give Felix another order for five full English. "I bloody love Saturdays, Diana!" he says and claps his hands, laughing.

I can't help it - I laugh too. I'm feeling okay, considering I nearly died yesterday. It feels safer to be near Gloria. It's like existing in the fog of her aura won't let me be sad, somehow. I'll be buying crystals next.

Around 9am the bell rings and I shout, "I'll be right with you!" while I fill two water glasses at speed.

"Hello again," he says, standing in front of the counter. I look up and wish I hadn't. "Where do you want me?" he says. "I was hoping we'd get some alone time."

"Umm, anywhere that's free," I say, and walk back through the curtain. It's like I can feel his fingers on the back of my leg again. The black grape of a bruise from his thumb has only just disappeared. "Get a grip, you're being silly," I say to myself, out loud.

"What?" Gloria says behind me, and I jump. I didn't know she was there.

"Oh, it's nothing, don't worry about it." I try to walk past her, but she takes a step to the side, and blocks my way.

"Two English ready!" Felix shouts.

"What's going on? Why do you look all weird and zombie - are you ill?" Gloria says, narrowing her eyes.

"No, I'm fine, it's nothing, Felix is waiting," I say, not meeting her eye.

"Felix *can* wait. Tell me, Diana." She actually stamps her boot.

"Okay, fine! It's just, that guy."

"What guy?"

"The guy that just walked in."

"The fit dad guy? That guy?"

I shudder.

"You dropped his sandwich last time, right? Is he being a dick about it? Did he say something?"

"No, nothing like that. It's nothing, really." I try to get past, but she still won't move.

"Diana, tell me." She stares at me, unblinking.

"He touched me, okay?"

"What do you mean, he touched you?"

"Look, I know it's stupid, but when I dropped his sandwich, it's because he stroked my leg and, just, kind of, put his hand up my shorts. But, you know, nowhere really bad. Just at the back of my thigh. I know I'm being silly." I brace myself for the roll of her huge eyes, but her jaw locks.

"Why didn't you tell me this last time?" she says quietly.

"Um, because you hated me? And it was just my leg. I know I'm being silly."

She looks like she's just downed a shot of crazy.

"Gloria, please don't say anything," I say, grabbing her arm.

She shakes me off. "Fuck that," she says. She grabs the two full English from Felix and approaches the table directly under the lemon. I follow at a distance.

"Get out," she says to him quietly.

"Hi, finally. I'll have a bacon...sorry, what did you say?" He looks properly shocked.

"We're closed," Gloria says, still holding the two breakfasts.

The bell rings and a young couple walk in.

"Grab a table, I won't be a second," she says to them with a wink and a full Gloria beam. She turns back to him, and her smile disappears.

"Is this a joke?" he asks, looking over her shoulder at me. I look down at my feet.

"No joke. We're closed and you're leaving. We don't serve deviants here." She hasn't blinked.

"What did you say to me?" His face is turning red.

She leans in, close enough to stain him with her lipstick. "The staff aren't on the menu," she says.

"What are you talking about?" he scoffs, but closes his eyes. Classic CIA tell.

Gloria looks at me, and back at him.

"Oh Christ, I didn't touch her." He laughs like I'm ridiculous, or I've made it up. If he hadn't done it to me, I'd believe him.

"You bruised my leg," I say quietly.

"Oh, for God's sake." He turns back to Gloria, the picture of innocence. "She's just a child. She probably had a dream about me or something."

"If she's a child, there's a perfect word for what you are when you touch her up."

He shoves his chair back and storms out, swearing insults under his breath, slamming the door.

There is a second of silence, and then everyone just starts eating their breakfast again.

"What?" Gloria says to me. She isn't embarrassed. Her neck isn't red and blotchy.

"Thanks," I say. I want to tell her that she is everything, but she just shrugs.

"What are friends for, right?"

4

The morning rush is over and Gloria and I are leaning on the counter, so close that the hairs on our arms touch, watching Peppa Pig on mute. I feel different, bigger. More important, somehow.

"What's the name of that generation, the rubbish ones?" Gloria says, without looking away from the TV.

"Which ones?" I say, hypnotized. Madame Gazelle is skiing.

"You know. Our parents."

"Oh. Generation X," I say.

Gloria nods and sucks on a piece of bacon wisely. "It's like they just wanted to screw us up. My dad left. My mum went to Australia. Your dad is in prison. Your mum topped herself. Even Richard's parents left him. It's rubbish."

"Tell me about it," I say, taking a slug of tea.

"I didn't ask to be born," she says.

"Tell me about it," I say.

She sighs and pulls out her phone, reading aloud. "You're in the driving seat today, Scorpio, where you like to be, but the best things in life aren't always straight ahead. Turn off the engine and walk into the woods. That's where the surprises are hiding." Gloria whistles, as if she completely understands.

"I'm a Taurus," I say.

"I know," Gloria says, scrolling. "Open your heart today, Taurus. Love is for the brave. Dream big." She nods wisely. "See," she says, nudging me.

See what?

5

When I get to the shop Aunt Vita has her backpack on, like a beautiful, angry turtle. She's panicking about something, again. "Richard is knee deep in new bags, thank Christ, but Eileen has had a fall, so I'm running to the home. I'll go with her to the hospital if she needs me."

"So, you're just popping out again?" I ask. "Shocker."

Richard doesn't even come out to say hello, and I'm glad. We haven't spoken since the beautiful comment. I'm worried he thinks that I'll think he likes me.

I'm buried in my book, my head swimming with politics and swords, when Jamie Beltrome walks in. He's holding a huge box, overflowing with clothes. Sunlight pours in behind him, like he's religious. I wait for his nose to turn up at the smell of the shop, or his face to twist to full grimace, but nothing happens. A strand of thick, dark hair falls over one of his eyes. He looks so serious and sad. I think he's *just* realized that some people are poor.

"Hi," I say, removing my feet from the desk.

He looks over at the counter, and his smile could power a Teslar. "Hi," he says.

His voice is so expensive. Maybe I'm in love with the sound of him?

"We met on the beach," he says, placing the box down on the counter. "I have a donation, if you'll take it?"

"That's so decent of you." I don't normally say that to people who come in with their bin bags and boxes of CDs. I usually say, "Leave them in the corner."

"So, Seagulls and this as well? Two jobs must keep you busy," he says, looking around.

I nod earnestly. "I think it's really important to give something back."

I hear Richard coughing in surprise. Whatever dude.

"I've read that book," Jamie says. "You know there are about seven more of them?"

"Well, I've got all summer." I gesture around at the empty shop.

"You are staying for the whole summer, then?" He says.

I nod. I can't put my book down, in case I reach over and touch him. I want to run my finger down the middle of his neck. I want to put my palm flat on his T-shirt and feel his heart beneath it.

"Jamie, old man, let's get a wriggle on. What the fuck?' Angry Guy walks in, actually covering his nose. He is so loud; he fills the shop with noise. It's like he thinks he owns every space he enters.

Jamie looks like he wants to die. "Josh, this is my friend Diana," he says.

Josh shrugs, disinterested. He is ridiculously hot, but it's not nice. He looks like an older version of Jamie, but his hair is blond, and his nose is bigger. Their eyes are different, too. Jamie's eyes are kind.

"Come on, Jam. This place stinks."

I hear a nervous cough behind me and Richard walks out from the back room. "Thetis scum aren't welcome here," he says, and I almost choke.

Jamie looks down, embarrassed, but Josh sneers. "Oh, but we are rich scum at least, Ricardo."

"Your money doesn't mean anything here," Richard says.

"Who the fuck cares?" Josh says. He holds his middle finger up behind him as he walks out. Jamie follows, but stops at the door. "It was nice to see you again, Diana."

By the time I've cooled down Richard is sitting on the floor of the back room, eating his homemade sandwich.

"Why did you say that - Thetis scum? That was really rude."

Richard swallows a mouthful of food. "They're all arseholes, Diana." His glasses have misted up and he starts wiping them on his T-shirt. He won't stop, round and round, harder and harder.

"Jamie was making a donation. I don't see what's so arsehole about that?" I stick out my chin, indignantly.

Richard looks sad, but I don't care. "They are all the same," he says. "They think they own this town and everyone in it, and they can do whatever they want. We are all just specks to them."

"Jesus, Richard, you're seventeen! Lighten up!" I storm through the curtain with maximum drama.

He doesn't come through to the front again, and I leave early without saying goodbye.

The weather turns as I walk down Beach Road. Clouds move in, the sky goes dark, and the wind picks up. Surfers appear from everywhere with boards under their arms, heading for the big waves.

The tables outside of Breakers have emptied as the first raindrops hit my nose. I glance inside. Sitting at the prime table by the window are Josh, Virginia and Audrey. The girls suck their milkshakes and flick their hair. Then Jamie appears, parting the wave of kids waiting for tables, sliding on to the bench next to Audrey. My heart stops. I stand still, desolate, staring in. Jamie looks up, but he doesn't smile. Audrey knocks on the window, mouthing 'Pound Shop' and waving. She whispers to Josh, who smirks and says something, and the girls laugh too hard. Jamie picks up a menu, pretending to read it. The rain stings my skin as I walk away.

6

I get changed three times. I throw myself down on my bed and open my book, but I keep re-reading the same sentence so I slam it shut.

Outside, the rain has stopped but the bench in the garden is still wet, soaking my shorts. I don't care. I can't stop thinking about Jamie. My throat tightens. "I feel stupid," I whisper to the ocean. "I actually thought he liked me."

Boys are predictable, that's what Betty says, what everybody knows. They just want the prettiest girl.

My dad would always make us watch these films on Saturday evenings, from when he was growing up. He called them 'classics'. They were about these super geeky guys who fall in love with the most popular girl, and end up getting her. We are supposed to be happy and cry tears of joy. But the girl was always really pretty. What about the geeky girl? Or the fat girl? The world is so busy telling girls we should love ourselves now, geeky or fat or whatever, but nobody is telling boys they should love us too. Skin is just skin, and the insults get through eventually, no matter how hard you try to protect yourself. It's like everybody wants to tell girls to be stronger, but nobody really wants to talk about how boys treat girls they don't want to sleep with. Nobody is telling *boys* to change how they think or behave. It's girls that have to do all the work.

"It wasn't even anything," I whisper to the ocean. "We'd just read the same book, and he said he liked my hair. I'm such an idiot."

The rain comes again.

When Aunt Vita gets home, she shakes herself off like a wet dog and turns on the radio.

"Joni Mitchell is perfect for stormy days," she says, smiling. She spots my red eyes.

"What is it?" She says, reaching for my hand, but I bat her away.

"I want to leave," I shout. "I hate it here!" I run upstairs and slam my door.

Aunt Vita knocks but doesn't wait for me to answer. I hug my knees as she curls up behind me and strokes my hair. My pillow is damp with tears.

"I'm being stupid," I say.

She pushes her fingers into my hand, hugging us both.

"Nobody wants me," I say. "I'm too weird, or too much, or something, or nothing. I'm unlovable. My mum literally chose to die rather than stay with me. My dad has gone to prison rather than be with me."

"No," she says into my hair, hugging me so tightly I think I might stop breathing, but I don't want her to stop. "No, Diana. You *are* loved. And you are exactly the right amount. Don't dilute yourself, Diana, for anyone. Don't pretend to be anything other than yourself to please someone else. If they don't get you, so what? Someone else will. If they don't understand why you care about something, go and talk to somebody else who does. If your passion makes them feel uncomfortable, who cares? You will *inspire* someone else. You must never pretend to be different, Diana, to make someone else feel better. You are you, and that is all you should be. And you have to love you. You *have* to."

Aunt Vita's breath smells like wine, and her hands smell like butter. It gets dark outside. I can hear the wind pushing through the window frame, but her breathing in my ear is more powerful than the wind. It sounds like safety. Howard shuffles in, circles our feet and collapses. The storm rattles the windows, and Aunt Vita breathes in my ear, as I fall asleep.

7

Ralph and Richard are playing hide and seek in the shop. Seriously.

"I'm going in," Ralph says, disappearing into a rack of old man trousers that occupy the length of one wall. I gag at the thought of it.

"Ready," he shouts, muffled by polyester. His small, grey, trainers poke out like shiny mice.

"I'm turning it on!" Richard shouts behind me.

"Do it then!" Ralph shouts, from the trouser forest. "Shit!" He jumps out, shaking his hand.

Richard emerges holding his phone and a small, metal box.

"It really hurt," Ralph says, examining his palm up close.

"On a scale of one to ten, ten being the time you had food poisoning?" Richard asks.

Ralph turns his hand over, checking it still works. "Maybe a seven?"

"Hey, losers?" I say, putting my book down.

"Yes, geek?" Ralph says.

"How are you getting on with your investigation about that missing girl?"

Richard sighs.

"You seriously want to know?" Ralph says, excitably.

"I seriously want to know."

Ralph holds his hands up in surrender to Richard, the victim of my incessant questions.

"Fine," Richard says. "Tell her."

Ralph's face lights up like an arcade. "Well, we are going back to her house tonight, to see if we can get into her old bedroom. You can come if you want, if you really are serious?"

This sounds mildly dangerous, and highly illegal, neither of which I'd associate with Richard and Ralph. "And you're sure she hasn't just moved? I mean, have you checked her Instagram and stuff?"

"Have we checked her Instagram?" Ralph says, laughing. "Do we look like amateurs?"

"Yes," I say, but he ignores me.

"Of course, we've checked. She hasn't posted anything, anywhere, since the day she disappeared."

"But guys, seriously, the police wouldn't just let a young girl disappear."

Ralph shakes his head, and Richard suppresses a smile.

"Poor, sweet, naïve Diana," Ralph says. "People go missing all the time. They just don't go to your school."

"What does that mean?" I say. Ralph treats everybody but Richard like an idiot.

"Try white privilege, for starters? How often do you see missing black faces on the TV?"

"Was Julie Peters black?" I say. It hadn't occurred to me. I'd just pictured her as me, as white.

"No, she was white, but she was poor, and she was expendable."

"But if there was really anything suspicious-"

"She left everything behind Diana!" Ralph says, desperate for me to understand something vital.

"What about her phone?"

"Yes, admittedly that is gone, and her bag too, but that's it, apart from the clothes she was wearing."

"And they haven't found any of it, her purse or anything?"

He shakes his head dramatically. "Now she's just a face on a poster at the police station. They've already stopped looking."

"Well, they obviously think she's just moved, so…"

"Look, do you want to come with us or not?" Ralph snaps, irritated.

"I'll come."

"Good. They are moving Mrs. Campbell into the old people's home next week, so we are running out of time. It's now or never." Ralph shakes his hand again, staring accusingly at his palm. "I'm getting aftershocks. It's still throbbing."

"You know it's still in its beta phase and you're the lab rat," Richard says, twiddling a dial on his box. "Let's try it again, but this time go outside."

"What is it, in his hand?" I ask, as Ralph scuttles off.

"Just a thing I've been playing with at home, a kind of tracker. It doesn't really work yet."

He shakes his head. That's Richard's tell that he's disappointed himself.

8

I jump off Snoopy as the boys flip up their skateboards at the end of Julie Peters' street. There are rows of pale, sand battered, almost identical bungalows, most with ramp access to the front doors. Every window is obscured by net curtains.

Ralph walks off nonchalantly down the road, his arms swinging; an impression of being carefree. He disappears behind a bush on the opposite side of the street. I wait for him to emerge on the other side, but he doesn't.

I laugh out loud, but Richard follows him, in exactly the same fashion. Okay, I get it. Tonight, we are spies.

The leaves are thick and there are dozens of huge, pink flowers, but we find three small holes just big enough to watch through.

"Which one are we looking at?" I whisper, because that's what spies do. We are pressed so close together that I can smell the washing powder on Richard's T-shirt.

"That one," he says, pointing. It's a pale blue bungalow with grey net curtains at the window, and two concrete steps up to a porch patrolled by potted geraniums. Old, orange rose bushes sit below white, plastic, double glazed windows. A ramp leads slowly upwards to a side door. A ginger cat is snoozing on the doormat. Everything about this house is almost dead.

"What do you think really happened to her?" I say.

"Thetis," Ralph says, peering through a set of children's binoculars.

"Thetis what?" I say.

"Thetis killed her."

"The guys from the school? Are you crazy? It's just a school!"

"Just a school, Diana? Tell me, have you seen their bodyguard?"

I think about the crowd outside the library and picture the yellow-eyed man, leaning on his car, blowing me that kiss.

"Do you mean the old guy with the cowboy boots?" I ask.

"Yes, him. Thetis boys refer to him as The Mayan," Richard says.

"The Mayan?"

"They were an ancient people, from the Yucatan Peninsula, in Mexico," Richard says.

"That's racist then, isn't it?" I look from one to the other, for affirmation.

"I don't know, is it?" Ralph says. "If it's his spiritual ancestry? It would be like if you lived in Mexico and people called you The Viking. Would that be offensive?"

"I'd rather they just used my name. What if they called you the…the…" Damn! I don't even know where his ancestors are from.

"The Vedic?" Ralph says, rolling his eyes at my stupidity.

"Yeah, what if they called you that?"

"It's more menacing than Ralph," he says. He's got a point.

"If Thetis are anywhere in a group, The Mayan is always close by," Richard says, "to sweep up any trouble. He's their cleaner, but he cleans up bodies."

"Isn't he a bit old for that? He must be at least fifty," I say.

"He's incredibly fit," Ralph says. "They say he was an Olympic swimmer when he was young. They say he's nocturnal. They say he goes swimming in the ocean every night. Then he sleeps for four hours each morning, with his eyes open."

"Who says this, who are *they*?' I say.

"People," Ralph says. "The internet. Us."

"Do they say anything else?"

"That bone he wears in his ear…" Ralph says.

"He wears a bone in his ear?" I say, shuddering.

"Yes. They say it's human, a child's finger bone - the middle phalanx of one of his victims." Ralph tries not to smile, but he clearly thinks this is cool.

"You're crazy. You can't just be a killer, it's totally illegal. You'd go to prison."

Ralph shrugs. "Depends on who you know."

"What? No, it doesn't," I say. "Rich people get sent to prison for murder too, all the time."

"Do they?" Ralph asks.

A car drives slowly past and we all duck further behind our bush.

"Open your eyes, Diana. If you have enough money, you can do *anything*."

"So, you think this *Mayan* (I do bunny ears; it must be racist) killed Julie Peters?" It's not cold but I shiver.

"No, not exactly," Ralph says, dropping his binoculars. They hang heavily around his neck on a pink strap. I recognise them from the WHSmith's kid's explorer section last summer.

"We think a Thetis did it. She was dating one of them in secret, and when it ended, badly, The Mayan covered it up. Maybe she was blackmailing them. Maybe it was just a sex game that went wrong."

Ralph says *sex game* like something abstract but factual, with no hint of embarrassment. On the other hand, Richard's neck goes bright red.

"And how do you know that she was seeing a Thetis guy anyway? If it was in secret? Were you following her?"

Now it's Ralph's turn to look embarrassed.

"Oh my God, you were! You were stalking her," I say.

"Keep your voice down," Ralph whispers. "No, I wasn't stalking her. I just saw where she was sometimes."

"Ralph, what do you think stalking is?"

"I like to think of it as unrequited love."

"Seriously, Ralph, it's not romantic to follow someone around. It's just fucking creepy."

"Okay, but I didn't kidnap her though, did I?"

"I don't know, did you?"

He ignores me. He's not strong enough to lift a bag of potatoes, let alone a grown woman.

"So, which one of the Thetis guys was she seeing?" I ask, as innocently as possible.

Richard side-eyes me. He knows what I'm thinking.

"That's what we're looking for tonight. I saw them kissing, but rich white boys all look the same to me. The same haircuts, the same clothes, and I didn't see his face properly in the dark."

The door of the house opens suddenly, and we all duck again. A large, black woman comes out, singing, in a vast, flowery dress. She carries a small bag of rubbish.

Richard grabs the camera around his neck and starts taking photos.

"Is that the woman who lives there?" I ask. She's hitting all the high notes to Amazing Grace and it's actually *amazing*.

"No, Mrs. Campbell is bedridden. This is her new carer. She's only been here a couple of weeks. The previous one kept the windows locked, but this one likes the fresh air. After dinner, she and Mrs. Campbell play cards for an hour, with the TV on. She doesn't close the windows until she leaves at 8pm, so this is our chance. We just have to wait for her to take the rubbish out." He points as she opens the dustbin. "That's the last thing she does before they play cards."

The woman goes back inside and shuts the front door.

Ralph checks his watch. "We're running out of time. Come on." He scuttles off, head first and down, around the back of the house.

Richard follows.

I dart out before common sense can take over.

There are two windows at the back of the house. A small, high, square opening that maybe Ralph could squeeze through, but not without falling onto the window ledge of bathroom bottles below.

The other window is much bigger, with drawn curtains. But it's locked.

"Damn it!" Ralph says. He is furious.

"What happens now, do we smash it?" I say, and Richard looks at me like I'm crazy.

"I think someone is getting carried away," Ralph says, eyeing up the bathroom window again. We all know that won't work.

"That's it then," Richard says.

Ralph nods sadly. "There's no way in."

9

I ring the doorbell and adjust my hair as the boys' heads poke around the side of the house simultaneously, one above and one below, like they've practiced it.

"Diana, what are you doing?" Richard whispers.

"Come back," Ralph says, beckoning me away furiously.

I hear footsteps padding heavily on the carpet behind the door. The woman in the flowery dress opens it, looking confused.

"Yes darlin'?" she says, holding her fan of playing cards close to her chest.

"Hi, I'm so sorry to bother you, but I was a friend of Julie's, the girl who used to live here. Would you mind if I just looked in her room quickly?"

"Why darlin'?' she says. Her huge eyes narrow with suspicion. Her bosom is vast and covered in the bright, yellow flowers of her dress, interrupted by a tiny, blue sticker with the outline of a fish on it. I've seen that fish before in car windows. It means 'I love Jesus', or 'God loves me', or something like that. We don't do religion in my house. I mean, we discuss it, we just don't believe in magic.

"Julie was a friend of mine and-"

"No darlin', come back another day, it's not convenient right now," she says, closing the door in my face.

I panic. "But she had my best church dress, that's all. It will take me two minutes to find it. I have to wear it to my grandmother's memorial service on Sunday." If there *is* a Hell, I'm going. Irony.

The door stops, an inch before closing. "A dress for church?" she asks.

"Yeah, I'll be really quick, I promise." I give her my best Gloria smile.

"You've got five minutes." she says from the bedroom door.

I open the wardrobe, desperate for her to leave.

"Ruth!" I hear an old woman call from the other room, then a bump, and the sound of crockery smashing.

She bustles off and I yank the curtains back.

Richard and Ralph stare in, mouths open. I unlock the window and Richard gives Ralph a foot up. He tumbles in noiselessly, a little bag of bones.

"Dead grandmother? Inspired!" he says, putting his child sized hand up for a high five.

I slap it, quietly. "What are we even looking for, a diary or something?" I say.

"No, you look for the dress, for plausibility, and I'll look for... whatever else," he says, smiling like it's Christmas morning. He starts rummaging around Julie's bedside table. "Shout something to keep her away," he says after a minute.

"I think I've found it, I won't be long," I yell.

I close the bedroom door quietly. There is a key in the lock, and I turn it. I work my way through Julie's wardrobe, full of cropped T-shirts, tiny skirts, short shorts, and super skinny jeans. Julie Peters was thin and proud, but I can't find a single dress. I pull at the drawers. It's a jumble sale of socks, and skimpy pants, and tiny bras, but no dresses. I search the room with my eyes. Hanging on the back of the door, hidden behind a dressing gown, I spot it. A solitary, short, blue dress. It's not black, I definitely wouldn't wear it to a memorial service, but it will have to do. I hold the dress up against me and look in the mirror. If I didn't breathe, I could button it up, but it would barely cover my bum.

"Nothing," Ralph says, throwing his hands up in the air. "You're a girl, where do you hide stuff?"

Suddenly the door handle yanks up and down. Ralph darts under the bed.

"Open the door!" she says.

"Sorry, sorry, I'm coming!" I shout.

I open it and she pushes it fully open, peering inside.

"I found it! I'm nearly done." I wave the dress at her.

"Why was the door locked?" she says.

"It must have just slammed shut when I was searching behind it." I shrug, giving her my Gloria smile again.

"What a mess," she says, disgusted at the drawers hanging open, and the T-shirts thrown on the floor.

"Yeah, sorry. I'll just tidy it up and get out of here," I say.

She nods and walks back to the sitting room.

Ralph scrambles out from under the bed. "There's something under there, help me move it," he says, grabbing hold of the metal bedpost.

"Ralph, we don't have time, she's getting suspicious."

"Come on, this is our last chance."

The bed is cheap and we pull it away from the wall easily. Ralph is right. There is a visible lump in the carpet, in the corner by the wall, and it comes up when he pulls it. Underneath is a loose pile of letters and papers. He beams, snatching them up greedily like fifty pound notes.

"Push the bed back," he says.

I do as I'm told. When I look back up, he's holding a photo in front of my face. It's a picture of a young, blonde girl. She's pretty and *really* tiny, in denim shorts and a string bikini top. She's got glitter on her cheeks and flowers in her hair, as if she's at a festival. She leans back against a tree. Behind the tree is a house made of glass.

"Where have I seen that house?," I say.

"Duh, where do you think?" Ralph says, stuffing the letters into his backpack. "It's on the cliffs. It's Poseidon. It's the Thetis house."

My stomach lurches.

Richards shoves his head through the open window. "Get out," he says, loudly.

"We've found something," Ralph says excitedly.

Richard glares at us. "Get out. The Mayan is here."

10

I scramble out of the window, scratching my legs on the latch, but I don't care. Richard reaches over and literally yanks Ralph out by his backpack. We press ourselves flat against the side of the house. The doorbell rings.

"She's in here," the woman says.

The front door closes, and we sprint for the bushes on the other side of the road. Richard makes it first, and Ralph and I land heavily next to him seconds later.

The Mayan comes back out of the front door. "Please call me if she returns."

His accent is Spanish, like Tito Matias, but lower, like something is pressing down on his throat. Or maybe that's just what evil sounds like?

He walks into the middle of the street and closes his eyes. I'm breathing so loudly he must be able to hear me. I can see the small, thin bone in his ear. The burns covering his neck are paler than the skin on his face and look smooth, like silk. I almost want to touch them. He climbs into an old, red, American looking car. The engine comes on like a jet plane. He drives away, and we all breathe out.

"So, what now?" I say, swinging my leg across Snoopy.

"I read the letters," Ralph says, "and tell you what they say."

I ride so fast that my front wheel shakes. I've never been so relieved to shut the kitchen door behind me.

~

"Find any bullets?" Aunt Vita calls from the sofa, with a newspaper in front of her, Howard spread-eagled on her lap, and a glass of wine at her lips. A massive bar of chocolate has been smashed carelessly to bits in front of her. She picks up a chunk without even looking and throws it in her mouth.

"Yeah, we found something this time," I say.

"Great," she says, barely listening, engrossed in her paper. She slaps a page, and shouts, "Ha!"

I bolt the kitchen door behind me.

11

Gloria calls the café to say she's not coming in. She sounds terrible. "Tell Felix it's period pains, that will shut him up," she says.

I find him in the kitchen. His shirt is orange and pink, with dancing parrots on the pockets.

"Gloria just called, she's not coming in," I say, throwing an egg from one hand to the other, absentmindedly.

"Eh? Why not? She'll 'ave to come in, I'll call 'er." He starts untying his apron.

"She said it's period pains," I say.

"Okay, fine," he says, tying his apron back up.

My dad bought me a book called 'What's happening to me?' when I was about eleven, with a picture of a confused looking girl on the front. He read it, then he sat me down and told me what was coming. He told me that, as I got older, I'd bleed every month, and why. I got my first period a year later. I just woke up one morning with blood in my pajamas. Dad said I could stay home from school if I wanted – I didn't – and he asked if I'd like to talk to the female doctor at the surgery, if I had any questions that I didn't want to ask him. He bought me sanitary towels and then, when I asked, he bought me tampons. I know my dad is crazy, but he's pretty amazing, too.

When I get to the charity shop it's locked, and two new bags of stuff are sitting outside. I have to scramble around under the dustbins to find the key.

Richard is working at the library all day. The new structure is already built, and now it's his job to move every book back.

Aunt Vita is visiting Eileen at the hospital, so it's just me and my book, again. It's not right. I laid awake in bed for an hour last night, my mind racing, checking my pulse every few minutes to make sure I wasn't having a heart attack, getting up to check out of the window to make sure the Mayan wasn't lurking in the garden. The thought that he might have caught us in Julie's room was so scary it made me want to be sick, but now, I think, I liked it. The memory of fear, after the fear has passed, is exhilarating. I shouldn't just be sitting behind this counter for four boring hours again today. Something should be happening!

I ignore the bags for at least half an hour. I keep glancing over, hoping they'll have dissolved or disappeared. I'll get in trouble with Aunt Vita if I just leave them for Richard to sort out tomorrow, but I HATE sorting the bags.

After another hour has passed, I locate a fresh pair of rubber gloves and drag the bag out in to the back room. The trick is to jump back before you inhale. I get to work.

I hear the whistling first. It's a nursery rhyme, but I can't make out which one. Then I hear the footsteps, like tap shoes, dancing their way slowly around the shop.

I walk through and stop.

The Mayan is standing in the middle of the floor, holding an old plate, turning it over slowly in his hands. He looks up and smiles. He puts the plate down carefully and picks up a woman's wedding hat from a shelf. It's small, and round, and red, with a yellow flower and a short veil. He stands in front of the mirror and places it on his head, and it almost fits. He smiles at me in the mirror, raising his hands, inviting me to tell him what I think, but I can't even speak. He takes the hat off, putting it back where he found it.

I have never been so scared in all my life. I wonder when I should start to scream.

"You look concerned, Estrella," he says. "Don't be. We've been through worse than this, Diana."

My throat is tight, like there are hands around it, squeezing, as he walks towards the counter slowly. "Can I help you?" I manage, but it's a whisper.

He leans across the counter, resting on his elbows, cupping his face in his hands. Close up, the burnt skin at his neck is almost magnetic.

"I've missed you," he says.

"I don't know you," I say.

He makes a pretend sad face and tuts. "Diana, you've been making some new friends and that makes me happy, truly, but there are no mysteries here, just sand and sunshine. I want you to relax and enjoy your summer. Don't go digging, my darling."

"I don't know what you are talking about. I don't know you. Stop calling me those names."

He's twirling something between his fingers, like a magician. "Be careful, Diana, you might hurt my feelings." His hand shoots up suddenly and swipes at his face.

I literally jump back.

A match sparks against his cheek, and he holds it between us, blowing the flame out just before it reaches the skin of his thumb. He winks at me. "Don't worry little one, it didn't really hurt then, or now. Be a good girl this summer, for me and all the people that love you, Diana, por favor. And stop skipping breakfast, it's an important meal." He blows me a kiss.

I'm so scared I actually want to be sick.

The smell of smoke lingers as he walks out. I need my fucking phone back.

12

"Gloria, I need to ask you something."

She is wearing cut offs, and a long white T-shirt that says 'Choose Life' in big black letters, and her red DM's. Her hair is part pink, part brown, and one black sparkly earring creeps all the way up her ear.

I'm wearing leggings, a short, white, lacy vest I found in Aunt Vita's wardrobe, and her trainers. I've piled my hair up on my head in an attempt to stay cool. My face is covered in freckles, and now I wear pink lip gloss, and mascara, every day.

We sit, facing each other, one leg on either side of the wall. She bought new neon blue Ray-Bans yesterday, so I'm wearing her red ones.

"So ask," she says, leaning over and taking a thoughtful lick of my ice-cream.

"Do you know anything about Thetis?" I say.

"Yeah," she says, "but I assume you mean more than are they all arseholes?"

I nod.

"Well, they've been here for years, since we were kids. Every year it gets worse."

"But have you heard anything really bad? I ask.

She is about to answer when we hear a loud, deliberate cough behind us.

"Pound Shop," they say, pretending to cough again, walking up the beach towards us.

Gloria looks around, confused, and back at me. "What are they saying? Are they talking to us?" she says, shaking her head.

"Let's just go," I say, swinging my leg over the wall.

"But I haven't finished my ice-cream yet," she says, putting her hand on my leg.

"They go to my school." I say, but I can't look her in the eye. I haven't seen them for over a week. I thought they might actually have left. I knew it was too good to be true.

"What are they saying? Is it Pound Shop? Is that it?" Gloria looks genuinely perplexed.

"It's because of my scholarship. Please Gloria, can we just go to the beach?"

"No. Diana, look at me. Look at me!" She demands quietly.

So I do. There are tears in my eyes.

"Do they call you that?" she says.

I didn't want her to know. "Don't worry, I've got to go now anyway," I say, jumping down from the wall. I don't want her to be embarrassed to be seen with me, or worse, embarrassed FOR me.

She jumps down too, grabbing hold of my arm.

"Gloria, honestly, I can't be bothered with the fight. I've got to get to the shop anyway, and they'll get bored soon."

She turns to face Audrey and Virginia. "Not today they won't."

13

"Are you talking to us?" Gloria says, completely up in Audrey's face.

Virginia actually looks scared.

"Do I look like I want to talk to you?" Audrey says

Gloria sighs loudly but doesn't back away an inch. "Your pupils have dilated. You know that means you love me, right?"

"Fuck off," Audrey says, but she looks confused.

I know she is wondering if her pupils have really dilated. Also, what dilated means.

"Well we are going to go actually, but not because you've told us to. It's just in case it's catching. I wouldn't want to get it."

"Get what?" I say, and Audrey glares at me like I've changed the rules of our game without consulting her first.

"The dirt," Gloria says. "Walking round town, calling people names to make yourself feel less bad about yourself. Is that literally all you have to do? Fuuuuuuck, I'm glad I'm not in your head. Come on, Diana. Don't get too close to them." She grabs my arm and we walk off, towards the beach.

"High-rise whores!" Audrey shouts after us.

"You're dirt!" Gloria shouts back over her shoulder, flipping her the finger.

"Why do you let them talk to you like that?" Gloria says, piling up pebbles in front of her.

"I don't know," I say. "It just happened. And now it's gone on for so long, I don't know how to make it stop. I get so scared before they've even said anything."

Gloria sighs and faces the sun, closing her eyes. "Don't the teachers do anything?"

"They don't know, properly. They never say anything really bad in front of anybody important. They save it for when I'm on my own."

"Bitches are dirt," she says. 'And they can't even see what they are doing. They think other girls are the enemy. They literally give themselves a bad name." She shakes her head and throws her pebbles away in disgust.

"I think I just need to toughen up a bit," I say. "I just need to be a bit more...Gloria."

She gives me one of her huge Gloria smiles. "I'll put that on a T-shirt," she says.

"Hey, who is the enemy?" I say, as she pulls me to my feet.

She shrugs. "Monsters, I guess?"

14

I hear the music before I see the party. It's already in full swing, at Mandalay, the big white surf house. I slow Snoopy down and jump off. A couple of guys are playing guitars in the garden, and a bonfire is throwing off dangerous looking sparks, but no one seems worried. I'm going to walk in, do one circuit of the house, and leave, but I AM going in, for at least five minutes. I take a deep breath and whisper to myself, "Be more Gloria." I *really* need that T-shirt.

A young guy in half a wetsuit and a red poncho passes me a bottle of beer from an ice-bucket. I walk past the guitars, up to the deck, and into a kitchen crammed full of people. I look around, searching the faces for the imaginary friend who came with me, but I don't stop walking. I carry my bottle through a big sitting room, with a huge dining table holding a surf board. Candles and pots of surf wax are everywhere. Bodies lounge on old, mismatching sofas, and literally nobody looks me up and down, or makes a face, or wonders why I'm there. I don't want anybody to talk to me, particularly. I just want to know that I did it. *I went in.*

Music is booming out from a large, dark room at the end of a corridor. My eyes adjust to the light as I hover at the door. Hip-hop blares from a set of huge speakers that sit precariously on top of wardrobes. Everyone is jumping straight up in the air. Beer sprays as they bounce, but still they jump.

A guy pushes his way in behind me, and suddenly I'm in the room too. Another guy jumps, and his beer drenches my vest. I've got two choices: leave or jump. So, I jump.

A dude with dreads and no shirt is next to me. He pokes out his tongue. His eyes are huge, and wild, and happy. People are shouting the lyrics, and my ears start to ring with the noise. The beat thuds through my chest. I close my eyes and keep jumping.

I fall out of the room, exhausted, dripping in sweat. My vest is soaked, and my leggings are stuck to my body. I don't know how long I was in there.

I walk outside and gasp in the fresh air. A skinny girl in surf leggings and a threadbare jumper waits at the bottom of some steps for people to come down in single file. She's carrying a tray of plastic cups, and a bottle of cider is shoved under her chin.

"Do you want me to carry that?" I ask her.

"Thanks, doll," she says, dropping the bottle into my hands.

I follow her up.

A girl sits on a chair playing a guitar. She's singing a song I recognise. The hip-hop thumps up through the floorboards. Most people are sitting in a circle on a large, orange rug in the middle of the deck, smoking joints and talking. They have crossed legs, or they lean on each other with their feet out in front of them.

A hot guy sits in the middle of the deck in a rocking chair. He's wearing half a wetsuit. His smooth, black chest is naked, but a blanket is draped around his shoulders. The pale soles of his bare feet face out, at the people sat around him, like a congregation. He strokes the small dog sitting on his lap, and occasionally swigs from a bottle of beer. He's not speaking, but everybody on the deck is half looking at him while they talk. He's more like the fire than the fire.

A blonde girl gets up from the circle and leaves, and the guy in the rocking chair actually beckons me over.

I sit in her spot and accept a plastic cup full of liquid from the girl with the tray. The guy smiles. "Hey," he says.

"Hi," I say.

"You new?" he asks.

I nod.

"You surf?" he says, gesturing towards the ocean with his beer.

"Not yet," I say, shaking my head. "I'm too scared, but I'd like to."

"It's good to be scared, sometimes. I'm Byron. This is President Bartlett." He gestures to the dog.

"How old are you?" I ask him, like I'm at nursery.

"I'm 28," he says, but he doesn't laugh at me. His accent is like a song.

"Where are you from?" I say.

"Jamaica. How 'bout you?"

"I live in London, usually," I say, "but I'm staying in Lattering with my aunt for the summer."

He nods, like he knows a lot of stuff.

"Well," he says, toasting me with his beer bottle, taking another swig, "it's nice to meet you…"

"Diana," I fill in the gap.

"Come around any time you want, there's always someone here. Maybe somebody can teach you."

"Teach me to surf?" I say.

"Yeah that. And when it's okay not to be scared."

I'm confused but he laughs, like everything is always going to be alright, and I just want to sit here and believe him.

Sunday is my day off. My room still goes full sparkle at dawn, of course.

The kitchen is empty, but the coffee pot is hot. A pack of small, thick, pre-made buttermilk pancakes have recently appeared on the counter, next to an unopened tub of chocolate spread.

Aunt Vita is on her bench, as Howard stalks her toes. I sit down next to her and she nods at the ocean. "Morning, darling," she says, squeezing my hand.

I sip my coffee. A lot of milk, but I'm getting used to it.

"Look at this beautiful morning," she says.

"Yeah, it's nice."

"Hey, how's Snoopy holding up?"

"Fine. Good. I like him." It's not even a lie.

"Are you cold?" She says, pulling off one half of her cardigan. "Put your arm in this." She reaches the cardigan around my back. Her right arm is still in the other side. "Better?" Aunt Vita says.

I nod and pick off a bit of the pancake. We sit on the bench, conjoined. I feel safe when I'm with her. I wish that was more often. "Can I have my phone back?" I say.

She nods. "You still have to talk to me though," she says.

"Of course," I say. But I don't say, "I only really need it for when psychopaths threaten me and I'm on my own in the shop," because that *might* make her freak out.

I cycle into town around lunchtime. The beach is full of tourists already. Gloria is waiting on our wall. "Finally," she says, jumping down. "Fancy a trip into enemy territory?"

"What does that even mean?" I say.

"Shall we go to Breakers? They do a wicked Oreo milkshake."

A queue of kids snakes out the door, and along the front of the shop window. They lean and take selfies, laughing and jumping on and off each other's backs. I spot Byron sitting on one of the benches, as Bartlett laps at the bowl of water that sits permanently outside for passing pets.

"Looooook at that dog!" Gloria says, running over, dropping to her knees, taking Bartlett's ears in her hands. "He's beautiful," she says to Byron, tapping her thighs for President Bartlett to jump up. He does, instantly and Byron lets go of his lead. "Hey," he says to me with a smile. "How you doing, Diana?"

"You guys know each other?" Gloria says, looking from me to Byron.

"We just met," Byron says.

She stands up, absent-mindedly stroking Bartlett's ears, giving Byron her full attention.

I feel like a spectator at a meeting of the beautiful people.

"What house you in?" She asks.

"Mandalay."

"How many this year?"

"Oh man, I don't count. Maybe five, maybe twenty, we come, we go."

The dog is rubbing his head against her leg, it's practically pornographic.

"I think you've found a fan," Byron says.

"I love him," she says, dropping to her knees again, but Bartlett loves Gloria more.

"Well, I'll see you around, ladies." Byron waves as he and President Bartlett amble towards the beach.

"He's new," Gloria says staring after him.

I can't tell what she's thinking. "You like him?" I say, trying not to feel jealous.

Gloria shakes her head. "Yeah, I mean, he's hot, but it's not that. Was he weird? I feel like he was weird." She shakes the thought out of her head. "Anyway, I'm pretty sure I'm not his type."

"You're everybody's type," I say.

"And you are crazy," she says, rolling her eyes. "Anyway, tonight, our first beach party Lady Diana. I'll bring the tunes, of course, and some drink. You bring something to eat that won't get sandy. Opposite the house with the ugly dolphins at 7ish, okay?"

Aunt Vita is standing outside Meat Market, talking on the phone, eyeing the window with disgust. She's agreed to buy me a steak, but she's not happy about it.

"That was your dad's lawyer, an old friend of mine. We can make another plea to the judge this week, but it's complicated. I'll talk you through it later."

She's pulling the pot of Vicks out of her bag, smearing two streaks beneath her nose. "Come on," she says, "let's get the abattoir over with."

16

I swipe a bead of sweat from my top lip as I trudge down the sand in flip-flops. The rhythm of the waves is the soundtrack to my life now.

Gloria sits, cross-legged, on a tartan picnic blanket, twiddling buttons on a portable CD player. She's wearing a bright red playsuit and battered, white converse, and her pinky-brown hair is plaited to one side. Her blue sunglasses have been pushed onto her head, and she's frowning in concentration.

"Retro," I say, pointing to the CD player with my foot.

She looks up and gives me a huge smile. "That's me! And it normally works, so…" She shrugs and presses a series of buttons until music comes on. She yanks up the volume, so we can hear it over the wind. "I thought we'd go classy," she says, crawling over to a Tesco carrier bag that's pinning down one corner of the blanket. She pulls out a bottle and two paper cups.

I drop, cross-legged, on to the blanket. I'm wearing jean shorts and a cropped grey vest-top that says 'FAME' on it, in yellow letters. It was on the top of a pile of clothes that mysteriously appeared by my bed this morning, with a Post-it that read 'wear me' in Aunt Vita's handwriting. There was a small, amber, beaded bracelet too, just like the one Aunt Vita has around her wrist that she uses for her meditation. I glance down at my wrist. The bracelet is pretty and it makes my arm look tanned. I'm not ready for chanting yet though. "Is that champagne?" I say.

"Kind of," Gloria says, popping the cork. Bubbles spurt out, and she takes a quick mouthful as a group of surfers walk back up the beach with wet hair and boards under their arms.

"Enjoy your evening, ladies," one of them says, in an American accent.

"We will," we say, in unison.

Two paper cups of Cava later, we are dancing on the rug. Eighty percent of Gloria's songs are about a broken heart. A slow song replaces a fast one.

"This is the best. Waltz with me." She throws her cup on the sand and grabs my arms. Diana Ross is Gloria's absolute favourite.

"Don't be weird," I say, trying to pull away.

"Don't *you* be weird! Dance with me to my favourite song, Diana. Oh my God, she's your namesake, I've only just realized. You *have* to dance now."

She lifts my arms up into an old-fashioned waltz position. We shuffle around the blanket as Gloria closes her eyes and sings. Within seconds her head is leaning on my shoulder, and I'm basically holding her up.

"Look, Diana, I know I'm not clever like you," she says, to the freckles on my shoulder, her deadweight arms hanging around my neck. "And I'm rubbish at exams, I mean, my mind literally goes blank, but I do know something. You are dealing with a LOT of shit right now, and you need to get it out. It's like when my Mum left. I genuinely thought if I asked her to stay until Nanna died, she would. But she went to Australia anyway. The other side of the fucking world, right? I know she doesn't get me, but I'm still her daughter. It made me feel horrible, and the only way to deal with it is to, you know, acknowledge it. So, I say it. Actually, I shout it."

She pulls away from me and faces the sea. She takes a massive breath. "I'm fucking sad my mum left me," she shouts into the wind. She fills her lungs again. "I'm sad I don't see her or my brother!" Gloria collapses on the rug and takes a swig of Cava.

"What about your real dad?" I ask.

We never talk about him, she always changes the subject.

She shrugs and drinks again. "I don't know him. He was around, when I was little. He left when I was four."

'Where did he go?'

"Dunno. Back to St Lucia maybe? Or London. He sent cards for a bit, but they stopped when Mum got married again, like that meant he didn't have to be my dad anymore."

"Don't you ever wonder about him?" I say.

"Yeah, of course. At least you've seen pictures of your mum. We don't even have any photos. My mum is short, and white, and jumps at fireworks, and look at me! But, you know, he wasn't interested." She shrugs.

I want to jump up and run off to St Lucia and find her Dad and tell him, "You should see her. She's everything."

"Do you shout about that too?" I say, picking at the straw in my drink.

"Yeah. I shout it all. I don't know if it works for everybody, but it might, you know? You have too much stuff in your head, Lady Diana. You need to get some of it out. Good or bad, just shout it! Declare it to the world!"

She laughs as I take a swig of Cava, and hiccup.

"I guess I do only say about ten percent of the things I feel."

"Well then, you need to be the change," she says, winking. "Talking of change, I totally love the glasses on you Diana, I do. I know it's part of your whole sexy librarian look."

"Um, no!" I say. Do I have a *look*?

"Um, yes, actually. But don't hide behind them, okay? You have amazing eyes. They are, like, twice the size of mine. And you could get those violet coloured contacts, so you look like that actress my nanna liked. That would look so good with your hair."

"Purple eyes?" I shake my head. "People would laugh."

"So?" she says.

"So, they'd be laughing *at* me."

"So?" She gestures to the sea. "Shout PEOPLE MIGHT LAUGH AT ME AND I DON'T CARE!"

I take a deep breath.

"No, stand up and shout it," she says.

I push myself up on to my feet and face the ocean. I feel like an idiot.

"Go on!" she says.

"PEOPLE MIGHT LAUGH AT ME," I shout, into the wind.

"And?" Gloria says, cross-legged on the blanket, swigging her Cava.

I take a deep breath. "PEOPLE MIGHT LAUGH AT ME AND I DON'T FUCKING CARE!" I collapse on the rug, laughing.

"How did it feel?"

"Okay actually." I do feel different. I feel like I've flipped a switch, and something has fallen out of me, down some emotional garbage chute. I want to cry, but I'm not sad. Of course, this could all just be the wine…

"You want to shout something else?" Gloria says.

"Okay!" I jump to my feet and face the sea again. I close my eyes and clear my mind.

"I'M NOT FUCKING PRETTY," I shout. I drop down on to the blanket, laughing, and look over at Gloria, but she looks so mad.

"Did you seriously just shout that?" she says, shaking her head.

"Yeah, I know. I don't want to talk about it, okay? That's just what I wanted to shout."

She glares at me.

"Why are you angry?" I ask.

"Diana Lind, I could beat the shit out of you. Of all the things there are to say! And yeah, so what if you aren't typical, skinny, blonde material? You are totally stunning."

I stare at my feet. When I look up thirty seconds later, she is sad.

"Diana, who are your friends?" She asks, pouring herself another drink then filling up my cup too.

"I told you, they are building walls in Cambodia."

"But didn't they ever tell you how amazing you are?"

"No! Why would they?"

"Why *wouldn't* they? That's what friends do. They tell each other the truth, and they make sure you know how important you are."

It's true that we've always talked about Betty's amazing hair, and Amy's amazing figure and how she always knows what to say. But, actually, we've never talked about me. We've laughed about my mountain of red, frizzy hair, and that my boobs suddenly got loads bigger one night, but nobody ever said anything *good* about me. We just laugh. It makes me feel weird. Why *didn't* we ever talk about me?

I turn on Gloria angrily. "Okay, I have a question. Where are the rest of *your* friends?"

She sighs. "Look, Diana, Lattering is…different. Kids don't stay here. There's nothing to do in the winter. I had a best friend, but she left. I should leave too, probably, but Nanna is too old. One day I will."

The music has stopped. I was happy, and now I'm sad.

Gloria contemplates her cup. She downs her drink suddenly, and claps. "What food did you bring?" she says.

I grab my bag and empty it out on the blanket, relieved by the diversion. "Pistachios and Haribo," I say proudly.

"Perfect," she says, ignoring the nuts, tearing open the sweets.

We lie on the blanket watching the clouds. The batteries in Gloria's CD player have died already so we listen to the waves, and the muffled conversations on the breeze from bonfire parties along the beach. The second bottle of Cava sits between us, with two straws sticking out of the top. We sit up and suck every few minutes.

"Look, I got a ring!" Gloria says, holding up her Haribo. She grabs my hand and pushes it on to my finger. "Now we are married," she says, lifting up my hand so I can admire the sugar diamond.

"Until death do us part," I say.

17

"Hey, do you want to see it?" Gloria says.

I thought she'd fallen asleep. "See what?" I say, pulling the straw towards me. I feel floaty.

"The school. Thetis."

I sit up too quickly, and my head spins. "Can we?" I ask.

"Um, yeah, if you can walk. I mean, we can't go inside or anything, but I know a secret way," she says, standing up, dusting sand from her bum.

"Let's go," I say, jumping to my feet.

The world is swimming. We walk along the beach for forever, away from town. When we finally reach the bottom of the cliffs, I notice a series of dark caves filling up with water. I hope, desperately, that Gloria isn't going to make us go into one of those. Caves, potholes, anything that only has one exit. I've seen enough horror films to know nature closes those doors.

"Don't worry," Gloria says, reading my mind. "They flood every night. I tried to hide from a storm in one once and nearly drowned, so, you know, don't do that. We are going this way."

She points to a set of tiny steps that I hadn't even noticed. They lead directly from the beach into the bushes. "I hope you've been doing your cardio, Lady Di."

There are one hundred and thirty-four steps, directly upwards. I know because I count them as we climb, to distract myself from the fires burning inside my thighs. The steps finish, abruptly, about half way up the cliff, but we keep going. It's rocky, but it's definitely a path. We scramble upwards.

Gloria yanks me up the tough bits. "Put your foot here," she says, expertly, as I navigate a ridge, "and also maybe don't look down."

Of course I do, as soon as she says it, and I want to throw up. We are so high. Waves smash against the rocks below, and there are no railings. This is definitely not safe. I've drunk more in the last two hours than I have in my entire life, and it's getting dark. The sun is setting behind the cliff at the other end of the bay. Something small and dark darts over the top of my head, and I stumble backwards, and scream.

Gloria reaches out a long arm and catches me. "Don't worry, it flattens out further up," she says, "and the bats don't bite."

We pass a huge tree with thick roots, like veins sprouting up from the earth. Stuck to it is a sign that reads 'Beware of Dogs'.

"Whatever," Gloria says, rolling her eyes, and keeps walking. "Here," she says suddenly, grabbing my hand, pulling me behind a bush.

Directly in front of us, without a wall or a fence to keep us out, is a large, wide courtyard the size of a hockey pitch. The paving is dark, and some squares are engraved with writing. Old statues of Greek gods patrol the edges. Beyond them is an immaculate lawn, framed by perfectly tended, white flower borders, that lead the way, like an aisle in a church, to a set of wide, grey steps at the back of the house. I'm practically *inside* Thetis. A fleet of dark Range Rovers are parked on a gravel driveway to our left, like army tanks. The metal gates behind them are as tall as trees. I spot The Mayan's monster car, parked in front of a huge, elaborate, dark wood front door. Next to it is a small gold sign, and I squint to read it. 'The Thetis School for Exceptional Young Men'. I can see an entry phone, and security cameras dotted everywhere like spiders creeping up the walls.

Half of the building is like an old castle, repaired ruins, but where the stone finishes glass takes over, merging seamlessly, bridging the gaps and the years.

"The stone bits are, like, 900 years old," Gloria says, reading my mind.

Bursts of white light glare suddenly from the low shrubs in the driveway, a metre apart, and the front of the house is flooded in light.

"Did we do that?" I ask nervously.

"No, they are solar powered. The sun did that," Gloria says.

When did it get so dark? My knee is shaking up and down.

Gloria puts her hand on it forcefully. "Calm down," she whispers. "It's just a school.'

"It's so beautiful," I say. What must it be like to be good enough to actually go here?

"Looks like a prison to me," Gloria says, disapprovingly.

Soft lights flick on in a series of rooms at the top of the house.

"Imagine if you went here, though?" I say. I can't help it, I think it's magnificent.

"Ummm, I'd feel like an inmate."

"I wouldn't," I say.

"So, you still in love with Jamie then?" She says, giving me a nudge.

"It doesn't matter. I saw him with Ginny and Audrey anyway."

"The rich bitches? I can't say I'm surprised. Thetis boys are all the same. They swim in the shallow waters."

"Yeah I get it," I say. "He is hot, though."

It feels good to admit it. He is the best looking boy I've ever met, and he talked to me. I guess they aren't the only shallow ones around here.

"But he was just born that way, Lady Di. It doesn't make you a better person."

I roll my eyes. Why does everyone keep giving me these speeches? Plus, this is from the most beautiful girl I've ever seen.

"It's true though! You shouldn't just like someone because they look good. It means nothing, Diana. Seriously."

167

"Oh God, you sound so much like Richard and Aunt Vita," I say.

"Hey, what about Vita, has she got someone?"

"Yeah, I think so."

"She should," Gloria says. "She's hot, for that old."

"I think she's, like, forty?" I say.

She nods. That's clearly what she meant.

"Well, she talks to some guy every night. He calls at the same time, and she has this little ritual. She pours herself a glass of wine, puts her feet up, waits for the phone to ring. It's kind of sweet. But I think she's avoiding him because of me."

A twig snaps twenty metres behind us, and I jump out of my skin.

"Calm down," Gloria says, laughing. "It's a rabbit."

Another twig snaps in front of us.

"A lot of rabbits," I say, but then I'm blinded by a beam of light shining directly in to my eyes.

Someone whistles in front of us, not far away, a long high note. In response, a pack of dogs begin barking like crazy.

"Shit," Gloria says. "Run!"

18

I'm running as fast as I can. I jump the roots of the old tree, but my foot catches. I fall forwards, landing on my hands and knees.

"Diana!" Gloria shouts, turning around.

"Keep going!" I say, scrambling to my feet.

The dogs are getting closer.

We sprint downhill, towards the path, as I try to stop my feet moving faster than my body, which would send me flying over the cliff into the waves below.

The outline of Gloria jumping tree stumps is in front of me, the pink in her hair like a torch in the moonlight.

Another whistle behind us drives the dogs crazy, and they howl like rabid monsters.

We scramble down the first steps of the path, clinging onto branches, but Gloria slips and tumbles forwards.

I scream.

She grabs a tree stump and stops herself. "Careful here," she says, breathing out with relief.

I glance over the edge of the cliff at the waves smashing against the rocks.

How did my mum walk out into *that*?

Two piercing whistles cut through the darkness, and the barking stops suddenly.

I look back up at the house.

A small figure stands above us, as three large dogs circle his legs. He whistles a low note and they all walk away.

19

I fall into freezing water. The cold stings my skin as I drag my legs towards the beach. My flip-flops keep getting stuck, so I surrender them to the ocean and continue barefoot. I collapse onto the sand, my legs weak, my heart banging in my chest. I definitely don't feel drunk anymore.

"What the hell?" I say.

"They take their privacy pretty seriously," Gloria says, holding her sides.

"Then why did we go up there? We could have been killed."

"Oh, don't be so dramatic, we're fine."

"Oh, okay! I actually lost my flip-flops but-"

"I'll buy you a new pair," she says, laughing. Her cheeks are flushed pink and her eyes are bright. I'm about to have a heart attack and she's exhilarated.

"Gloria, seriously. I think that was The Mayan, and someone told me he's...a killer."

She rolls her eyes. "Oh God, Diana, there are so many rumours about that place, but they're just stories. If you hang around here long enough, you'll hear them all, but it's boring people gossiping in a boring town."

"So, you don't think he's dangerous?"

"Look, I mean, he's a hired thug, sure, but he's never really done anything."

We reach the path and she takes her trainers off, shaking out the wet sand.

"Can I tell you something?" I ask.

"Yeah, of course. You want my trainers?" She offers them, but I shake my head and she leans on me as she pulls them back on.

"He came into the shop, The Mayan, the other day, and he said…"

"He said what?" she says, standing up straight. When Gloria gives you her full attention it's like standing naked under floodlights.

"He said he'd missed me, and he used my name, and kept calling me darling and stuff."

"And then?" she says.

"And then he lit a match against his cheek and left."

"Why did he light a match?"

"I don't know."

"Did he say anything else?"

"He said, 'It didn't really hurt.'"

"What didn't?"

"I don't know, lighting the match, I guess? But if I tell Aunt Vita she'll freak out, and I'm scared she'll lock me in the house, or make us leave town."

She nods and stares into the distance. "Well, look," she says finally, "*anybody* could have told him your name, so don't worry about that. This isn't London, everyone knows everyone. So maybe he just wants your arse? He is a seriously creepy old dude."

That hadn't occurred to me. When he blew me the kiss, it didn't feel romantic. It felt like a threat. "It was kind of more sinister than that."

"Well that's pretty fucking sinister. You're sixteen, he's, like, fifty?"

"I don't know…" I shudder. He's in my head. But I don't think she's right. It wasn't sex.

"Seriously, Diana," she says, grabbing my hand, "he's a puffed-up taxi driver. He's not going to hurt you. He's got his dogs, and his alarms, and his silly, scary nickname, but that's it. He's got a ponytail for fuck's sake."

"I know," I say, biting my lip.

"Look, if he comes in again, tell me, but he won't, I promise."

I glance back at the cliffs as we walk away. The shadows are moving, like someone following us in the dark.

BEFORE

He smells it first, the familiar stink of impending death. He looks up. A wisp of smoke, snaking away from the alley. He drops his newspaper and opens the car door. His boots crunch softly on the path.

He stops in front of the kitchen window. Smoke is rushing out through the rotten frame. No sign of movement upstairs. He scoops up a handful of gravel and tosses it gently at the window. Pressing himself against the wall, he listens. Nothing.

Their kitchen is a death trap. Old appliances, exposed wires everywhere. One morning Juan discovered their toaster smoking in the corner. He isn't surprised something has finally caught fire. He's just thankful it's a Tuesday. He always watches on a Tuesday.

A fire won't survive on its own. It needs accomplices; oxygen and fuel like paper, or rubbish, or curtains. It needs to burn SOMETHING. It might start nervously but, if it finds what it needs, it becomes psychotic. It runs screaming at the curtains, and the ceiling, and the sofa, exploding televisions, smashing glass.

He checks his watch. It's been thirty seconds. There are no sirens, yet, but the orange light dancing behind the window is growing...

He ties the sleeves of his jacket tightly behind his head. His eyes peer over the denim. Smoke will get you first.

He unlocks the back door quietly and locks it again from the inside.

The plastic worktop is bubbling. The flames have reached the walls. The old curtains are disintegrating to ash. The hallway door is open. The flames follow him into the hall. The fire breathes angrily behind him as smoke creeps up the stairs.

He checks her first. She is still asleep, breathing heavily, clutching her bear. The flames are turning the brown stairs red. The smoke is getting thicker.

He crosses the hall as the glass in the kitchen door smashes downstairs. Tom is snoring loudly, passed out, face down on his bed, drunk, fully clothed. A brick through the window wouldn't wake him.

He hears the first wail of the sirens.

Crossing the hallway to the bathroom, he pulls a large towel from the rail and turns on the tap.

She stirs as he presses the handkerchief over her mouth. He waits for the familiar relaxation of her head against the pillow. He lifts her little body easily, placing her down on the soaking wet towel in the middle of the floor, swaddling her like a newborn. The smoke is a blanket now, but fire moves sideways, there is still a little time.

He carries her in his arms down the stairs, as the flames lick his boots. The metal of the door handle burns his fingers.

He lays her gently away from the windows and checks his watch, listening for the sirens. He walks back inside.

The stink is everywhere now. The walls are on fire. He doesn't have time for another towel, but he submerges one anyway.

He grabs the body roughly from the bed and throws him over his shoulder. The stairs are ablaze. The sirens are close, screaming through the lash and crack of the flames. He reaches the bottom step and stumbles as the carpet gives way. He falls forwards, lurching sideways to protect the body. The painful lick at his neck tells him his jacket is on fire. The doorway before him rages with flames.

He drops the second body on the gravel, whipping away the towel that covers him. Walking quickly to his car, he tears off the burning jacket at his throat, and replaces it with the towel. He sinks into the seat of his car as two fire engines screech around the corner.

Fire keeps its secrets. Nothing will look extraordinary. They won't be looking for a hero. He'd locked the kitchen door behind him. The front door was still open, and the position of the bodies would demonstrate that Tom Lind had carried his young daughter down the stairs himself, and then collapsed. There was only one wet towel. They'd call Tom a hero, not a drunk passed out while his daughter was about to be burned alive. They'll call it a miracle. They will never know who saved them.

He watches them wake.

They sit on the wall, hugging each other tightly as blankets are draped around their shoulders. Firemen swarm in through the front door. The cannon of water explodes to soak what's left of the roof, and the memories of Lana that hide inside.

PART VI

1

I walk barefoot along the sea's edge, shoes in hand, until the flashing lights of the fair come into view.

The Thetis boys move around in a pack. There are at least twenty of them, and they all look different but the same. Josh seems to be the oldest, and the youngest must be about eight. They laugh, too loudly, and muck about, pushing and taunting each other like brothers do, and everyone just gets out of their way. They throw balls at coconuts, cheering each other on, howling at the throws that completely miss. They shoot plastic guns at targets, angling their pistols to the side like in films. Every time they win something, they hand the giant stuffed toy to a passing kid. "Public Relations," my dad would call it.

Gloria is standing in front of an old fashioned merry-go-round, wearing a pair of Minnie Mouse sunglasses, holding a giant stick of baby-pink candy floss. She looks like she's in a music video. Her white jeans are so high they reach her rib cage. A strip of bare brown skin underlines a gold sports bra, and her denim shirt billows open, three sizes too big. Her hair is straight tonight, dark brown, pulled over one shoulder into a ponytail.

She links arms with me and offers me her candy floss. It feels like a cloud of additives disintegrating on my tongue. Reaching into her pocket, she pulls out a bright red lipstick and stops walking. "Pout," she says, and smears it on my lips. "Now, open wide," she says, contorting her face for me to copy.

I want to see a mirror, but also, I don't. "Thetis are here," I say, as she produces a tissue and pushes it between my lips.

"Blot. Yep, I saw them," she says. "They look like a fascist boy band."

We join the queue for the bumper cars, tokens in hand.

"Separate or together?" I shout over the music.

"Separate, otherwise you'll just sit there!" she shouts, winking at me as the buzzer goes.

We stampede towards empty cars, knocking the previous drivers out of the way. I pick a green one. Green is a non-offensive colour. If you pick a red one you are asking to be hit. The buzzer goes again, and I tap the pedal softly, turning the wheel to inch out, but I end up even further in the corner.

"Mine's broken!" I shout, as Gloria thumps into me from the side, screaming with joy.

"Switch!" she says, jumping out.

"Oh fuuuuck!" I shout, leaping out of my car and into hers, terrified as the cars speed around us.

Gloria picked a red car, of course. I put it into reverse and it backs away, as Gloria magically turns the green car around and shoots off. I edge around the sides, like a toddler on ice-skates. Gloria gets rammed by a ten year old boy in a police car, and she screams with delight. Has anybody ever got this much joy from dodgems?

I'm still smiling at her when I'm flung to the side by a massive impact. "What the fuck?" I say, turning to face the driver.

Jamie Beltrome smiles at me from behind the wheel of a fire truck. His bare knees poke out from red shorts on either side of the wheel. "I'm coming for you, Diana," he says, speeding off.

I spot Gloria and drive towards her. She sees me and picks up speed, screaming, aiming for a head-on collision.

I shake my head, shouting, "No! I have to tell you something..." I get rammed from the side before she can hit me, and my glasses fly off. "Not again!" I shout, grabbing for them in the bottom of the car, turning to face my attacker.

Jamie puts his car into reverse, smiling wickedly.

"Go that way," Gloria shouts, pointing to the far corner, as she speeds off in the opposite direction.

Jamie's firetruck circles the edges, picking up speed, before turning and heading directly for me again. This is abuse.

I shake my head at him, mouthing 'no', trying to move out of the way, bracing myself for another smash.

Gloria ploughs into the side of Jamie's firetruck at full speed, just before he hits me, shunting him so hard he nearly falls out of his car.

The buzzer goes, and everybody jumps out.

"Come on!" Gloria says, grabbing me.

I look around, but he's disappeared.

"Okay, that was weird," she says, studying me evenly.

"I know, I'm going to have bruises." There are red marks already where the steering wheel dug into my flesh every time I got hit.

"So, Jamie Beltrome loves you back," she says.

I don't want to smile, but I do.

"God help us," Gloria says, shaking her head.

W e sit patiently on a waltzer, singing along, waiting for it to
start.

One of the fair dudes jumps on the back of our carriage, and
winks at Gloria. "Alright gorgeous, you wanna go faster?"

"No," she says, rolling her eyes.

He spins us around anyway and we are suddenly face to face
with Audrey and Virginia, sandwiched between Josh and Jamie.
The girls look like show ponies, their long, sleek hair draped
perfectly over their shoulders, their tiny waists visible beneath their
cropped tops.

"Yuk," Gloria says, loudly.

Audrey flips her the finger.

"Let's go on something else," I say, just as the buzzer goes.

"Too late," Gloria says. "Close your eyes instead!"

Every time I open them Jamie Beltrome is looking at me. He is
squished up against Audrey, but he's staring at me. She shrieks as
they spin, her silky hair flying out behind her, draping his face in
golden strands, her slim hand clutching his knee in delighted fear.
But he's looking at me.

~

"I need to wee," Gloria says, dancing on the spot behind the ride.

"I'll come with you," I say, but then I see the portable toilets, like a row of drunks in the corner. They look infested. I haven't gagged this badly for ages.

"So, you do that," she points to a ride called The Cyclone where people are literally stuck to the side of a circle as it spins, at speed. Their cheeks are pinned back against their ears by the sheer, awful force.

"Okay, if you want me to actually die," I say.

"Okay, grandma, do that then!" She points at an old fashioned Helter Skelter tucked away in the corner. Parents are holding the hands of little kids climbing the steps.

"I'll meet you at the bottom, I'm busting," she says, sprinting off.

It's windy at the top. I can see all of Lattering, and out to sea. Thetis is in the distance, on the top of its cliff, shrouded in darkness. There are a couple of parents in front of me in the queue, and little kids who are *so* excited they keep clenching their tiny fists and grinning madly. I don't even know why I'm up here, I could have just waited at the bottom. It's *literally* a big slide.

"Diana, how are you?" he says, and I turn around. Jamie Beltrome is standing behind me. His face is so perfect it makes me want to laugh.

I dig my nail into my leg, hard, and it works. I stop smiling. "Did you follow me up here?" I raise one eyebrow.

"Of course. Aren't you talking to me?"

"What, so you can laugh at me with your brother and your girlfriend? No thanks."

His smile fades, and he looks genuinely hurt. Whatever dude, it's all just fake.

"I haven't laughed at you, Diana," he says, and I almost believe him.

"Well, if you didn't actually laugh you sat there while they did, which is just as bad. Worse even."

He looks out to sea. Seriously, spare me the lost boy routine!

"Is Audrey your girlfriend?" I say.

"Absolutely not! You have to believe me, Diana."

"Why are you always hanging out with them then?"

"For Josh. I swear. I'm just his wing man."

"They go to my school."

"Yeah, they said. I'm sorry. They aren't very nice to other girls."

"Don't feel sorry for me. I can take care of myself." A lie.

"Well, you're a lot stronger than me," he says, daring to squeeze my wrist. It goes so hot under his fingers that I have to check the skin isn't burnt.

"You should stand up for people," I say, folding my arms.

"I know, but it's complicated. If Josh thinks for one second that I like you, he won't leave you alone. He'll bug me, and he'll bug you. Honestly, it's just so much easier if he doesn't suspect."

"Doesn't suspect what?" I say. My heart is beating faster than it did on the waltzers.

"Come on, love!" A young, tall, spotty guy in dungarees hands me a doormat, and points to a space at the top of the slide. "You're holding up the queue."

"I'm not your love," I say. Spotty guy just rolls his eyes.

"Is that it?" I ask. "I don't get strapped into anything, there aren't any safety barriers?"

"Nope," spotty guy says. "Are you doing it or not?"

I peek over the side. It's really high, just to be sitting on a mat. "Has anybody ever fallen out of the side?" I say.

"No, and there's a queue waiting, of children," he says.

I glance behind me. They are literally three year olds. I drop the mat down.

Spotty guy puts his foot on the back of it as I sit, but it slips forward an inch and I scream. "You want a push, Malala?" he says.

'No,' I say. But I just sit there.

"Come on, carrot, there's a queue," he says again, but I can't move.

Jamie suddenly drops on to my mat, pressing himself in behind me, his legs on either side of mine. "You can protect me," he says.

3

His arms are wrapped tightly around my waist as we slide. I feel his breath in my hair, his chin pressed on to my shoulder.

"This can't be safe!" I scream, and he laughs loudly. We tumble out at the bottom, landing with a thud on a gym mat, and I jump up. My hair feels huge and my cheeks are flushed from the wind.

Jamie stands up and grabs my hand, pulling me behind a doughnut van. "Meet me somewhere," he says. His eyes are brighter than before, and his pupils are massive. That's a classic tell but I don't trust him now.

"Where?" I shake my head.

"At the end of the beach. There's a house called Brizo. They are renovating it, but they always leave the back open and you can just climb in under the plastic."

"When?" I ask.

"Jam!" The awful but familiar voice of Josh shouts, from around the corner.

"I'll come to the café, tomorrow, we can sort it out then."

"You'll come to Seagulls? What if someone sees you?" I say.

"They won't," he says.

I look down. He is holding my hands.

"Jam!" Josh shouts. He can only be a few feet away, on the other side of the van.

I look into Jamie's eyes. He leans forwards, and glances down at my mouth. I actually think he is going to kiss me.

"I've got to go," he says, dropping my hands, running off.

"Where did you go?" Gloria asks, her lipstick reapplied, her hair plaited.

"Oh, there was a queue at the top, and then I freaked out," I say, as casually as I can.

"Why are you smiling like that?" she says, poking me in the ribs.

"It was fun, you should try it."

"It's literally a slide," she says, rolling her eyes.

"Yeah, but it's… high."

I open my purse an hour later, and the only coins left are silver. Night has gradually replaced day. The flashing lights seem faster, and the music is louder.

"I don't want to leave yet," Gloria says, checking her watch. "Hey, let's go in there!" She points at the façade of a house, tucked between the fishing and shooting games. The sign reads 'Dracula's Tomb: 50p' next to a shop dummy in a black cloak, with fangs. A plastic flying bat has been stapled to his arm. It looks so shit.

I can't see my hand in front of my face.

Gloria holds tightly to my arm as we edge down a thin corridor.

Every few metres is a new scene, the size of a small bedroom, enclosed behind a rope. Wax models shunt forwards and backwards on tracks, their arms moving up and down, their heads turning back and forth. Manic laughter plays from the walls every thirty seconds. There's Sweeney Todd, predictably, slicing away at some unsuspecting fat man's throat with a razor. There's Dracula, again, his fangs about to sink into some pale girl's neck.

Every time the canned laughter plays, Gloria jumps.

"Calm down, it's the same laughter every time," I say.

"It's freaking me out," she says, clutching my hand.

"But it's not even remotely scary."

"It's the wax. I don't like the wax. They don't look alive."

"They literally aren't alive, Gloria."

"How are you scared of everything else, but not this, which is genuinely terrifying?"

"Because it's so silly," I say, gesturing towards the Dracula scene in front of us, as it clunks back and forth.

We turn another corner, as Gloria hides behind me. Frankenstein's monster sits up on his table, then down, then up, then down. The laughter track plays, and Gloria jumps. It's comical.

"Damn it, I need to pee again," Gloria says, crossing her legs. "Let's go, I don't like it. Come with?" she says.

"You go, I'll see you outside," I say. "I want to see who else they have in here!"

"Alright, geek, I'll meet you in five minutes, but be careful!"

I laugh as she runs off. I follow the sign along the corridor. Marie Antoinette is having her head chopped off.

"I mean, come on! Revolutionary France, really?" I say.

I turn the next corner. There are four trees, but I can't see a figure.

"Brilliant," I say. "Couldn't even be bothered to put anyone in this one?"

I focus on the dark spaces between the branches. Something is hanging in between them. I squint, really hard. Is it...a noose? The laughter track stops, and I hear whistling. It's too dark. Is something going to appear out of the shadows? It's like a slow tune, but it's not the wind through the branches, which would make sense. It's just a series of low notes. I look around, at the ceiling, and the walls. I don't understand why the noose is swinging. Then I hear my name, softly, from the dark spaces between the trees.

"Diana...Diana..."

4

"Diana...Diana..."

This is all Gloria's fault, freaking me out and then running off.

I'm imagining things.

I walk quickly around the next corner. The space behind the next rope is completely empty, other than a lone figure at the back in a black cloak, wearing a bird mask. It's grotesque. The beak is three times too long and sticks out like a knife. The eyes are glassy and red. The laughter track doesn't play.

I wait for the figure to move, to clunk its arms upwards like a bird's wings, but nothing happens. He is completely still, his hands at his sides, and there is nothing behind or around him.

My hands are sweating, and I wipe them on my shorts. Something is poking out of the bottom of his cloak. I see the rounded tips of black trainers. I look up.

The head cocks slowly to one side, its long beak shining under a low spotlight. Its arm moves upwards, out in front, one finger extended, pointing directly at me.

"This isn't funny," I say.

I can hear my own breathing, fast and heavy. The emergency

exit sign is lit up in blue at the end of the corridor. I take one tentative step forwards.

The figure doesn't move, its finger still pointing ahead.

I take another step, and his arm drops as he sprints towards me.

5

I fly out of the exit, tears streaming down my face, straight into a young couple holding a giant teddy bear.

"Are you okay?" the woman asks, alarmed. "Neil, look at her, she's white as a ghost."

My hands are shaking, and I clutch on to her, sobbing, burying my head in her T-shirt.

"What is it, what's wrong?" she says, hugging me.

"It's behind me, a birdman, behind me."

"Love, there's nothing there," her husband says.

I raise my head slowly and look back at the exit to the house. He's right.

"Scary, is it?" the guy says, chuckling. "Maybe we should go in, Nat?"

She tuts at him. "Are you going to be okay?" she says, holding my hands.

"Yes, sorry, sorry," I say, walking away.

I find Gloria at the front of Dracula's Tomb, dancing on the spot to the music that's everywhere.

"What happened?" she says, grabbing my arms, feeling my forehead with her hand.

"Where did you go?" I say, looking back up at the house. Other people are going in and coming out. They all look fine, unimpressed even. It's just a silly funfair attraction.

"I went to the toilet, I told you. What happened to you?"

"Somebody chased me, I think."

"What? Okay, we're going back in!" she says, striding towards the entrance.

"No!" I grab her arm. Did I just imagine this?

"I think...I think it was just part of the house or something, and it just totally freaked me out because I was on my own. It just got loads scarier after you left!" I laugh, and wipe my eyes, relieved. "Come on, let's get some chips or something," I say, and drag her away.

"I told you it was scary, Diana," she lectures me, as we link arms. "Was it the wax? I bet it was the wax."

"Hey, what's going on over there?" I say.

The Thetis boys, and a cluster of locals, are standing in a circle, about fifty metres from the edge of the fair.

Gloria starts to walk faster, towards the group.

"Is there someone in the middle?" I say, squinting.

"It's Richard," she says, starting to run.

6

I see Virginia's hair first, long and dark against her little, white top. She is standing at the back of the group in denim cut-offs. The rest of them are mostly local lads interspersed with Thetis boys.

Gloria pushes through the outliers to the centre, where Josh is standing, swaying and sneering at Richard, whose cheek is bleeding.

Ralph is next to him, like a tiny, angry, guard dog.

"Give it back!" Ralph shouts.

Josh ignores him, and waves Richard's metal detector clumsily over the grass, banging the head against the earth on purpose. He staggers. He's drunk. "Oooh, I think I've found something, I think I've found something," he slurs in a high voice, which is bullshit. Richard doesn't sound like that.

"What's going on?" Gloria says, walking into the middle of the circle, standing directly in front of Josh.

Somebody wolf-whistles.

"Fuck off," she says to the crowd. "What's going on?" she demands again.

I edge around the circle, so I'm standing behind her. I can't see Jamie anywhere. Josh turns, muttering "Oh shit" under his breath, and stumbles a few feet away.

Audrey pushes past me in to the centre. "Where else has that mouth been this evening?" Audrey says to Gloria.

A couple of the crowd giggle.

Gloria grabs Josh's arm, spinning him around to look at her. "Don't be a dick, give it back to him," she says, pointing to Richard. "And sober up. I thought you were supposed to be a pillar of the community?"

"Careful Josh, you might catch something from skin to skin contact," Audrey says, and I step into the inner circle.

"Why are you such a massive bitch?" I say to Audrey.

Someone in the crowd says, "Catfight."

"Fuck off," I say to them, and look back at Audrey. "Seriously, what is your deal? Why do you behave like this?"

"Oh, go away, Pound Shop, we were just searching for treasure with our good friend Richard."

"It's gone too far," Gloria says to Josh.

"Oh, fuck this," he slurs, opening his hand, letting the metal detector drop to the ground.

Jamie appears, out of breath and sweating. "The Mayan says let's go," he whispers, pulling Josh away, whose shoulders slump as he's led away by his brother.

The rest of the Thetis boys immediately follow.

Audrey looks disappointed, and walks back towards the rides, as Virginia silently joins her.

"Is it alright?" Gloria says to Richard, who twiddles with the buttons, inspecting the base.

He nods. "I think so. Thanks, Gloria." Richard meets my eye and I smile, but he shakes his head. He hates himself.

When we reach the road, Gloria checks her watch. "I have to go," she says.

"Where?"

"I'm meeting someone."

"Who?" I ask. The moon is entirely obscured by a blanket of evil looking clouds.

Gloria ignores my question. "Are you going to be okay getting home on your own, Lady Di?"

"Yeah, of course," I say, but she isn't listening.

"Hey," she calls.

I turn and see Richard, thirty feet behind us.

"Richard!" she shouts, "Walk Diana home."

7

"You'll get your exam results soon," Richard says, kicking stones from the path. "Where will you go?" His board bangs gently against his leg with each step.

"Durham, maybe. It's where my mum and dad went, where they met. But it's still two years away."

"I was looking at Durham, too," Richard says.

"To do what?"

"Computer Science and Maths."

"What do you have to get?"

"A*, A, A."

I nod, like that's fine. It's so weird to be a kid, and be clever, and good at exams. My dad always tells me not to take it for granted, but I think it's the same as someone who's a fast runner. They can train to be quicker, or practice their starts in the rain, but they find that initial burst of speed easy, and it's the same with learning.

'Being intelligent is a gift, Diana,' my dad always says, but I'm not walking around like I won the lottery, and neither is Richard. It doesn't give us confidence. In fact, it's the opposite. Why *doesn't* it get you more friends? Richard deserves to be way more popular than Audrey or Josh.

"It would be cool to know someone already at Durham. You could show me around," I say.

He cleans his glasses with a handkerchief and dabs the cut on his cheek. He looks older without them.

It's so hot tonight, and we both have sweat on our top lips. I fan my face with my hand, and he pushes up his long sleeves absent-mindedly. A rumble of thunder makes me jump, and we both look up at the sky. How long have we got, before the storm hits?

"It's really cool, having you here this summer, Diana," he says, as we walk a little faster.

"Thanks," I say. Something in our chemistry has changed, since he said what he said about me being beautiful. We are different, but I don't know how it makes me feel, so I change the subject.

"You don't really think somebody from Thetis hurt Julie Peters, do you? I know Ralph does, but he's crazy."

We stop by the Shalimar sign. The lights are on in the kitchen. Aunt Vita is still up.

"I really hope she just moved away," he says sadly. As he puts his glasses back on, I see the fresh cuts on his arm. He pushes his sleeves down quickly.

"Hey, Richard, you can talk to me about anything that's worrying you, if you want? I get stressed out by exams, so, *so* much, and you're a year ahead of me. So, I'm just saying…you can talk to me, if you want to."

"Thanks," he says, but he's backing away.

"Thanks for getting me home safely, Richard."

"Any time," he says, dropping his board, skating off on his own in the dark.

8

"So, who even is this guy?" I say, as we wait for the toast to pop. I feel like a day old balloon. Everything about last night seems like it happened to somebody else, like I read it and then went to sleep, and now it's just words in somebody else's story.

Gloria, on the other hand, is radiant. "He's just a guy," she says, smiling, playing with my hair, pretending at shy.

"Do I know him?" I ask.

"Oh God, Diana, he's so bad for me. I don't even think I like him, when I'm not with him, but then when he kisses me...I swear, I can't help myself!"

What guy could be so special that Gloria loves him? Gloria, who is everything.

"Is he married?" I say, and she frowns.

"That's what you think of me - your best friend - after all we've been through?" she arches a perfect eyebrow.

I could count the weeks I've known her on my fingers, but also it feels like forever. "*Is* he married?" I say again.

"No, Diana, he isn't married, I promise. Hey," she whispers, as the bell above the door rings behind me, "I think this one's for you."

I turn around. Jamie Beltrome is standing in the doorway. The butterflies in my stomach explode.

"Hello, Sir, are you lost?" I say. I'm flirting?

Jamie runs his hand through his hair. I remember looking down and seeing that hand in mine last night. But something is wrong. His expression looks like someone shot his dog.

"I'm joking," I say, shaking my head, thinking: take it back! Start again!

"I'm so sorry about the incident with your friend last night, Diana, and the metal detector."

"Oh God, it's not your fault," I say, actually relieved. "It's your stupid brother."

He flinches. "Are you sure you're okay about it? I'd understand if you weren't." He looks so serious and sad. Is he actually for real?

"No, I'm fine! I mean, Richard was pretty upset, but…I'm okay."

I am officially a shit friend.

"Thank God," he says, and then leans closer to me, "because I can't stop thinking about you."

I inhale so sharply I make myself cough.

"It's the last house at the end of the beach, before the sign, called Brizo. Tomorrow night, at 9pm. Will you come?"

I nod as Gloria strides past us towards the window, looking alarmed.

"What's going on outside?" she says.

9

J osh circles Ralph and Richard in the middle of Beach Road.
Kids' faces are pressed against the window in Breakers,
tongues hanging out, mid ice-cream. A few have even come
outside to watch.

Byron jogs across the road towards us.

"We've got evidence," Ralph shouts, waving a piece of paper in
front of Josh, who grabs at it, but Ralph ducks out of his way. He's
little but he's quick. "Did you tell the police you were dating Julie
when she went missing?" Ralph shouts, jumping up and down like
an excitable kid.

Josh lurches forwards, but instead of grabbing for the letter he
throws a heavy punch at Ralph's shoulder, and Ralph hits the floor.
Josh pulls his leg back as if he's about to take a penalty in Ralph's
stomach.

"Hey," Byron shouts, walking calmly into the fray, standing
directly over Ralph who squirms and moans on the ground. Byron
faces Josh, and smiles. "Whatever is happening, this isn't the
answer, man."

"Get out of my way." Josh snarls. Saliva flies out of his mouth
like he's rabid.

"No can do I'm afraid, buddy," Byron says.

"Why don't you fuck off back to where you came from?" Josh says.

Gloria inhales sharply beside me.

Byron's smile disappears. "Here's some advice, man, from me to you," he says to Josh. "Your attitude needs some work."

"And who the fuck are you to tell me anything?" Josh presses his forehead against Byron's, his eyes wide and furious, but Byron's feet are cemented to the ground.

"Do something," I say desperately to Jamie.

He walks over to his brother and starts to whisper in his ear, like an unbroken horse.

Josh steps back, visibly calming down, but Ralph jumps to his feet and lands a pathetic punch into Josh's lower back with his child sized fist.

"Shit," Gloria and I say simultaneously.

Josh falls on Ralph like he's a punch bag at the gym, as Jamie and Byron desperately grab for his arms. They haul him off and Ralph rolls on the floor moaning. Josh shakes Jamie off, out of breath. He touches his nose and inspects his finger. Somehow, Ralph has managed to draw Thetis blood.

Suddenly the wind drops, like the seconds before a hurricane, and The Mayan steps into the circle. "Josh," is all he says, so quietly we barely hear it.

"I'm going!" Josh says, 'But you've got it coming, Paki!'

Everybody looks at Ralph, who is being held up by Richard. His eyes are red, and his chin wobbles.

Please don't cry, please don't cry, I think to myself.

He breaks free and sprints off towards the beach. Richard grabs their boards and follows.

"You have to tell Ralph to stop provoking him," Jamie pleads with me.

"Or you could tell Josh to stop being such an arsehole?" I say.

The Mayan coughs.

It is only when we turn to face him that I realise how close Jamie and I are standing. Our bodies are almost touching.

The Mayan looks us up and down, but his eyes fall accusingly

200

on Jamie, not me. He looks really angry. "Come," is all he says, and Jamie walks away.

Gloria, Byron and I are all that is left of the crowd, standing randomly in the middle of the road. The faces in Breakers have turned back to their ice-creams.

"Let me know if the little dude is okay?" Byron says, and walks away, shaking his head.

Gloria and I sit on the wall by the beach in silence.

"Hey, want to hang out later?" I say finally.

"Yeah, maybe," Gloria says quietly.

"You going to be okay?" I say.

Her eyes are red with tears.

"It's really shaken you up, hasn't it?"

"I'm okay," she says, as the town bell chimes. "I've got to go. I'll see you later."

Gloria strides off towards the beach, wiping her eyes.

I'm reading my book on my own in the square half an hour later, when a long shadow falls over me.

"Hello, Diana," he says.

He's wearing a grey suit and a blue tie, and a pair of sunglasses that look like they cost more than our car. He removes them as he smiles, revealing eyes that are so dark they are almost black. I feel like one of those frogs you throw into a pan of cold water and then turn up the heat, like I'm cooking from the inside. He holds out his hand to be shaken.

"I'm Hugo Beltrome. It's so nice to finally meet you."

"Yes?" is all I manage.

His eyebrows raise in surprise at his still outstretched hand. I have an awful feeling that it's infected, but I shake it anyway, and he squeezes, just a bit too hard, placing his other palm on the back of my wrist so I'm trapped.

"Well, you look just like somebody famous, don't you, with your fun glasses and your big autumn hair?" he says.

I don't reply.

He stares at me like I'm a statue, as if I can't see him doing it, and I was brought here purely to be appraised. I'm a curiosity. It's not creepy, it's not sexual, I'm just being completely judged.

"I'm Jamie's father," he says. "I thought I should introduce myself to his new friend."

I feel a fly, or a spider, or something tiny run across my cheek. I swipe at my face and my glasses fall off. I scramble for them on the floor.

"May I?" he asks, gesturing at the space next to me.

"It's not my bench," I say.

"No, actually, it's mine," he says smoothly, sitting down, straight-backed. He crosses his legs.

I don't look at him, but I can feel him staring. "Josh started a fight," I say. "Everyone is really shaken up by it. He's an animal."

He flicks a speck of dust from his trousers, but it may as well be me. "Josh will be dealt with. Tell me, what do you think of Lattering, Diana?"

"It's okay," I say, not that it's any of his business. I can feel my face heating up, my neck turning red.

He smiles and inspects his sunglasses. "Are you happy here, in our funny little town? Are you enjoying your summer?"

"It's okay," I say again.

"And how is it, living with your aunt?"

I don't reply this time. Why is he so interested?

"When I was your age I lived with my grandfather," he says, although I definitely didn't ask for his life story. "My parents were what we used to call hippies. My father died of a heroin overdose when I was seven, and my mother followed him shortly afterwards, when I was nine. I was sent to live in Lattering with my grandfather. It was a shock at first, because I was used to a very different experience, but then I grew to realise that I was meant to find this town. Sometimes you have to trust that life has a plan for you, Diana."

I don't know why he's telling me any of this - it's weird - so I shrug, as Byron walks past with Bartlett.

"Hey, Diana," Byron says, giving me a wink and a smile.

Hugo stands up, brushing himself off. "Well, it's been a

pleasure, Diana. I've heard so much about you. We'll see each other again soon, I'm sure.' He picks up my limp hand from the bench and kisses my knuckles. I swear he smells my skin.

~

A unt Vita is carrying four big boxes, stacked up in front of her face.

"Aunt Vita…" I begin. I'm going to tell her everything.

"Diana!" she says at the same time. She's actually smiling. Not stressed, or in a panic, or sad.

"Sorry, darling, I interrupted you. Did you want to say something?" she smiles again. She looks *genuinely* happy.

"No, I was just saying hello. It's nice to see you."

"Okay, I need to crack on!" She picks up her boxes and puts them straight back down again.

"Gosh, you look beautiful today, Diana, so much like…well, you just look beautiful. The seaside suits you."

She marches through the door in her paint spattered dungarees, singing to herself.

I don't want to tell her anything that will upset her. I don't want her to lock me in the house. I don't want her to make us leave.

10

We reach Mandalay, just as Ralph and Richard are flipping up their boards.

Gloria's carrier bag clinks cheerfully.

"Pretend champagne?" I say.

She nods and pulls me to one side. "Hey, is it weird that this Byron dude suggested we hang out at his place?" she says, looking up at the house.

"It's not his place, there are so many surfers here, nobody owns it, and I think he just thought we needed some fun, after everything..." I push the gate open, balancing two pizza boxes precariously, but she grabs my arm, and I nearly drop them both.

"But why does he care about a bunch of kids so much?" Gloria bites her lip, looking suspicious.

"What's wrong?" I say, irritated.

"Okay, don't take this the wrong way, but does it feel odd that he's so interested in you, though? I mean, I've never seen him in town before this summer, and then the open hangout invitation. He's ten years older than you. I know he's hot, but just think about this for one second...is Byron creepy?" she says, grimacing.

But I don't need to think about it. This is a good thing, and a fun thing, and I did it! I got us all invited to the cool surf house, and there is no agenda. This isn't lies, and subtext, and secrets, this is just fun.

"He's not creepy. Besides, I walked into his party, not the other way around."

She shrugs, staring up at Mandalay like she doesn't trust it, as the bottles clink in her bag.

We walk through the kitchen and the lounge, and out on to the deck that overlooks the front garden. We drop on to beanbags, popping open tubes of Pringles, doling out the re-heated takeaway pizza I found untouched in Aunt Vita's kitchen this morning, ripping into big bags of Maltesers. The waves are huge this evening, so the house is almost empty.

Byron saunters in twenty minutes later, zipping up his wetsuit. "Hey guys, I'm so glad you came, but I can't miss those waves tonight." He turns to Ralph, 'You okay, man?'

Ralph nods, with a mouthful of Maltesers. His swollen eye has gone down already. A Malteser drops out.

"Okay, you guys hang for as long as you want. I'll be back."

Bartlett follows him off through the house. We hear the front door slam shut, and the dog comes padding back moments later, settling down at Gloria's feet instead. She strokes him absent-mindedly, and bites on the neon pink straw sticking out of her bottle of Cava.

"See," I say to her.

She shrugs and sucks. "Hey Ralph," Gloria says, moving her hair out of her face.

Another Malteser falls out of his mouth.

"How do you know Josh was dating Julie?" she says.

Ralph sits up, swigging from a paper cup full of Cava like it's lemonade. He burps loudly, on purpose. "Well, I knew she'd been seeing a Thetis…" Ralph says.

"But *how*?" Gloria says.

"Ralph was stalking Julie," I say from my beanbag.

Ralph crosses his arms indignantly. "It wasn't stalking! I never even spoke to her."

"Okay, spying then, that feel better?" Richard says seriously.

"Et tu, Brutus?" Ralph says to Richard.

"I never saw you, not once," Gloria says.

"It was after you two had stopped speaking," Ralph says, and I look from him to Gloria.

"You knew Julie?" I say to Gloria.

"They were best friends," Ralph says.

"*Were* being the correct term," Gloria says, making a face at her Cava. "Does this taste weird to you, tonight?"

We look at our cups thoughtfully.

"We don't know what it's supposed to taste like," Ralph says, burping again.

"What happened?" I say to Gloria.

She rearranges herself on the beanbag. She's been fidgeting ever since she sat down. "She just got weird. She started doing loads of coke, and got really secretive, and then she stole my tip money."

"Fuck," I say, involuntarily.

"Yeah, fuck," Gloria says. "And she wouldn't even admit it, even though I saw her do it. I said I'd lend her money but she couldn't steal from me, obviously, and we didn't speak again." Gloria sips her drink as everybody goes quiet.

It's the first time I've ever felt embarrassed for her, and I don't like it. "Shall we play a game?" I say to break the silence.

"What kind of game?" she says.

"Do you know Pancake?" I say.

"Do we have to eat pancakes with no hands?" Ralph says, licking his lips.

"No, it's basically truth or dare," I say, "except in Pancake you can face it, flip it, or swallow it."

"What's swallow?" Gloria says, alarmed.

"*Facing it* must be answering the question, obviously," Ralph says.

"And *flipping it* is getting somebody else to answer it?" Richard asks.

"But you get to add something to the question," I say. "To make it tastier."

"Can you flip a flip?" Ralph says.

"No, you can only face it or swallow it. And you can only flip three times in the whole game, so flip wisely."

"So, *swallow it* must be a dare, right?" Richard says.

"Who needs instructions when you hang out with the mathletes?" Gloria says. "I'm going to need more drink." She pours the rest of the Cava into our paper cups and pops another bottle.

Ralph downs his, burps, and says, "Hit me again, sister."

Gloria rolls her eyes but fills it up, offering a top-up to Richard, who declines. His cup is still full. "So, who starts?" Gloria says.

"The youngest, normally," Ralph says.

"That's Diana," Richard says.

"Okay. Gloria," I turn to face her, "have you ever stolen anything?"

"Oh God, face it. Of course, like, a thousand lipsticks, when I was younger. And a few hearts as well." She winks at me.

Ralph coughs 'ego' really loudly.

"Shut up, Ralph," Gloria says. "Okay, my turn."

"Diana," she turns to face me, seriously, "have you ever kissed a girl, with tongues?"

I cough up the Cava in my mouth, and bubbles stream out of my nose. "Face it! Umm, no!" I say, like it's obvious.

"Okay, your go again, then," Gloria says, refilling her cup.

"Ready, Ralph?" I say, turning to face him.

He downs his drink and slams his cup on the deck. "I was born ready!" he says.

I look over at Richard, who is smiling at me, and we affectionately roll our eyes at Ralph.

"Have you ever kissed anyone, with tongues, ever?" I ask, and Ralph immediately blushes.

"Flip to Gloria," he says, "but I want to add, tell us the name of the last person you kissed, and everywhere on their body you kissed them!"

"Ooooh, that's good!" I say, sitting up.

Gloria surveys her audience, opens her mouth, but shakes her head. "Swallow it," she says evenly.

"Damn it!" I say, drinking my Cava.

"So, I get to name the dare, right? Right?" Ralph looks excitedly at me for confirmation.

"Sure." I nod my head.

"Okay," he says, lowering his voice. "Gloria. Kiss Richard, right now, with tongues."

"Oh, easy," Gloria says, putting her cup down.

I look over at Richard, sitting against the wall. His neck has gone bright red and the tomatoes in his cheeks have exploded. He's digging his nails into his arm, hard.

"Ralph, that's so stupid, just pick something else," I say.

"No, it's fine," Gloria says, oblivious to Richard's embarrassment. "Richard's a good looking guy, I'll kiss him."

She genuinely thinks she's being nice, but Richard just stares at the ground.

"Seriously, Gloria, I don't think he wants to," I say. This is getting strange.

"You better dare her to kiss me next!" Ralph shouts at Richard, clapping with glee.

Gloria is on all fours, moving towards Richard seductively like a cat. Ralph is hypnotised, mouth hanging open, but Richard won't even look up. Gloria crawls over his long legs, dropping down into his lap, her bent knees on either side of his chest, but Richard hasn't moved. She puts her hands on his cheeks and pulls his face up, to meet hers, closing her eyes. She opens her mouth a little, and her bright pink lips touch his gently. She presses her body into the kiss. I look away.

"Please don't," Richard says suddenly, turning his face, pushing her off.

Gloria falls clumsily, her fingers splayed into a slice of half-eaten pizza, her hair drenched in an upturned cup of Cava.

Richard jumps to his feet.

"What the hell?" she says, wiping her hand on her jeans.

"I didn't ask you to," Richard says.

"Alright, calm down, I didn't know I was repellant," she says angrily, wringing the Cava out of her hair.

"I didn't ask you to do it," Richard says again.

"Yeah I heard you, Richard. It's a fucking game. Just because I'm not Diana…"

"Uh oh, you gone done it now!" Ralph slurs, too loud. He's pretty drunk.

"Shut up," Richard says quietly.

"It's not my fault she likes Jamie and not you," Gloria says under her breath, but we all hear.

"Can you both shut up?" I say.

"You don't even know what they are capable of," Richard says, glaring at Gloria.

"It's all gossip and you know it!" She snaps back, "You're just jealous."

"Girls disappear, Gloria! Julie disappeared!" Richard is actually shouting, I've never seen him this angry.

Gloria stands up, wild eyed. "Julie was a druggie and an idiot, I know that better than anyone. She moved to London. She was always talking about it. She hated Lattering! Stop trying to frighten Diana into liking you instead, and stop making stuff up. She just doesn't fancy you, deal with it!"

Richard's face is the reddest it's ever been. His fingers press hard into his arm.

"Gloria, don't," I say, shaking my head.

She's furious, but when she looks at me it's like her anger disappears. "Shit," she says, guiltily. She turns to Richard. "I'm sorry, I didn't mean that. I just lost my cool, because I got showered in Cava…"

Richard just stands there, staring at the floor, shaking his head.

"Seriously, Richard, I'm really sorry. Friends?" Gloria holds out her hand to shake.

He looks up at me, but I don't know what to say.

"She said she's sorry," I say, weakly.

He grabs his board and walks out. We hear the door slam behind him.

"Well, I'm going home," Gloria says. "All of a sudden I feel pretty sick."

"Ralph, seriously, just walk home instead," I say. Ralph tries and fails to stand on his skateboard, falling on the floor, waving his arms and legs in the air. "Look, I'm a turtle!" He's giggling uncontrollably.

"Do you want me to call somebody to come and get you?" I say, but I'm swaying too. What idiot put me in charge?

"No, I'll be cool, loooook." He clambers on to his board and stands up uneasily, his arms out like he's surfing. He wobbles dangerously but rights himself at the last moment. At least he doesn't weigh anything; it won't hurt *that* much when he falls off. "Later gurl, sorry it got weird!" he shouts, pushing off, still giggling.

When I fail to jump up onto Snoopy for the third time, I realise I'm drunk too. It's got really dark, but I don't really care. I walk past the big houses where the rich families stay, pushing the heavy, old bike that now I kind of love. I see a couple of huge television screens flickering in the darkness inside, but it's so peaceful. All I can hear are the waves crashing onto the beach, and the footsteps on the path behind me…

11

I straighten my back and try to walk faster. I'm so drunk. Why am I so drunk, on my own, in the dark? I'm an IDIOT.

I'm walking faster, but so are the footsteps.

I look ahead and try to focus. I'm coming to the stretch of empty houses. There are four of them, detached, boarded up, in total darkness. Shalimar is still a football pitch away. Should I turn around? Should I scream? Dad always says shout 'fire' and people come running. Shout 'rape' and you're on your own. That's so fucked up.

I see an opening in between the houses ahead, one of the narrow grass alleys that leads to the road, and probably cars, and streetlights, and people. With the empty houses looming ahead of me, and the footsteps quickening behind me, I turn on to the path, ditch Snoopy, and start to run.

I'm dizzy, my feet falling heavily. I bounce off the fence, stumbling forwards, just managing to stay upright. I'm sprinting as fast as I can, but the ground keeps coming up to meet me, and drifting away again. I close my eyes for a second and feel sick. I open them as I hit the other side of the fence. I roll off and trip forwards, twisting my ankle, landing on one knee.

I cry out and scramble to my feet, bursting out on to the road.

It's wide and open, with no trees or obstructions. The pavements are clear and visible.

A car slows down as it passes me, then speeds up again. I can see the headlights of another car approaching from the opposite direction. I'm safe.

Gasping for breath, I turn around.

At the other end of the alley, standing on the beach path, is a man. He's looking down at Snoopy. He stands up and I see his face, but it's not a face. It's a bird mask.

The car ahead of me turns left. All the houses around me are dark. I look back down the alley.

The birdman is walking towards me quickly.

I start to cry. I turn and focus on the postbox in front of Shalimar, limping forwards.

I can hear myself sobbing. I'm too scared to look behind me. I'm focusing on the postbox. The pain in my ankle comes like stabs, hot slices in to my muscle. I can't support my weight. But the kitchen light is on. Aunt Vita is in. If I can just get there…

Someone grabs my arm, their fingers wrapping themselves tightly around my wrist.

I scream, trying to yank myself free.

"Diana," he says, "it's me!"

Richard lets go of my arm and steps back. "What's going on?" he says, alarmed.

"Richard?" I look behind him, but there is nobody there.

Richard is wearing jeans and a long, dark T-shirt. Not a bird mask.

"What the fuck are you doing?" I shout.

"I wanted to make sure you got home safely," he says, confused. "Why are you limping? Are you crying?"

"Were you wearing a mask?" I say, trying to catch my breath. The guy looked tall. Richard is tall.

"What are you talking about?" he says. He's carrying his board. The guy wasn't carrying a board, I think.

I shake my head. "Where did you come from?" I say.

"Down there," he says, pointing at the grass alley past the

empty houses. "I was waiting to make sure you were okay, but then I saw you run down that alley."

Richard wouldn't hurt me, would he? I'm so drunk. Was it even real?

"God, I'm so stupid!" I say, hitting my forehead with my hand. "What was I thinking?"

"It's okay, Diana, it doesn't matter." Richard is holding my hands, squeezing sober sense in to me. "I'll walk with you the rest of the way."

"I don't know what's going on with me, Richard," I say. "I keep imagining things, and drinking too much."

"Well, you've got a lot going on," he says, but I don't think that's enough of an excuse. Outside Shalimar, I look up at him. His eyes are red. I think he's been crying, too.

"Look, about what Gloria said, Richard..."

He shakes his head to make me stop, but I don't. "Just ignore her, you know what she's like. She was in a weird mood tonight anyway, and you pissed her off when you wouldn't kiss her back. I know you don't like me like that, it's fine." I smile. I stand still and close my eyes, and try not to sway, but I feel sick.

"But you already know, I do like you like that," he says quietly.

Richard presses his lips gently against mine. They are dry, and smooth.

I fall backwards into Aunt Vita's wall and my ankle screams with pain. I open my eyes, and he is staring at me bleakly.

"Oh, Richard, I'm so sorry," I say.

He drops his board and skates off.

"What's wrong?" Aunt Vita says, as soon as I walk in. I'm aware that I'm still drunk. Just keep it together, I think to myself. She's sitting at the kitchen table. Two plates of half eaten pasta are by the sink, beside two empty wine glasses. Her pink lipstick is smeared around the top of one of them, but there is none on her mouth.

"Nothing," I say, as brightly as I can. "It's just been a strange night. Can I talk to you about it tomorrow? I'm so tired, I want to go to bed."

I don't wait for an answer and head towards the stairs, concentrating on walking in a straight line, trying not to limp.

"Of course," she says to me. "But what happened? Nothing bad? You'd tell me if it did?"

I turn on the bottom step and nod my head. It's all I can manage.

I am going to tell Aunt Vita everything tomorrow. Everything. When I'm sober.

12

So, this is how terrible feels? It's like that time I had flu, but worse. I feel sick, constantly, and my head feels heavy, like somebody has pumped it full of water. But my eyes are dry, like they've been hoovered, and I can't keep them open for more than a few seconds at a time. And, no matter how much water I drink, the inside of my mouth won't stay wet. My cheeks keep sticking to my teeth, and my tongue feels like it's been dipped in sand. My throat feels like I've swallowed crushed glass.

Snoopy was at the end of the path, exactly where I ditched him, and I cycled nearly all the way to work with my eyes closed. I think I hallucinated. I've had nightmares about the man in the bird mask ever since the haunted house. It was just that, plus the booze, and the dark. It wasn't real. But I'm never drinking alcohol again.

I get to Seagulls on time, somehow, and Felix takes one look at me and laughs his loudest laugh, like Big Ben chiming in my head. My eyes practically vibrate with the noise. His shirt hurts my eyes.

"I know how that feels," he says, waddling off, still chuckling.

I rest my cheek against the cool plastic of the counter, as five fat fingers place two Nurofen and a glass of fizzy orange water in front of me.

"I'll just be in charge of Elvis and water today, okay?"

"Nope. Gloria's called in sick."

"Nooooooo, how can she do this to me?" I say, as the bell above the door rings. "And why is the bell louder?"

"Chin up, Diana, it's only an 'angover," Felix says.

❧

Richard is already at the charity shop when I get there, re-organising the shoes in the corner. He looks normal, but then he barely drank anything last night, of course. Sensible.

I've drunk so much water this morning I was actually starting to feel better, but when I see him I feel sick again.

"Hi," I say quietly.

He looks up, and his cheeks go full tomato. "Hi," he says, and walks straight through the curtain and out the back.

"What's going on with you two?" Aunt Vita says, looking up from the broken Barbie house she's trying to rebuild in the corner.

"Nothing," I say, sitting down behind the counter, pulling out my book. I've decided I'll talk to Aunt Vita tomorrow, when I know I'll get through the conversation without gagging, or breathing alcohol fumes all over her, or throwing up, or passing out.

"I'm going to the bank, and the chemist, and then I'll get snacks," she announces, striding out of the shop an hour later.

"Just a Coke, please," I say, trying for a smile.

"I don't know what's up with you today," she says, but I don't care.

As soon as she leaves, I curl up on the carpet behind the counter and close my eyes. I fall asleep immediately.

I wake up when I hear Richard cough. He's standing at the end of the counter.

"Look, Richard, about last night..." I say, grabbing on to the counter to haul myself up.

"I'm sorry," Richard says at the same time.

We look at each other, and we both smile.

Gloria walks in. "You two," she says, frowning, standing in the doorway, and I am *outraged.*

"Where the hell were you this morning, Gloria, when I had to work the whole damn shift on my own?"

"You have to come. Now," she says, walking straight back out.

13

Two police cars are parked at the end of Beach Road. They are silent, but their doors are wide open, blue lights flashing.

"They're on the beach," Gloria says, as we catch her up.

"Who are?" I say, but she doesn't answer.

We jog along the path, away from town. A cluster of policemen gather in the distance. I look up at Thetis as it sparkles on the edge of the cliff. I feel present, and sober, but sick.

A policewoman is standing in the middle of the path ahead of us, in front of a small crowd of locals. We slow to a walk, as she holds out her palm, blocking our way.

"No further please," she says.

A line of police tape flutters in the breeze, on the beach below the cliffs.

"What's happened?" Gloria asks, taking another tentative step forwards.

"Move back," the policewoman says.

"Look," Richard says, pointing.

An ambulance skids off Beach Road and onto the sand, towards the tape.

"What's going on?" I ask an old lady standing next to me.

"There's a body," she says. "At the bottom of the cliffs."

"Oh my God." I turn to Richard. "Julie Peters?" I say, horrified.

"No," the old lady says. "It's a boy. Indian. Terrible thing." She shakes her head, making the sign of the cross.

I look down. My hands are shaking. "Richard?" I say.

His skin is white, almost transparent. His blood has drained. "Where's Ralph?"

BEFORE

The temperature dropped suddenly at 3pm. Two feet of snow fell in four hours. It's beautiful, but not without its problems tonight. It may mean more bodies, but the footprints will help. He ran the park perimeter after dark, checking the exits. It's an enjoyable ritual, even with snow underfoot. He found one problem - a busted fixing at Sheen Gate - but he carries bike locks for a reason.

Now, he cradles a black coffee and watches them from the shadows in the corner of the room. Their faces are gargoyles in the candlelight, drunk and grotesque. One hundred Thetis employees, men and boys, collars stiff, ties bowed at their necks. His employer, Hugo Beltrome, sits at the end of the third table, surveying his kingdom. There are three new boys tonight, or Hunters as the ritual dictates they are called for the evening. Three sixteen-year-old Thetis sons from the schools in Geneva, Atlanta, Hong Kong. There will be no Lattering boys this year, and Juan is thankful. He understands the purpose of the Hunt, but he does not like it.

He checks his watch and walks quietly to the third table, whispering in his employer's ear, before slipping back into the shadows. Hugo stands and raises his glass. Quiet descends like a November mist, as Hugo clears his throat. "Gentlemen. If you'll follow me."

The race of life is won before the pistol is ever fired. It's all just luck, and the three boys in the van – the Foxes, for tonight- weren't born with *any. They are naked, drugged, beaten and bleeding, about to be torn apart. Juan checks the dogs, who are as hungry as they are angry, then leans against the van, lights a small cigarette, and whistles. Streams of his breath float away in the dark.*

In front of the lodge, Hugo speaks. "Good evening. A warm welcome to you all on this snowy London night, and thank you for coming. A very special thanks goes, of course, to my friends and colleagues who have flown in from across the globe to be here. This is a special year. It marks the tenth annual Thetis Hunt. Some of you have experienced our meeting before, I know, and will remember your own hunt. Some of you are here for the first time, meeting new brothers. Believe me my sons: you will never forget tonight."

Hugo turns to face the three sixteen-year-old Thetis boys, wild-eyed and frenzied on the coke Juan has been giving them all evening. "You enter these woods as boys. You will return as Thetis men, ready to rule. Tonight will prepare you for the rest of your lives, to place the success of the family above all else, to be ruthless, to be fearless, to know without doubt or question that you are leaders of men, that you are kings of the world. Tonight, you will learn that the rules of life do not apply to us. The family will always protect you. Thetis will always protect you. Life is the hunt. We are the hunters my friends, my sons. And the hunt begins... now."

The audience of men begin to bark.

The stench of piss hits him as he opens the van. Three luckless teenage boys – delivered last night by Lattering CID from the Chichester young offenders' remand centre - stare out from the shadows of the van. They are woozy from sedatives and blood loss, shaking with cold and fear. Two of them speak no English at all, as requested. The third is a problem.

"Run," the crowd screams. "Run. Run. Run. Run. Run."

Their bruised faces are terrified as they clutch at the small, sliced, knife wounds in their thighs.

He drops his cigarette and jumps up into the van. One boy inches forward from the back, his skinny, brown body falling out of the doors and on to icy dirt. The crowd cheers. He turns and limps quickly into the woods. Another boy follows him. But the last boy, the biggest, sits at the back of the van, staring out at the baying mob of black ties and testosterone.

"What the fuck is this, man?" the boy says, this English one. His voice is low. He is sixteen, but his size makes him look older. Juan specifically asks for the refugees. Ford has messed up bringing him, but it's too late now.

"It's life," Juan replies. "You have done something to bring to you this place. You have made a choice. Now you must run. Or I'll kill you myself."

But the boy doesn't move.

"Run!" Juan says, pulling out the knife from his boot.

The boy swears and stumbles out of the van, sprinting off into the trees. He notes their direction.

The mob stops baying. They look to their father. He nods.

"HUNT!" they scream at their three wild-eyed young brothers. "HUNT! HUNT! HUNT!"

The Thetis boys sprint and scramble into the woods, screaming for blood.

The crowd staggers back inside, drunk, swaying, patting each other on the back, remembering their first time.

Juan finds two of them quickly, as they beat the first boy out of the van unconscious. The young Hunters scream at the sky and run off, searching for another victim.

He checks for a pulse. The boy is still alive, just. Juan gently lifts and carries the body, placing him under a blanket in the back of the van, holding the handkerchief to his mouth for thirty seconds, for a maximum dose.

One of the Hunters emerges from the trees, dragging another boy to the van, and collapses. Juan carries the Thetis boy into the house first, to the doctor, and then throws the second unconscious boy in the van.

He hears shouting to the north, and sprints towards the noise.

The last Fox, the big one, is cornered. The two remaining Hunters face him in a clearing.

"You touch me, I'll fuck you both up, man. I'll fucking kill you," he says.

The Thetis boys look unsure. They edge forwards, but their confidence is gone, even with their coke, and their knives, and their unfair advantage.

Juan knows he will have to help. He whistles, and the dogs go crazy.

"FUCK YOU, MAN!" the boy shouts at him, running off. His only chance would be to make it to the perimeter, which feasibly he could do, if he was quick and knew exactly where he was going. But the park is vast and dark, and the dogs are hungry.

The two Thetis boys collapse, exhausted.

Juan has to carry them both back to the lodge. "Go and see Doctor Cole," he says to them, as he hears the first screams from the woods. The dogs have found their dinner. That will be a bloody mess, he thinks, reaching for his gloves. The device on his belt throbs.

"Wolf One, this is Wolf Two. Come in. Over."

"This is Wolf One. What is it please, Wolf Two? Over."

"We have a problem, at Sheen Gate. Over."

"What is it? Over."

"Somebody is trying to climb in. Over."

He checks his watch. It will take him twenty-five minutes to get there at a full sprint.

"No, wait. He's just fallen off the gate again. I think he's drunk. Shall I leave him there? Over."

"Wolf Two, yes, leave him there. If he climbs back up, knock him out, break his back, and call it in to someone friendly at Richmond CID. Over."

The screaming in the woods has stopped.

Juan whistles, long and high, and the dogs bark, leading the way. He drags what's left of the boy back and throws him under the blanket.

~

At 5am, he pulls the van to a halt in front of the cliffs.

As he tosses the bodies out to sea, he thinks again that he must find a new way to dispose of remains. A burial perhaps, or some kind of supervised dig, without threat or obstruction. They'll need a reason to make some really big holes. The ocean is getting too risky. It's started giving body parts back; last week he found a foot on the beach.

As he drives back through the gates at Thetis, Juan's mind refocuses on *the drunk climber at the gate. He had climbed again, and Ford had indeed broken his back, as instructed, and called it in to Richmond CID. A thought occurs to him then, and he smiles, even though it means trouble.*

"Was that you, Tom Lind?" he says, to the November dawn. "What have you found out?"

PART VII

1

The sky is purple. A low blanket of dark clouds has fallen over the beach.

A line of police officers trudges heavily through the sand, from family to family, towel to towel, apologising, asking folks to pack up for the day. As they lower their heads and recite their police lines, I see mothers' glance anxiously at the area below the cliff, and the cluster of detectives with their white gloves and dead expressions. The fathers don't wait for the police to finish talking. They jump up, urgently commencing the tug and roll of windbreakers, the shake and fold of beach blankets. The mothers pull their kids towards them, wrapping them in towels, getting their tiny, vital bodies close. The kids squirm to be set free, of course. They don't know how important they are.

I cover my ears against the noise of the sirens as the ambulance speeds back up the sand, easing over the curb before racing off, wailing, blue lights flashing. We are all thinking the same thing: he must still be alive. But how can he be alive? I look up at the cliff. You can't fall from that high, down, all the way down, onto wet sand that's as hard as concrete, and survive. It's physics and biology. It's all the science that I've ever learnt, and every fact I've ever known. Unless he didn't actually fall?

"Must have been drinking," says the old woman next to me. She sniffs and tuts. I want to scream.

"He never drinks," I say to her. "This was the first time."

Richard looks at me, and I can see the glassy fear in his eyes. "We don't know for certain. It might not be him," he says.

I nod in agreement, but we know.

"Terrible thing, drinking at that age. Anti-social. Where are his parents? My father would have used his belt on me for drinking that young." She knows I can hear her. She's prodding me with her old lady spite, trolling me in plain sight.

"I don't think parents should hit their children," I say.

She sniffs again and turns away, muttering, "It didn't do me any harm,"

"Yes, it did," I say loudly.

"Look," Gloria says.

A policewoman is pushing sticks into the ground, cordoning off another small area of sand. She pulls police tape from pole to pole.

"What is it?" Gloria asks, straining to see.

Richard has a vantage point, a full head and shoulders above us. He visibly stiffens, like a cardboard cutout. "It's his skateboard," he says.

"What hospital will they go to?" I say.

"St John's, in Chichester," Richard says. "We should go too, now,"

"Shouldn't we talk to the police first?"

"Why?" Gloria asks, her eyebrows knotted in confusion.

"To tell them about Josh threatening Ralph?" I say.

We are the only ones who will tell, who *can* tell. Ralph needs us.

Gloria's shoulders droop. She looks back at the crime scene, but she doesn't reply.

"Richard, shouldn't we go to the police?" I say.

He's scratching at his wrist, harder and harder, smearing blood up and down his arm like a finger painting.

But why am I asking their permission to do this? I have a voice. I can use it.

"Excuse me?" I say to the policewoman in front of us. She raises her eyebrows.

"I'd like to make a report, about that." I point down the beach.

"Go to the police station then," she says, flatly. Helpful.

"I'm going to the police station," I say, to her and my friends. "Come if you want."

We walk back to The Fish Stand in silence. I feel a drop of water hit my nose, but I don't look up. I know it's going to rain and I don't care. I *want* it to rain.

"I've got to check on my nan," Gloria says as we reach the road, but she hovers beside me as if she has something else to say.

"Is she ill?" I say, but she doesn't answer. She's just staring back at the beach.

"Is she ill, Gloria? What's going on?" I say.

"Nothing's going on," she says, shaking her head, but she grabs me, and hugs me so tight that I gasp for air. She lets go, and squeezes Richard's hand, too.

"See you later," she says, pulling out her phone and walking away.

2

The ride through town is eerie. The sound of the wind drowns everything else out. The rain is incessant and fine and soaks us. It only takes ten minutes to reach West Lattering police station. It's fancy but old, imposing but brown, with two hastily erected portacabins stuck to its sides, like a pair of cheap wings. Huge sycamore trees guard the entrance, shading concrete steps and a ramp so steep that wheelchairs won't get up it without a push, so what's the point? The modern sliding glass door looks out of place.

A kid in baggy jeans is sitting on the steps only just under cover, inspecting his bright white Nikes, smoking a cigarette to its very end.

I push wet hair from my eyes, and prop Snoopy against the railings, as Richard turns the corner, skating all the way up to the bottom step really fast, only flipping up his board at the last moment.

He takes his glasses off, wiping away the rain, and his eyes are red. We stand together at the bottom of the steps in silence, side by side, looking up. I don't know what we are going to say, but we are going to say *something*.

The sliding glass door opens above us. A distinguished man in a police uniform walks out, pulling on his hat and chuckling. His chest is covered in so many medals it looks like he's going to a fancy dress party. Emerging from the darkness behind him, patting him on the back and laughing too, is Hugo Beltrome. They stop at the top of the steps and shake hands like old friends.

"Do send my love to Jane," Hugo says.

"Of course," the Chief Constable says. "I'll let you know if anything comes up."

"Thank you, Edward, as always," Hugo Beltrome says.

The Chief Constable walks rigidly down the steps, pulling on his gloves, and passes us without a second glance.

Hugo Beltrome sees Richard and his smile disappears, his face twitching with anger, but he looks right through him, to me. He stops on the step above me and looks down.

"Diana. I hope you aren't wasting your summer on conspiracy theories and gossip, they are not a productive use of your time."

"I'm just here to…" I can't speak.

His eyes bore in to me, and I immediately doubt myself in the face of his confidence. How is he so sure of everything?

"I'll see you again soon, Diana," Hugo says, and walks past us to the car that has silently appeared behind us.

We stare after the shiny ghost monster as it pulls away.

"Should we still go in?" I ask eventually.

"What's the point?" Richard says, digging all of his left fingernails into his right palm.

"What then? We can't just do nothing?" I say.

Thunder rumbles above us, and bigger, fatter raindrops begin hammering our heads.

"We need to get to the hospital," he says, dropping his board. "And we need to find Vita."

3

We ride back to the shop to dump Snoopy, but there is no sign of Aunt Vita. I spot the familiar brown and pink mass of Gloria's hair poking over the wall in the square.

"I'll be one minute," I say to Richard.

Gloria is sitting on her own, staring at her phone bleakly. Dirty mascara smudges look like bruises, and a thick streak of black runs from her right eye to her hair, where more tears have been swiped away.

"Did you see your nan?" I ask.

"What did the police say?" Gloria says, ignoring my question.

"We didn't go in," Richard says, climbing over the wall, standing in front of Gloria, and offering her his hand.

She takes it and he pulls her up. I feel weird.

"Why didn't you go in?" she says, looking from me to Richard.

"Hugo Beltrome was there," I say. 'He knows the police chief, there was no point. How's your nan? Have you been crying?"

She sighs heavily. "You should have gone in. You should have told them what you know."

"Well, you could have come too and gone in with us," I say, spoiling for a fight.

"We're going to the hospital, and we need to find Vita," Richard says, shutting it down.

"What about the shop?" Gloria nods at the rack of rain soaked paperbacks behind us, flapping in the wind. We all stare blankly at them. Like a modern art exhibit on a school trip, we can't make sense of what we are seeing.

"I'll go to the hospital with Richard," Gloria says. "You stay and wait for your aunt."

They climb over the wall. It feels odd watching them leave together. Nobody says goodbye.

4

I scrawl KNOCK LOUDLY on a piece of paper and stick it in the window.

I lock the door and curl up on the floor behind the counter, covering myself in a huge puffer jacket that I know is clean. My teeth chatter as I peel off my rain-soaked top. I'm about to pull a Thetis-donated sweater over my head, my arms already in the sleeves, when I change my mind and grab a scratchy, old football top instead. I don't want them next to my skin. I close my eyes and try to clear my mind, but I can't stop thinking about Ralph...

Ralph wobbling off on his skateboard last night; I should have stopped him.

Ralph lying on the ground, waving his legs and arms in the air, so drunk that he was pretending to be a turtle; I should have stopped him.

Ralph hi-fiving me in Julie Peter's bedroom, and waving the letter in Josh's face, and standing up for Richard, and punching Josh in the back.

My lips start to tremble. I gasp my first sob. It feels like my head will explode if I don't cry. My head rolls back and hits the floor, and I cover my eyes with my arm as the tears come until I fall asleep.

I dream that Gloria, Richard and I are running down the steps of the cliff, taking it in turns to carry Gloria's grandmother. Barking dogs circle us, snapping and snarling. We look down at the beach and see Ralph standing with The Mayan. They both wave and smile. I raise my hand to wave and drop Gloria's grandmother off the side of the cliff.

I wake up with a jolt and find a Post-it stuck to my hand. It's from Aunt Vita.

'I've gone to the hospital to find out what's happening. You looked like you needed the sleep. The door is locked with a key, you'll have to unlock it.

Come straight home please. V x'

It's stopped raining but it's cold, and really windy. The paperbacks are ruined anyway so I leave them outside. Beach Road is freakishly quiet. There are no barefoot surfers in the middle of the street, and no families with screaming kids being tugged home, but I'm not ready to go back to Shalimar yet.

Police cars are still on the beach under the cliffs, the crime scene tape whipping about in the wind, the ocean creeping in. Soon, there will be no evidence left. I walk towards Seagulls, and the vast comfort of Felix, but as I get closer I cross the road and head for Breakers. I see them, sitting at their window table as usual. I knew I would. Three of them are laughing. Jamie is looking down at his phone seriously. He may as well be sitting at another table but, the point is, he isn't.

I shove my way through all the other kids until I'm standing in front of them. My glasses have steamed up and I rip them off. I can still make out the expressions on their faces, just. Virginia coughs nervously, but Audrey titters and smirks, incredulous at this fresh confidence.

Josh sneers but runs his hand through his hair.

Jamie puts down his phone, and shakes his head at me, once. Screw him.

My hair is wet on one side, and frizzy on the other. I've probably got mascara smeared under my eyes. I'm wearing a Bournemouth FC sweatshirt, and jeans so damp they are starting to smell. I don't fucking care.

"He could die," I say.

Virginia looks away, as Audrey sighs dramatically. "The fun police have arrived," she whispers under her hand to Josh.

"He could be dead, and you think it's funny!" I shout.

Everybody in Breakers stops talking. They all look at me, the crazy girl being crazy, making a fool of herself in front of the cool kids, but I *genuinely* don't care.

Jamie reaches out, putting his hand on my arm, but I shake it off.

"Is he that bad?" Virginia says. She's white as a sheet. Good. You *should* be scared.

"Oh, calm down, Pound Shop, we *obviously* weren't laughing at that," Audrey says, rolling her eyes.

I face Josh. "What have you done?" I say to him, my body and my voice shaking with rage.

"Let's go outside," Jamie says quietly, taking hold of my arm again, but I throw him off.

"Well? What have you got to say for yourself?" I slam my hand on the table, and their milkshakes jump. A spot of milk lands on Josh's navy Thetis shirt.

"I haven't done anything, darling. It sounds like your little buddy got drunk and fell of his skateboard," Josh says.

"Bullshit."

Josh turns towards Jamie. "Jam, will you tell your librarian friend to fuck off before I get really angry."

Audrey laughs into her hand.

I grab the nearest milkshake and throw it in Josh's face.

5

J osh screams the worst word through the window at me, his face dripping in milk like a snowman in the sun.

I allow myself to be carried around the corner, but the rage rises up in me like vomit, and I wrestle myself free. "And you!" I say, turning on Jamie. "You're the fucking worst. You just sit there while they say everything they say, and you *let* them laugh. You're a Nazi guard! You're complicit!"

"I was just about to say something," Jamie says, "and then you threw the fucking milkshake."

The tops of his ears are bright red. Does that mean he's lying, or telling the truth?

"You're so fake," I say. "You don't believe in anything, you don't stand up for anyone. You're so shallow, like a...pretty puddle."

I want him to cry, or apologise or something, but when he looks up at me again, he's mad.

"You think you are the only one who has problems Diana? Have you thought for one second that I might hate my life, too?"

"Oh, spare me your poor little rich boy act, please."

He steps forward and looks directly into my eyes. "It's not an act. This is me! I hate them. Let's assume for one minute that Josh did do something to Ralph. He's my brother, Diana. How do you think that makes me feel, being related to someone like that? Having to spend all of my time with someone like that?"

I stare at him but I don't know what to say, so I don't say anything.

"Meet me tonight, please," he says.

I shake my head, unconvincingly.

"You think you're such a good person Diana, and I'm asking for your help. I need to talk to someone. I need a space where I can just be me. Please, say you'll be there, at Brizo, tonight."

He's either telling the truth, or he's the best liar in the world.

6

When I open the door Aunt Vita actually jumps. She practically chucks my phone at me. Irony.

"Take it. It's charged, and topped up, and working. I'd rather you didn't log into the photo one, or any of them really that require a password."

"Thanks," I say, pushing it into my pocket. 'How is Ralph?'

"They wouldn't tell me anything, it was a waste of time. Always answer that phone if I call you," she says.

"Okay," I say, wide eyed, like I'm talking to a toddler mid-tantrum.

"There's one other condition," she says, swiping off her glasses, rubbing her eyes.

I sit down at the kitchen table. One of us should be calm.

"I want you to text me every hour that you're out of the house," she says.

"Are you serious? You haven't seen me all afternoon, Aunt Vita. You leave me on my own all the time. You actually left me asleep in the shop today."

"The bloody doors were locked!" she shouts, outraged. "Diana, I assumed that you didn't *want* your aunt following you around all day like a stalker, but I bloody can, if that's what you think I should be doing. You do know that I spend huge swathes of my time calling people, every day, asking them, 'Has she left yet? Have you seen her go past? Has she just cycled by?'"

Now it's my turn to be outraged. Also, swathes?

"Everyone is spying on me? I don't need a town full of babysitters!"

She throws her hands up in the air again. "Don't be so dramatic, Diana, it's not spying, it's just *noticing*, and everything is different now, you must understand that? Be reasonable, for Christ's sake."

Her hands meet in prayer, and her pleading eyes beg me to agree with her.

I grab her cardigan from the back of one of the chairs, and wrap myself up in it like a blanket.

"Why are things different now, because of Ralph?" I ask. "What about Julie Peters, she's been missing since before I got here?"

She turns away and begins opening and closing cupboard doors. "Julie Peters left six months ago, and she moved! You think I wouldn't care about a missing girl in my own town, Diana? This is totally different. And now Hugo Beltrome is back, too!"

I want to tell her he's been back for days, but I don't. I think that will tip her over the edge.

"Ralph was *drunk*, Aunt Vita, we *all* got drunk. I've literally been hungover all day. He could have fallen off the cliff. He could have just skated onto the sand and wiped out and banged his head! Maybe nothing sinister has happened, and everything is just the same?"

She pulls a bottle of wine from a cupboard and slams the door, rounding on me. "Do you think he fell, Diana?"

I should just lie, but I don't.

Growls of thunder keeps interrupting us. Howard is curled up in his basket in the corner, jumping in his sleep.

"All I'm asking is that you send me a message that says 'ok' once an hour. Why is that such a big deal, if it keeps you safe? Also, I'd like us both to be home by 8pm, every night."

I feel my throat tightening. Let's call it what it is - a curfew. I flick at the beads on my amber bracelet. It's become my nervous

240

habit. "Aunt Vita, please, this is so unnecessary. You can have my phone back, I don't even want it."

I yank it out of my pocket and thrust it towards her, but she turns her back, walks over to the sofa, and starts leafing through newspapers.

"It's your choice, Diana. You can text me on the hour, or we leave Lattering tomorrow morning. I've ordered us pizza," she says.

Is that it, conversation over? I was genuinely about to tell her everything. About the man in the bird mask, and The Mayan in the shop, and Hugo Beltrome in the square, and Josh threatening Ralph, but she'll spontaneously combust. So it's her own fault I'm not telling her. I wish she knew *that*.

"By the way, we have to go to the police station on Thursday," she says, "for an interview." She takes a huge glug of wine, breathing out in relief, like it's medicine. "And, terrible timing, but we are going to a party tomorrow night."

"What kind of party?" I say. 'If it's past eight o'clock I assume that's breaking the rules, so…' I look at her smugly. I'm not going.

"It's the Lattering Women's Refuge Support Group annual summer cocktail party. In Chichester Library. I forgot all about it. We have to go. The rules don't apply to this."

"Oh how convenient! I don't feel like going to a party."

"We are going together. The invite is for both of us. You don't have to enjoy it, we just have to show our faces."

"Is Richard going?" I say, but she ignores that.

"I don't have anything to wear to a party."

"I'll lend you a dress," she says. She takes another slug of wine. She just filled her glass, but it's almost empty already.

I hear the pizza boy's steps on the path.

"I'm not hungry," I say. "I'm going to have a shower and go to bed."

"They confirmed Ralph's name on the radio by the way," she says, grabbing a twenty-pound note from the kitchen table.

"Goodnight," I say.

"Goodnight," she says, walking to the door as the pizza boy

knocks again. "And thank you for understanding about the texts. I know it's a drag, but it won't be forever. We just need to keep safe, until we know what's going on."

I blow dry my hair on the lowest setting with my door closed. This is a mistake, I think.

"I shouldn't go. I shouldn't go," I whisper out loud, as I draw black flicks in the corner of my eyes.

"I shouldn't go," I say to the bathroom mirror, as I brush my teeth. Then I brush them again.

I should sit and think about Ralph. I should cry myself to sleep. I shouldn't go.

I hear another bottle being opened downstairs as I shut the bedroom door from the inside. I position two pillows under the duvet, up against the wall, the way that I sleep, and turn off the big light.

Edging the bedroom window open as quietly as possible, I climb out on to the roof of the porch. I sit and turn, my legs dangling beneath me, my feet searching for the top rung of the ladder that I propped against the side of the house before I came in.

I scuttle down the path on my tiptoes, keeping my head low until I'm through the gate.

It's not raining but the wind is fierce, and I pull my hood up anyway. A murky layer of clouds obscures the moon.

I walk quickly along the beach path, and away from town. I'm heading for a house that I've never seen, with a boy that I barely know, in the pitch black, while my friend lies in hospital in a critical condition. The butterflies in my stomach are on crack, flipping and flying and freaking out. I don't know if I'm hungry, or excited, or terrified. It's probably all three. The one thing I do know is that I've made better decisions than this.

7

Somehow I know it's Brizo, long before I can read the sign.

The gate at the top of the path is twice my height. I hesitate, my hand resting on the wet metal of its twisted iron vines. The house is three stories high, and at least five times the size of our home in London, but it feels familiar. Big, black windows lurk at the back of a white, wooden deck that's as wide as a tennis court. The top floor and roof are framed by scaffolding and wrapped in sheets of plastic that flap angrily in the wind.

I push the gate open and it creaks. It's sinister as shit. I run my fingers along the outline of my phone in my pocket.

The path up to the door is wide, broken, brick. It splits the garden in half. Wooden beams and bags of sand are on one side, and breeze blocks and a cement mixer are on the other. I hear the sound of my own footsteps on the steps up to the deck. I try the front door, but it's locked, so I follow the porch around the side of the house, with one hand pressed against the wall in case the planks beneath me give way. It's almost completely black tonight.

I stop walking.

Where am I?

WHAT AM I DOING?

Have I lost my fucking mind?

243

A flap of plastic breaks free from its binding above me and claps angrily at the sky. It's like a gunshot, and it makes me jump.

At the other end of the deck, a dark figure moves around the corner.

I catch my breath. Why am I here?

"Diana?" Jamie says.

Oh yeah. *That's* why.

8

Four fat, white candles burn in glass lanterns, dotted around the floor. A checked picnic blanket is laid out neatly in the middle of a vast, almost empty room. A pizza box sits in the middle, next to two Cokes. The plastic sheeting beats like angry wings above us.

He looks nervous. I shiver.

"Here," he says, as he tugs his Thetis hoodie over his head.

I glimpse the flat brown board of his stomach beneath his T-shirt. All the hairs on my arms tingle at once. "Thanks," I say, pulling it on. It smells like soap. "I nearly didn't come. This house gives me the creeps."

"Yeah, but I don't think anybody else even knows you can get in. You want a Coke?"

I nod. He grabs one from the floor and opens it, passing it to me. He's even brought napkins. Breeding.

I take a sip and look around. I don't know what to say.

"We can sit, if you want?" He gestures at the blankets.

I position myself on the opposite side of the pizza box to him, like it's going to protect me. Like I want it to. "This house is huge," I say, looking around. A wide wooden staircase, three times the size of anything at home, leads to a landing with a huge glass chandelier dripping down from the ceiling above it, like a frozen water leak. Two flights of stairs extend on either side, leading up to a hallway that circles the whole house.

We start to eat.

"The builders keep starting, then stopping" Jamie says, wiping tomato from his cheek. "It was sinking into the sand when they found it. The foundations had totally gone."

"Do you know who owns it?"

He shakes his head. "Probably my dad." He rolls his eyes.

"Does he own most things?" I ask, picking off a piece of onion and throwing it back in the box.

"Most things I know about. Do you want another slice?"

"Maybe in a bit." I cross my legs and try to relax. "So, did Josh order another milkshake?" I say, doing my best impression of innocence.

He laughs and throws a slice of half-eaten pizza back into the box. "He was pretty angry, but more with me than you."

"Why? You didn't throw it."

"Yeah, I know, but...let's not talk about my brother, is that okay?"

Awkward. I swig my coke and look up at the ceiling. There are angels carved in a circle around the chandelier. I wonder if they'll protect me. The waves have got bigger, crashing on to the beach. They sound too close. The plastic claps in the wind. I think I want to leave.

"What do you normally do with your summer, in London?" he says.

"Just normal stuff. Hang out with friends. Go to Westfield. Get a job."

"Where are your friends now?" he says.

"Cambodia. Annoying orphans."

I push myself on to my knees. I should go before he decides to leave first. We can both feel the awkwardness in the room. A gust of wind rushes through the house and blows out a candle. A shadow covers half of his face.

"Are you okay?" I say.

"Is Ralph okay?" he says.

"We don't know yet. Richard and Gloria went to the hospital this afternoon, but I haven't spoken to them. Aunt Vita says he's stable."

"God, I hope so. You know he likes you, don't you?"

"Ralph?" I say, confused.

"No, your friend. Richard."

I remember the kiss, and it makes me sad.

"But I think you like me," Jamie says, without looking up. He folds up the pizza box, moving it to one side.

I'm still kneeling, still half-thinking I should go. I could have pizza in my teeth. I rock back on my heels to stand but my bad ankle gives way, and I literally collapse. "Oh shit," I say, flailing, desperately trying to get up, but my legs are caught beneath me.

He grabs me and pulls me to my feet. I look down. He's holding my hands. It feels like I've injected skittles directly into my bloodstream. Something is happening...

Jamie's thumbs are drawing circles on my palms, but his expression hasn't changed, like he doesn't even know that he's doing it.

Everything about me feels like it's shaking.

"Can I see you again tomorrow?" he asks.

"My aunt is taking me to a party." I roll my eyes.

He reaches our joined hands behind my back. His chest is pressed against mine. Our faces are so close that I notice a tiny spot of tomato sauce on his cheek. He closes his eyes and kisses me softly.

I don't close my eyes. It lasts for at least ten seconds.

He stops. "What is it?" he says.

"I could have pizza in my teeth."

He laughs out loud and shakes his head. "You are different to any girl I've ever met, Diana, I swear, no bullshit."

"Good different?" I say.

"Perfect different." He takes hold of my face and looks into my eyes so deeply that I have to fight the urge to look away.

"Am I the first boy you've ever kissed?" he says.

I think quickly of Richard, but I nod. "Do you mind?" I say.

"Do I mind?" he repeats, raising his eyebrows, incredulous.

~

W e are twenty feet from Shalimar.

"Take this back," I say, peeling off my coat, tugging off his hoodie. I don't want Aunt Vita to find it. My hair whips around in the wind.

"Will you meet me again?" he says, zipping me up, pulling my hood over my hair and holding on to the sides so that all I can see is his face.

I nod.

"Well I must have done something right then. Was it the pizza?"

I kiss him this time. I can't believe he wants to kiss me back.

The ladder rungs are wet. The window opens easily, and I drop back into my room.

The pillows are in the same position, but the door is ajar. I spot Howard, asleep at the end of my bed, and breathe a sigh of relief. I stare up at the neon stars on the ceiling, and I think: what if I hadn't gone?

9

I need to tell Gloria so desperately that I leave *early* for my shift at Seagulls. I'm almost blown off Snoopy three times on the ride into town. The rain soaks my jeans. I'm the only person smiling.

Huge waves crash against the bottom of the cliffs, one after another, barely a breath's gap between them, and that's when everything from yesterday comes flooding back. My smile disappears. But the memory of Jamie, standing outside Shalimar holding the hood of my coat, burns through my mind like a flame through an old photograph. A smile corrupts my face before I can stop it. I hate myself.

I fill the water glasses. I wash and refill the ketchup tomatoes. I wipe the tables. I sweep the goddamn floor. I flip the sign at 6am, and peer down the road. There is still no sign of Gloria.

Felix isn't himself, but then, nobody is. I think everyone is just waiting. We all need to know if Ralph is okay.

The day stretches out ahead of us, full of seconds, and minutes, and hours that could be vital. It only takes a moment for a heart to stop. This is torture. Someone just needs to call and say he's fine. His little body survived the crash, or the fall, or whatever it was that left him on the beach, unconscious and broken. Then I think, what if the tide had come in and just washed him away?

My hands are full of mugs when Gloria rushes in, finally, twenty minutes late, headphones already swinging by her sides, Ray-Bans in hand, no lipstick, no eye-liner, no smile. She looks naked, and so young.

"How was he, did they let you see him?" I say, following her through the curtain to the back room.

"No, he's still in intensive care. He's stable but critical," she says, washing her hands furiously. She's scrubbing so hard I think she'll take the skin off.

"That's what the radio said too," I say, nodding.

"Then why ask?" She pushes past me, back through the curtain.

She's sorting the change that I've already sorted.

"I've done that," I say quietly.

"Is the urn on?" she says.

"Yes, it's all under control Gloria, I've had to do this on my own loads recently, I know what I'm doing."

"I can't help it if I'm sick," She looks up from the change and I think she's going to cry.

"I didn't...I wasn't saying that. Gloria, are you okay?"

She nods furiously but doesn't speak.

"Is it Ralph?" I say, and she shakes her head.

Yesterday's curls look tired and matted. She hasn't even styled her hair. "Does that make me a bad person?" she says, biting her lip. Tears swell dangerously in the corners of her eyes. I reach out for her hand, hoping she won't shake me off, but she clings to it, squeezing my fingers. Her arm tenses up. She sobs and stares at the neat piles of change obscuring Elvis's face, for what feels like forever.

"It's over, with him," she says finally. She looks up and tries to smile but tears are streaming down her cheeks.

I feel so angry I want to scream. "How? Why?" I say, but she just shakes her head and shrugs, as the bell above the door rings.

"I'll be right with you," she says, as breezily as she can manage, but her voice cracks. She gives my hand one last squeeze and walks over to the table.

I glance up at the clock. It's 6.30am. I pull out my phone and text Aunt Vita 'ok'.

~

A hand grabs me as I'm walking past Surf's Up, pulling me into the space between two full-size boards.

Jamie starts kissing me so passionately that I think we might knock them all over, like giant dominoes. We don't stop until we run out of breath.

"Come with me," he says, and darts around the side of the shop.

I wait ten seconds and follow.

He grabs me as soon as I turn the corner.

"Hey, I meant to tell you last night, I got my phone back," I say. "I can give you my number."

He ignores me, kissing my neck. He's actually licking me. "I've started dreaming about your face, Diana," he says, between kisses. "Why do you smell so amazing?"

His lips and tongue are so soft, and his hands are so smooth.

"Why can't I stop thinking about you? What IS it with you?" he says, leaning back. He bangs his head against the wall once.

It's alarming. I don't know the answer.

"It's because you are so good. And it's our secret. I love that," he says, kissing me again.

I kiss him back because then I don't have to think about what *good* means. My anxiety dissolves and I forget everything.

Jamie lifts me up and turns me around, pressing me against the wall. I wrap my legs around his waist, my chest pressed against his, our bodies together. I feel his jeans harden. I feel the inside of my jeans tingling. One of his hands is on the back of my neck, his tongue in my mouth.

I can't breathe. I pull my head away and shake my head.

"I'm sorry," he says, lowering me to the floor. "It's just…I swear it's like I'm a different person with you, Diana. You're so pure. You make me think my life could be different."

10

Richard is sitting on the floor in the back room of the shop. Silver CDs and their plastic cases litter the space around him. Seriously, what's the point?

"You should go home," I say.

"What else am I going to do?" He opens a Steps case and closes it again, placing it on one pile.

"How did it go at the hospital?" I say.

"It didn't, really. They wouldn't let us into his room, it was family only. I heard one of the doctors say that his legs are both broken, but not his back."

"He's still not awake?"

"No, he's in a coma."

He opens a Fugees case but there is nothing inside. He throws it in the corner with uncharacteristic anger.

"He'll know you were there, Richard. You're his best friend," I say, but it's lame and he doesn't even answer. "Hey, I got my phone back, do you want my number?" I say.

He nods and hands me his phone, and I tap it in. His wallpaper is a picture he took himself, of the Thetis cliffs at night. I hand him back his phone.

"You want some help?"

He shakes his head. "I just want to be on my own I think."

"Of course, no problem," I say, and go and sit behind the counter.

I had nine messages. Nine. In all that time. Half of them were from Betty and Amy at the airport the day they left, and the others were spam. I've had nothing from either of them since.

I feel like a fool. I was so desperate to get my phone back, but for what? Noise.

I type in 'ok', and press send. I throw it back on the counter and pick up my book.

11

Byron is sitting outside Mandalay, sipping a cup of tea. He's
wearing a grey sweatshirt that says 'ILLINOIS' in orange
letters, and checked pajama trousers that remind me of Christmas,
and trying to stop the bits of paper he's reading from blowing
away.

I jump off Snoopy and sit down next to him.

"Hey, how's the little guy?" he says.

"He's in a coma. His legs are broken. They won't let us see
him."

Byron nods thoughtfully. "How are you?"

I shrug.

"What was that?" I ask, pointing at the papers.

He's put them face down under his cup, so I can't read them.
"Just work," he says.

"I thought your job was surfer."

He smiles but doesn't say anything else.

I get my phone out and press send on another 'ok'.

"What's that about?" he says.

"Aunt Vita being mental," I say.

He chuckles as my phone buzzes.

I glance at the incoming message.

'We are leaving for the party at 7pm, don't be late home, Vita'.

"I feel weird," I say to Byron after we've sat in silence for a while.

"Good weird or bad weird?" he says, watching me.

"Bad weird. It feels like everything has changed."

"Some things have changed," he says.

"I don't know what to do about anything, not that it matters what I do of course."

"Why not?" he says. "You are important, Diana."

I shake my head. "Gloria has split up with her boyfriend. Richard is so sad he doesn't even want to talk to me. Ralph is in a coma. I'm definitely not the important one right now."

"But you're the glue," he says. "You created this group of friends. It didn't even exist before you got here. You made something, and you need to help it survive because you all care about each other now. So you must take care of yourself too. Now is not the time to be reckless, Diana."

I shrug. I don't know what he means. I'm so tired.

Cycling back to Shalimar, I think about Gloria crying. I think about Richard, full of anger but with nowhere to put it. I think about Ralph plugged into machines at the hospital. I think about Jamie, holding me up against the wall, his mouth pressed over mine, so I couldn't breathe. I think about Josh shouting at Ralph, and Audrey smirking.

Maybe I am the glue? Or maybe everybody would feel so much better if I just wasn't here.

12

Every dress that Aunt Vita owns lays sadly on her bed, in a heap of sequins, and silk, and leather, and mesh. Actual *leather* and actual *mesh*. Pink and blue scarves dangle from picture-hooks instead of art, and a huge red and orange silk tiger prowls along the main wall, pinned up at its corners like some kind of hunting trophy. The floorboards are a sea of newspapers and half opened post, nail varnish bottles, and discarded T-shirts. The window is big and white and draughty. I can actually feel the wind pushing through the sides, but beyond it is a perfect view of the sea.

Aunt Vita stands next to me, hands on her hips, biting her lip. "Well?" she says.

"They're a bit...fancy," I say.

"There must be something you don't hate, surely?"

I pick up what looks like a plain black shift, but then I see the giant pink bow on the bum and place it back down. I *may* have grimaced.

"Diana, just pick a bloody dress," she says.

∿

I pop the contact lenses out of their plastic containers. I've had them for two weeks. Gloria marched me into the optician in town one afternoon. I put my chin on the little paper shelf and took away three strips of five lenses to practice with. There are only two left. Putting them in is getting easier, but the really strange thing is the world. It's bigger. I'm used to seeing everything with a hard edge. I didn't even recognise myself in the shop mirror. My face looked like a wide open space, blank and vast.

"You look hot," Gloria had said. "Stop hiding."

13

As we walk through the main doors of Chichester Library, I hear somebody whisper, "Vita's here".

I count three men in total, all versions of the same: thin, glasses, beards. There are at least one hundred women of every size, shape, and colour, with more pouring in behind us. There are more black women in this room than I've seen in the whole of Lattering since I arrived.

A short, stocky, Indian woman in a ball gown stands before a wall of boxed wine. She passes us two fizzing glasses.

"Vita," she says, smiling. Her voice is high, like she's sucked helium.

"Neelum, this is my brilliant niece, Diana," Aunt Vita says.

"Good to meet you, Diana. Your aunt is a rock star. She helped me after my divorce. She's helped everybody here. She's a legend."

"A rock star? Like Green Day?" I ask, as Aunt Vita steers me through the crowd.

"The cynicism of youth. Some people think I'm pretty special," she says, smiling.

The next hour is a cocktail of raw finger food, and women gushing about how amazing my aunt is. Everyone wants to talk to her or talk to me *about* her. "After my husband died Vita got me a job/Vita painted my house/got a restraining order against my ex-husband/walks my two-legged dog."

At 9pm we reach the other side of the room, where three elegant women (all taller than me), and one of the bearded men, greet us with open arms.

"Diana, these are my friends," Aunt Vita says, dropping down onto the arm of a chair, taking off one shoe and rubbing her foot.

A black woman in a flowing white dress, with a bright red head wrap and lipstick to match, offers me her hand.

"Hello Diana, I'm Mariam. I teach economics at the university. We've heard so much about you."

"Hello," I say, trying to match the firmness of her handshake.

The woman standing next to her looks a lot like the Mona Lisa. She holds out both her arms and pulls me in for a hug, squeezing me, then holding me at arms-length, appraising me like I'm the painting.

"I'm Helen Cohen. This is my husband Anthony," she says, smiling at the handsome man to her left.

"Hello Diana, I'm Anthony Odebywa, Helen's lesser half." Anthony shakes my hand and reaches around me to kiss Vita's cheek. He is incredibly tall and wearing a dark red suit and tie.

The last woman in the circle is a bit younger and super slim, with shoulder length white-blonde hair, and skin the colour of the expensive vanilla at Two Scoops. She's wearing skinny black trousers, black sling-backs, and a fitted black shirt. She looks like a Swedish pop star. She's wearing no make-up or jewellery. She gives me a massive smile.

"Hello Diana, I'm Susan," she says, with a faint accent that I can't place. "How are you?"

"I'm good," I say.

"Susan is a surgeon at St John's," Aunt Vita says.

"The hospital where Ralph is?" I say, looking between them. Susan nods.

"Yes, I've seen Ralph today, Diana. He's made it through the first 36 hours, that's really positive."

Mariam, Aunt Vita, Anthony, and Helen start chatting, and I scan the room for more food.

"Vita tells me you are interested in the law?" Susan says.

"Well, I thought I was."

"You've changed your mind?" she asks.

Everyone I've spoken to this evening has wanted to get to Aunt Vita; I felt like Taylor Swift's boyfriend. But this genuinely feels like a conversation about me.

"I think I'm a bit naïve," I say.

"Really, why?"

"I don't know. I just don't feel certain, like I did at home. I feel like I don't know anything anymore."

Susan sips her drink and considers what I've said.

Aunt Vita laughs and throws her head back, grabbing hold of Anthony to stop herself from falling.

"I'll let you in on a secret Diana," Susan says. "Nobody knows anything, really. We are all guessing, hoping for the best, riding our luck, and trying to be happy. And you are luckier than most people, of course."

I pull a face. I'm not lucky at all.

My aunt is listening to Anthony talk, but looking over at us. She points and mouths at Susan, 'Tell her I'm amazing'. Susan smiles.

"But you have Vita," she says. "And your aunt would go to war for you, Diana."

We ride home in a taxi in silence, at midnight. I put my head on Aunt Vita's shoulder as she stares out of the window. She squeezes my hand, but she looks sad.

14

The regulars keep asking me why Gloria isn't singing, and I say the tape machine is broken. None of them tell her to cheer up, to give them a smile, it might never happen. Everybody knows about Ralph. There's still no good news from the hospital. I can't even contemplate what bad news might feel like.

I'm sitting in the square, opposite the library. A huge sign advertises the official reopening in two weeks' time. It's taken them less than two months, not even a full summer. I'm pretending to read my book with my eyes half closed, when I hear a noise behind my head, like a bird whistling. I turn around.

The Mayan takes his sunglasses off, and smiles. I see the bone dangling in his ear. His hair looks wet.

"Good morning, Diana," he growls.

"What do you want?" I say. Rude.

"Mr. Beltrome would like to speak with you," he says, pointing to the monster car parked twenty feet away.

I didn't even hear it pull up. "I'm not getting in there with him," I say.

"It is a private conversation, that is all. I will leave the door open."

"Where will you be?" I ask him.

His lips twitch, trying to suppress a smile. "Where would you like me to be?" he says.

"Getting me an Oreo milkshake from Breakers."

He nods his head. "Consider it done. Follow me, please, Diana."

He opens the car door and I stand well back, and peer in.

Hugo Beltrome is sitting on the opposite side, reading a report. "Hello Diana, it's so nice to see you again." he says, placing the papers on a small table in front of him. His car has a wooden *table*.

"You have to leave the door open," I say, not getting in.

"Whatever makes you most comfortable. I simply have something I'd like to discuss with you, an educational proposition, that's all."

"I will get your milkshake," The Mayan says, walking off towards Breakers.

Hugo Beltrome raises an eyebrow in surprise.

The seats are leather and the colour of blood. It smells of new.

"Thank you for taking the time to see me, Diana. I hope I didn't interrupt anything important?"

I shrug, because shrugging is bad manners and he'll hate it.

"Did you get everything done at the police station in the end? It was so nice to bump in to you again, and it reminded me that I needed to talk with you. You'll be getting your exam results soon," he says, patting down his tie.

I don't reply.

"You attend a very good school, Diana; your father chose well. But St Jude's is very expensive, too."

"I have a full scholarship," I say.

"You do. But do you know how much it costs to attend one of my schools, Diana?"

I shake my head.

"It's completely free. They are by invitation only."

"For boys that are related to you," I say. Sarcasm. He ignores it.

"They were founded as boys' schools, it's true. It was easier from a regulatory perspective. Single sex is far simpler for boarding, and I know very little about young girls I'm glad to say. But I'm making a change. Would you like to know what that is?"

I shrug again. I've gone maximum petty.

"I've always known I would make an exception, when the exception came along." He smiles at me. "Let me be clear, Diana. I think *you* are the exception."

"But you don't know anything about me," I say.

"Don't be naïve Diana, I know everything about you," Hugo Beltrome says, without blinking. "I know the opportunities I can give you. Everything will be paid for. You will receive an allowance for your own interests. You will have a car, when you are old enough. Can you imagine the pressure that would take off your father, Diana? The financial burden of raising you must put such a strain on him, emotionally. Think of the good you'd be doing both him, and you."

"Where would I have to live?" I say, surprising myself.

He smiles. "You would travel between the Thetis schools, with the other students."

"But I live with my dad in London," I say.

He stares at me so intensely that I have to look away.

"Have you considered that your father may not be released from prison?" he says softly. "You cannot continue to attend St. Jude's with no London address, and no money for essentials."

"He didn't do anything wrong. They are just holding him on a technicality."

"Perhaps," he says, like he already knows the answer. "Or perhaps, due to terrible circumstances, your life is taking the shape that it should."

"Why do people hate you so much?" I say.

He flicks an imaginary speck from his trousers. "Are you referring to your aunt?"

"Among others," I say.

He smiles. "Well, Vita and I have a complicated relationship."

"You were her ex-boyfriend. Did you hurt her?"

His expression suggests I've answered a question he hadn't asked.

"Aunt Vita has told you a white lie, Diana. We have never been romantically involved."

"I don't believe you," I say, but I feel like an idiot.

"Come to dinner at Thetis on Thursday," he says. "You can see the house and ask me your questions. I'm sure you must be just a little curious and, who knows, you may even enjoy it. And now Juan has returned with your dessert."

The Mayan stands five feet away, holding an Oreo milkshake.

"I'll expect you for dinner at 6pm on Thursday, then. Juan will meet you here and drive you up, it's quite a steep walk."

I climb out of the car, and look back in.

"Do come to the house, Diana. If nothing else, you'll have a nice dinner. On the other hand, it may just change your life."

I'm eyeing the milkshake with suspicion when I see Gloria walking towards me.

"Hey, want to share my milkshake?"

"What were you doing?" she says, crossing her arms tightly.

"What do you mean?" But I know *exactly* what she means.

"In that car. What were you doing?"

"It's not what you think, Gloria."

"What do I think?"

She hasn't smiled once.

"He just wanted to talk to me about school."

"And what will Vita say, when you tell her?"

I don't want to say out loud that I'm not going to tell Vita, but Gloria already knows that anyway. She looks up at the sky, stamps her foot, and screams with rage.

"What is going on with you?" I say, alarmed.

"What is going on with YOU, Diana? Vita took you in, have you forgotten that?"

"You don't even know why he was talking to me and, actually, he's right! What if I can't go back to St Jude's? What if my dad stays in prison? Aunt Vita hasn't even thought about that. Maybe he's just looking out for me?"

"Oh please!' Her expression is pure disgust. "This old, creepy guy, that you've just met, is suddenly looking out for you more than your own family?"

"Maybe he thinks I've got potential!" I hear myself, sounding like an idiot.

"There are normal schools in Lattering, Diana. You could go to one of those."

I shake my head, because she doesn't understand, and she laughs, but it's not nice.

"Oh, I forgot, you're too *good* for a state school."

"It's not about being too good, Gloria. It's about me, and what I need to do to get into the right university."

People are turning to watch us arguing in the street. My head feels hot and angry. We glare at each other through tear-filled eyes.

"I thought you were better than this," she says quietly. "Ralph might die, and you are getting into cars with Hugo Beltrome."

"We don't even know what happened," I whisper so quietly that I can barely hear myself.

"Exactly," Gloria says, and walks off.

15

Aunt Vita is pulling on her sweatshirt when I get to the shop.

"We are going to the police station," she says, rifling through her bag.

"Jesus! Why?"

She looks up at me like I've lost my mind. "To talk about your dad. I told you yesterday."

"Of course."

I don't know why I'm relieved.

∼

The mirror behind their heads takes up the whole wall. My chair is metal and uncomfortable, and the room is surprisingly cold.

Aunt Vita has a notepad and pen, and she's wearing her glasses. They've offered us both a can of Coke, and a plate of digestive biscuits is in the middle of the table. There are two officers sitting across from us, both in suits, no uniforms. They are a bit younger than Aunt Vita maybe.

Inspector Blonde is the whitest man I've ever seen. His eyes are so pale, they are barely blue. His hair makes him look like he's had a terrible shock.

Inspector Brown has black eyes, black hair, and a mole on his cheek. They are both smiling at me and ignoring Aunt Vita, whose eyes have narrowed to half their normal width, and they haven't even said anything yet.

"What did your father say to you the evening before his arrest, can you remember?" Inspector Blonde says.

I'm going to call his tone *professionally kind*.

"He wasn't himself," I say. "He was having an episode. He has them sometimes, but then he's fine. He isn't dangerous."

They both smile at me.

"Can you remember what he said?" Inspector Brown says.

"Badgering," Aunt Vita says.

Blonde sighs, and Brown rolls his eyes.

"Remember, this isn't court," Inspector Blonde says to me wearily. "We are actually trying to help your father and establish his thoughts or motives."

"Motives for what?" I ask. "He didn't do anything."

Aunt Vita coughs down a laugh.

"Can you remember what he said?" Inspector Blonde says.

I close my eyes and try to think back to the kitchen. "It was just muttering really. A typical episode."

"And then?" Inspector Blonde says.

"And then…" I squeeze my eyes shut to think, and drop myself back into that space. "He was holding a letter and he just kept saying Aunt Vita, over and over. That's it."

All four of their eyebrows go up at once.

"A letter?" Inspector Brown says.

They turn to look at Vita, like synchronized swimmers.

She is already packing up. "Diana looks unwell. I think we are going to leave it for today." She pushes back her chair.

"Are you sick, Diana?" she says, feeling my forehead, widening her eyes for my agreement.

"I'm sick," I say. I don't know what's going on.

She shoves her pad in her bag, and strides to the door.

Inspector Brown smiles knowingly at Aunt Vita as we leave.

"Aunt Vita, do you know what that letter was?" I say, as we drive home.

She shakes her head but closes her eyes. Another lie. I'd bet my scholarship she has it.

16

I've typed fifty messages and deleted them. It's like wearing an overcoat that's ten sizes too big for me. I feel physically weighed down by the fact that Gloria is out there, hating me. I need to talk to her, but I feel sick at the thought of it.

Felix is writing on the blackboard when I walk in. A stripe of his hairy back is visible beneath a cerise shirt swarming with yellow birds.

"Glo's called in sick, again," he says, without turning around.

~

"I told Richard to stay at home today," Aunt Vita says.

She puts down the bottle of furniture polish and the cloth she's been using to clean an old-fashioned metal picture. There's a woman on it, in a bathing suit and a flowery swimming hat. At the top it says, 'Welcome to Lattering: the surprise of your life!'

"I spoke to Susan this morning," she says, walking over to the counter, so I'll pay attention.

"She said Ralph was the same. Critical, but stable."

"That's good, right?" I say, and she nods.

"Aunt Vita, how will we know what happened if Ralph doesn't wake up?"

"I think we can only focus our vibes on him getting better."

I notice she doesn't say 'our prayers'. She never says prayers.

She picks up her polish.

"Aunt Vita, do you think rich people get away with things other people don't?"

She smiles sadly, as if I've just guessed the answer to the universe. "Absolutely."

"But what about murder?" I say.

Mid-spray she turns, alarmed, and a fine sheen of polish fizzes over her leg. "What about murder?" she says.

"Ralph said that rich people get away with murder."

I've never seen the look on her face before. It's like she's in physical pain.

"All I know is that life definitely isn't fair," she says. "Hey, you look so sad, and it's been a rough few days. Take this afternoon off. Go and lie in the sun. Try and relax, if you can."

I pick up my bag, and she gives me a hug. She smells of vinegar.

"I'll text you when I get home," I say, as she kisses my head.

Aunt Vita finally mowed the lawn at the weekend. The garden is like that uncle you've always known with a beard, who shaves it off and has a totally different face. Tiny solar lights wink from the borders when it gets dark. Even Aunt Vita had forgotten they were there.

Howard wants to play so I get his chewy snake. He has so many toys now. Aunt Vita brought home a baby teddy bear from the refuge, and he carries that around with him everywhere. We've called it Huggie. Howard has started cuddling Huggie in his sleep. It makes me want to cry.

It's so quiet. Howard gets sleepy and we lay down for a snooze on the grass. My eyes are closing, and I'm drifting in that space where your dreams are your life, when Howard sits up, ears pricked. He barks at the fence between Shalimar and next door's garden.

The house has been empty for a week, and all the shutters are closed. The plastic toys are packed neatly away in the shed, by the side gate, but the gate itself is wide open, which is odd.

Howard runs over to the fence, still barking, and I follow. I step into the dirt of our border, and lean over, bracing myself. If it's a dismembered mouse I'm going to freak out. I look down and want to cry.

Laying on the ground, on the other side of the fence, is the bird mask.

17

I lock Howard inside with Huggie, and ride like hell to Richard's house.

His grandfather answers the door. He looks like the wise old elf. I've never been inside their bungalow before. It's spotless. They have a big, paper phone directory, on a tiny glass table, next to a plastic phone and a pen. On the wall there's a photo of Richard with people I don't know. He looks happy, it's weird. They must be his parents.

Richard's granddad taps gently on a bedroom door. "Jeremy, there's someone to see you," he says.

"Come in." It's Richard voice behind the door.

"Can I get you a cup of tea?" his granddad says.

Richard stands up from his bed, bleary-eyed. He's in a T-shirt, and it's the first time I've seen his naked arms. They are covered in tiny cuts and plasters. We'll never really know what's happening in each other's heads, no matter how much we describe it for the counsellors.

"Sorry, I didn't mean to wake you up," I say, looking up at the ceiling as Richard grabs a long sleeved sweater and pulls it on. He reaches for his glasses on the desk.

"Why did your Granddad call you Jeremy?"

He gestures at his desk chair, and I sit down. He straightens the duvet and sits on the side of his bed. "It's my real name. But I hate it. Richard is my middle name."

"Have they let you see Ralph?" I ask, looking at the posters on his wall. The Force Awakens *and* The Empire Strikes Back.

Richard shakes his head. "Mr. Srao won't let anyone see him but family."

"Ralph would hate that," I say. "You *are* his family."

"Why are you here Diana?" He looks uncomfortable.

"I need to show you something." I reach inside my rucksack and pull out the bird mask.

"What's that?" He takes it from me, turning it over in his hands.

"I found it in the garden next door. Howard was going mental, and their gate was open, and this was on the ground."

He holds it up in front of his face, looking it in its red eye. "It's fucked up," he says, trying to hand it back.

I nod towards my rucksack. I don't want to touch it again.

"The night we got drunk, when I was running away, I saw somebody behind me, and he was wearing this mask."

I've buried the memory in my brain, but now the thought of it keeps rushing out. I cover my eyes, as if that will stop it, but he is walking slowly towards me down the alley.

"Why didn't you say anything before?" Richard looks genuinely shaken.

"Because I thought I was drunk. And another thing. The night of the fair, in the haunted house, somebody was wearing it, and he chased me."

"What the hell?" Richard says, his back straightening. "Have you told Vita?"

"No. Shit!" I grab my phone and text 'ok' and press send.

"But you *aren't* okay Diana. Someone is following you."

It's like spiders are crawling around inside my head and I want to shake it, and shake it, until they all fall out.

"What do you think will happen if I tell her, Richard? She'll go mental."

"Maybe she *should* go mental."

"I need to speak to Gloria. She'll know what to do. Will you come with me please?"

∼

G loria's flat is three floors up. I'm out of breath by the time we reach the front door. The doormat has a cat on it, and there's a hanging basket full of plastic flowers.

Richard stands behind me, holding his board.

I hear movement inside and wait. I glance over the railings at the car park below. Snoopy is propped against a skip at the bottom of the steps, and it's the first time I've worried he might actually get stolen.

Nanna Gloria's stooped frame slow shuffles, slippers on carpet, towards the door.

"Hi Nanna Gloria," I say.

A mixture of confusion and faint recognition on her face. She glances up at Richard behind me.

"This is our friend Richard. Is Gloria here?"

"Yes dear, she's in her room."

She shuffles away, leaving the door wide open.

We take off our shoes and walk down the narrow hallway. Gloria's flat *always* smells of roast dinners. Richard has to duck beneath a shelf with two ceramic squirrels on it.

I take a deep breath, knock, and open the door.

Gloria is laying on her bed, clutching a teddy bear. Her eyes are red from crying.

"I have to talk to you," I say, sitting down on the bed.

"How are you?" she says to Richard, who is loitering uncomfortably in the corner.

"I'm okay. How are you?"

"I've been better," she says, sitting up, wiping her eyes. She's wearing a huge pink T-shirt that falls off her shoulder, and tiny bed shorts.

"Richard, would you mind if I talk to Diana on her own for a minute?"

274

"Of course. I'll wait outside." He practically runs from the room.

I sit opposite Gloria and wait for her to speak, but she is silent, inspecting the ears of her teddy bear, pulling at loose threads.

"I think Richard is cutting himself," I say quietly.

"Yeah, I've seen it too," she says, not looking up.

"And I think I'm being followed. I found this in next door's garden." I unzip my bag and point to the mask. "It's the same one from the haunted house at the fair. And the night we got drunk, I was followed by someone wearing it too."

"Why didn't you tell me?" Gloria says, horrified, pulling the mask out of the bag by its awful beak.

"I thought I was drunk, and then, well, Ralph…"

"Have you told Vita?" she says.

"No. I will. Also, I've kissed Jamie Beltrome. Twice."

She wears an expression I've only seen once before, in Seagulls, just before she threw that creepy guy out.

"I'm sorry I shouted at you," I say, "and you were right. I was just flattered by Hugo Beltrome. It was stupid."

"I'm sorry too," she says, twisting a thread so tightly around her thumb that the tip starts to go white.

"What's going on with you, Gloria?" I say.

She puts her bear down and stands, lifting up her top. She looks weird. Her belly is completely sticking out. My mouth literally falls open.

"Oh, Gloria. You're pregnant?"

BEFORE

*S*he walks quickly, glancing back over her shoulder. She senses someone following her in the shadows. As she turns the key in her front door her shoulders visibly relax. She's home. She's safe.

He walks quietly around to the back of the house. Taking the pregnant women was the part of his job Juan liked the least. No: killing them was worse.

The bathroom light flicks on. He can see the outline of her through the mottled glass. She stands before the mirror, examining herself. He can picture her face. Her blood-stained toothbrush. Her grubby unicorn slippers. The bin, where he found the first test, under the used cotton wool balls and yellow stained cotton buds. He found all five tests, with their bright pink lines. She took some convincing.

He'll wait until she's asleep. He doesn't like to frighten them. The bathroom light flicks off and seconds later the pink twinkles in her bedroom come on. He opened her window earlier, just an inch, and pulled her curtains shut. She won't check it, she doesn't check anything. He hears a muffled cry.

'Julie! Julie!'

The hallway light flicks back on. She's checking on the old woman, making sure she hasn't fallen out of bed again. She fetches her a fresh glass of water sometimes. He was behind the kitchen door once when that happened, caught by surprise, but she was practically sleep-walking and he understands shadows. It wasn't a problem.

She's a sweet girl really. She just makes bad choices, as young girls do. He's learned them, as they stand in front of bathroom mirrors, bedroom mirrors, pulling faces, staring at themselves but never really understanding.

They all believe the big pink lie: be prettier, show more skin, starve a little longer, be chosen. They dream of handsome boys and stolen kisses and being the one, but Juan knows that there is one fundamental truth, and that truth is so simple: man cannot exist without woman. They have the power. But the lie is too big, and too noisy, and too old.

Her bedroom lights finally go out. He'll give it another thirty minutes. He sits casually on the back step and studies the stars in a clear, perfect sky. He's wearing his gloves anyway, of course, but they are useful tonight. The air is sharp with cold. The ocean will be bracing.

Half an hour later, he places his palms flat on the windowsill and pushes up. He takes his weight on his hands, like a gymnast. He bends his back and his legs, squatting to the side of the open window. He pulls it open and drops in lightly, two-footed. She turns over in her sleep, and murmurs, but in one step the handkerchief is out of his boot and over her mouth. Ten seconds. Her head relaxes gently against the pillow. He pulls the duvet away. Her pajamas are covered in smiling faces.

The bump of the baby pops out at her stomach. She hasn't bought any new clothes yet, she is still forcing her tiny frame into her regular clothes. He spreads his palms flat on her belly, fanning out his fingers. He presses a little and feels a tiny kick against his finger.

He finds the blanket in the corner and lays it on the floor, wrapping her in it. He tucks her phone and charger in her bag, checking that her purse is already there. He scans the room but there are no tubs of expectant vitamins, or week by week baby guides. He finds her diary in her underwear drawer and takes it. He shuts the window and makes the bed, removing any trace of himself. Throwing her bag across himself like a bicycle messenger, he lifts and carries her out of the front door to his car.

All these poor girls. Why do they let it happen? But he knows why: the world will always forgive a handsome man.

PART VIII

1

I can't stop staring at it. She drops her T-shirt and sinks back on to the bed. You can't even see it when she's sitting down.

"How many months?"

"I don't know. It could be anything."

"Haven't you been having periods?"

"I just lost track." Gloria rolls her red eyes.

"Have you been to the doctor?" I take her hand.

"No. I convinced myself it was too many ice creams with you," she says, "but then it kept popping out more and more, and now I feel it moving around inside me like an alien."

"Weren't you careful?"

"Most of the time. He didn't want to be, though. And there was this one time when we just..."

"Well, you can't be that far. It might only be, like, five months?"

"I dunno. Nanna always says she didn't even know she was pregnant with my mum. She just fell out in the toilet one day." Gloria laughs sadly and it breaks my heart.

"You have to go to the doctor tomorrow. Do you want me to come with you?"

She nods. I pull her towards me. Her head rests under my chin. I hug her as tightly as I can and stroke her hair.

"Hey," I say, twenty minutes later. "Will you tell *him*?"
She nods into my shoulder.

R ichard is peering into the hanging basket. "Is she okay?" he
says.
"Not really. I've left her to sleep."
"Will you come with me somewhere, Diana?"
I nod but I'm exhausted. "Where?"
"The old people's home."
It's where Eileen lives, Aunt Vita's *muse*.
"Why are we going there?"
"I have to know what happened to Julie. Mrs. Campbell won't
talk to me, but she might talk to you."

I spot Eileen straight away. She's kneeling on a garden mat,
wearing flowery rubber gloves and a hat with a veil, cutting
roses. Her hands shake with each snip. It's risky business for the
roses.
"Hi Diana," she says, waving. "You've just missed your aunt."
"Shit," I say, and she laughs out loud. I grab my phone from my
pocket and send my text.
"Sorry Eileen," I say, helping her up off her knees. "We've come
to see Mrs. Campbell, she's quite new, do you know what room
she's in?"
"Oh, I know everyone. She'll be in the day room, dear, it's
Pointless time. I'll walk with you. I'm so bored of gardening. Is this
your boyfriend?" she says, smiling at Richard.
"No," we both say, at once.
Richard's cheeks go full tomato. "I'm going to wait outside," he
says as we reach the entrance.
"Why?" I say. He's the reason we came!
"Because she's more likely to talk to you on her own."

"You know, you can come and see me any time you want. I've got an iPad. We can watch YouTube," Eileen says. She points to the corner of a pale yellow dayroom, where a woman is sitting on her own in front of the TV.

"Can I sit here?" I ask.

"Have you come to do my nails?" Mrs. Campbell says. "I've got my own colour here." Her purse rests in her lap. She fumbles with it and clumsily pulls out a ten pound note.

"No, I'm sorry," I say.

She puts the money away, looking sad. Her fingers shake trying to snap the clasp shut.

"Actually, I will do them today, but for free," I say, and pick up the small bottle of red varnish on the table.

She smiles and places her shaking right hand flat on the table. I'm good at nails.

"I'm a friend of Julie's actually, the girl who used to care for you," I say, as I swipe three stripes of varnish onto her thumb. "Do you know what happened to her?"

"She was such a lovely girl, but she moved away, dear."

"Did she tell you that she was moving?" I say, blowing softly on her fingers.

"No, she didn't tell me anything, but the fellow did."

"What fellow was that?" I say casually, lifting her other hand, placing it gently on the table.

"The foreign chap with the bone in his ear. I'll never forget. He came with the policeman. The policeman gave me his card. It's in my purse, but I don't want to smudge."

She nods at the purse in her lap, and I pick it up. Inside is one solitary ten-pound note, and a business card with Lattering CID on it, with a mobile number written on the back.

"Can I have this card?" I say.

"Of course, dear. I won't see her now, shut up in here."

"Thank you," I say, inspecting her nails. "Let's leave it a few minutes and I'll do the second coat."

We sit quietly next to each other, watching the TV. Occasionally she says an answer like "Frank Sinatra," or "Oooh, that's too hard."

She keeps her hands flat on the table. Every now and then she looks down at the colour and smiles.

The credits are rolling on Pointless and the second coat on her nails is dry. I get up to leave.

"It was really nice to meet you," I say.

"You too, dear. You've done a lovely job. I'm sorry Julie left you but it was such a nasty business, and it was scaring her."

"Sorry, I don't know…what business?"

"It was that ex of hers," she says, pursing her lips. "He didn't like her seeing that new fellow. She was such a tiny little thing."

"She had two boyfriends? Do you remember their names, Mrs. Campbell?"

"I didn't meet the new one. The first one was tall. I don't know why she split with him really, other than the new one had a big car."

~

Two wheelchairs are parked together on the grass, with a view of the ocean. I've never seen so many old people in one place before. What's the collective noun for a group of old people? A denture? A doily? A memory? I recite the conversation to Richard on a bench outside the home.

"So, that's it. She had two boyfriends, not one, and it could have been either of them," I say. "We know one of them was definitely Josh, because of the letters, and because The Mayan went to see her. But maybe they were both Thetis?"

"We need to go to Ralph's house," he says, standing up.

"Won't the police have taken the letters, if they've searched Ralph's room?" I say.

"Nope. Ralph is better at hiding than anybody."

2

Children are screaming and playing on the other side of the door, so we ring the bell again. Mrs. Srao finally answers, after five minutes. She doesn't even look at us.

Richard disappears into Ralph's room.

I make a cup of tea and sit with her silently in the living room. She has a pink stone in the middle of her forehead, and her sari is green and blue. She's young and so beautiful. She hadn't even occurred to me until now. Her husband has just come out of prison, she's got twin toddlers, and her eldest son is in a coma. She is broken. She's a whole other story.

The twins stagger around the room, gurgling. I rescue a choking hazard statue that one of them is sucking.

Richard comes out ten minutes later, and nods. His backpack looks full and heavy.

"We should go," he says to me.

"We can't leave her like this, it's not right. The kids could put anything in their mouths, one of them was just eating that china monkey."

"We'll call social services or someone," he says.

"We can't, she'll get in trouble, and it's not her fault really."

"It's not theirs either," Richard says, pointing to the twins.

"There must be another way," I say.

"We can tell Vita, she'll come and visit. But we have to go," Richard says walking into the kitchen. He washes out the teacups, putting them back in the cupboards, erasing our visit.

Mr. Srao is standing, key poised at the lock, when we open the door.

"What are you doing here?" he shouts at Richard. "You're a bad influence, both of you! Where are your parents? Look at his mother, she's having a breakdown!"

We move around him on the step, backing away.

"Inspector Ford told me this morning you're a bad crowd, you're using!"

"Using what?" I say, confused.

"Drink, and drugs!" Mr. Srao shouts at Richard.

"Ralph doesn't use drugs," Richard says quietly. "And he only drank that one time."

"And then he fell off a cliff!" Mr. Srao screams. "You are to blame! You corrupted my son!" He takes a step towards me, but Richard moves between us.

"You won't see him again," Mr. Srao shouts from the doorstep, as we walk away. "They are moving him, and you'll never hurt him again!"

Richard stops and turns around. "Where are they taking him?" he says.

"Away from you! He needs intensive treatment for his injuries."

"Where are they taking him?" Richard says again.

"I'm not telling you! You can't sell him your drugs anymore. Leave! Leave!"

~

"I need to get to the hospital," Richard says. "I need to find out where he's going."

"It's getting late Richard, I should get home, or Aunt Vita will wonder where I am."

My phone buzzes, but it's not Aunt Vita.

'Dr, 11.30am tomoz. Pickering Rd, behind Tesco's. C U outside? Heart U D, G xxx'

"See you tomorrow," he says, as the bus pulls up.

"Message me if you hear anything," I say, as the doors close behind him.

I cycle back through town. The inflatables are still swaying in the breeze outside Dave's Toy Emporium. Inside it's so packed full of plastic that there's only enough space for one person to walk down the aisle. A grumpy lady with corkscrew curls reads a newspaper behind the counter. Her boobs spill out of her top like porridge.

"Do you sell fancy dress?" I ask.

"On the back wall." she says, without looking up. "But I'm closing in five minutes."

The bird mask is hanging on its own. I pull it down and take it to the counter. She closes her newspaper and smiles. "Some kind of fashion, is it?"

"What?" I say.

"They've been on that wall for two years. I sold two last month, and now you."

"I don't want to buy it. Do you remember who bought the others?"

She tuts and sucks her teeth. Rude.

"Well if you aren't going to buy anything…" she says, opening her paper again.

"Fine." I pick up a bottle of bubbles.

She tuts again and taps at the till. "£1.50," she says.

"Well?" I say, giving her the change.

"Sorry, I don't remember love. Might have been a boy from the school. Tall. Very polite."

I thank her but we both know I don't mean it.

Jamie is leaning on Snoopy outside the shop. The sight of him makes me gasp.

"I've missed you," he says.

My cheeks burn but I don't know if it's attraction or anger. He looks like Josh today. I picture Ralph's body laying on the sand.

"If you took my number you wouldn't need to miss me."

"Josh looks at my phone all the time. I don't want him to know about us." He smiles and stands up, into my body space, too close.

"Are you that scared of your own brother?" I say, stepping back.

"Diana, what's wrong?" He reaches out and runs a finger down my hand.

My body tingles and I feel pathetic. Is this what love feels like? Because I HATE IT!!!

"Meet me tonight," he says, stroking the palm of my hand with his finger.

"I can't," I say, and I don't even know why, really.

"Diana, please?" he says. It's like I've kicked a disabled puppy, I've never seen anyone look so comically sad.

"Excuse me," I say, pulling my hand away, grabbing hold of Snoopy.

He steps forward. I feel his breath on my face. His lips graze my cheek when he says, "I need you, Diana. Please. You're my only hope. I'll be at Brizo at 9pm."

The urge to kiss him almost overwhelms me, but I walk away.

3

resh fat candles are burning inside the lanterns again. The blankets are already on the floor.

I wasn't going to come, but I put the ladder against the house earlier anyway. I positioned the pillows under the duvet, still thinking I wouldn't go. Then I found a reason, as I stuffed the mask in my rucksack and dropped out of my window, along the path, and through the gate.

At least it's not raining. The moon is bright, and the sky is clear.

Brizo looks different, less creepy, more peaceful. Half of the plastic sheeting is gone.

I walk in wearing the mask.

"Fuck, what the hell is that?" Jamie says, jumping backwards.

A wave of relief sweeps through me, as I pull it off and chuck it on the blanket. He's clearly never seen it before.

"It's nothing, just a joke."

"I got pizza." he says, pointing at the unopened box.

"I'm not hungry," I say.

He walks forward until he's standing over me. I look up at his beautiful face. It's like invisible cabling wraps itself around us and binds us together and I *have* to touch him.

"Thank you for coming, Diana. You are the most important

person I've ever met," he says, taking my face in his hands, studying me.

"You don't even know me," I say, and kiss him.

Twenty minutes later, we are lying on the floor. He has the most beautiful chest, completely smooth and tanned, and I can't believe I get to touch it.

"I wish we could just disappear," he says, contemplating our laced fingers.

"Aren't you cold?" I say.

"I like the feel of you on my skin. It makes me feel real. I know that sounds like some bullshit poetry."

"Have you had many other girlfriends?" I say.

"Not really. A couple of summer things. Nothing that felt like this."

"Jamie, did you know Julie Peters?" I don't know why I ask, except I have to know.

His fingers stiffen in mine. "Why are you asking me about her?"

"She was gone before I got here, and she and Gloria used to be best friends. I just wondered if you knew her?"

He coughs uncomfortably and drops my hand. I want to scream.

"I didn't, really," he says. He stands, pulling on his top, covering up. "It's getting late, we should get back."

"Why are you acting like that?" I say, trying not to cry.

"Like what?" he says, but he won't look at me.

"Like you did something wrong!"

He clenches his fists, and his face tightens like there are strings sewn into the back of his neck and someone is pulling them.

"Can't it just be enough that I actually like you, Diana?"

His fists are still balled, and it's all I can focus on.

"Can't we just ignore everyone else? I thought you liked *me*, Diana, like I like *you*."

"Of course I like you! Look at you!" I say, and it's like I spat in his face.

"Do you even care who I am? Or is it just about how I look?" he says.

"Oh, bullshit Jamie! You *do* look like that, and that makes you who you are, as happy as you are, as confident as you are. The world loves you *because* of how you look Jamie, don't be naïve."

"And who are you, the elephant man? Because you wear glasses and you've got red hair? Stop pretending you don't know you're pretty, it's so fucking fake!"

"I'm fake? Coming from you and your friends Audrey and Virginia?"

"You think you know so much, Diana, but you don't understand anything about my situation, at all. You're just jealous of the money."

"I hate money!" I scream.

"No, you don't. Nobody does!"

He grabs the blankets up of the floor, and kicks the uneaten pizza box in to the corner.

"Look, maybe we shouldn't see each other for a while," he says, blowing out the lanterns. "Come on, I'll walk you back."

"I don't need you to walk me anywhere!" I shout and run out.

4

"Hello," Aunt Vita says, as I climb back through my window. She's sitting on my bed in the dark. My heart sinks.

"I came to find Howard," she says evenly, "but I found this instead." She holds up the pillows that were supposed to be me.

I pull my phone out of my pocket, still on silent. I keep forgetting I've got it back. Twelve texts, ten missed calls.

"I was about to call the police," she says calmly.

"I'm so sorry."

"Where were you, Diana?"

I don't reply. She'll hate it. She'll hate me. I stare at the ground instead, waiting for it to end.

"You're a bloody silly girl," she says, standing up. Her eyes are furious with tears.

"And you're not my mother, so stop acting like it!" I shout. "You've known me for five minutes! Where were *you* for the other sixteen years, if you really care about me?"

She wipes her eyes furiously as fat tears spill out.

"I thought being around you would hurt too much, but-"

I don't let her finish. "And if you had cared about my mother enough, she wouldn't have killed herself!"

I run into the bathroom and slam the door shut. I slump to the floor in the dark and burst into tears. I hear her walk across the hallway into her bedroom and quietly close her door.

"I take it back," I whisper to the dark. "I take it back."

~

I can't just sit on my bed forever. I take a deep breath and walk downstairs. Howard has biscuits and water already. The blinds are up in the kitchen and early morning sunshine pours in, uninterrupted. The radio is off. Aunt Vita's Hillary Clinton mug is in the middle of the table, filled with tea. That's a good sign at least. Steam is still rising from the middle. The Post-it reads 'Speak tonight'. No kisses.

The wind has changed. Sheets of sand blow through town and everybody rubs their red eyes. I check my phone: 11.40am. Still no sign of Gloria. I walk up a neat path and push the door. It opens into a small, brown room that smells of old magazines.

"Excuse me, I was supposed to meet my friend here for her appointment. Gloria Dennett. Has she already gone in? I'm afraid I might have missed her."

"No, she hasn't arrived yet, dear."

Standing with my legs on either side of Snoopy, I message her again. I wait 30 seconds for a reply, but nothing comes.

I stop halfway along Beach Road and call her. It goes straight to voicemail. I leave a message and ride Snoopy to the flats. I knock loudly, and wait for ages, but nobody comes. I peer through the kitchen window, and then the letterbox.

I spend the rest of the afternoon looking out of the shop window, waiting, but I don't see her. I text her again, before I climb back on Snoopy for the ride home. 'PLEASE tell me u r OK xxx'.

There's another party at Mandalay. I drop Snoopy on the grass and walk straight in. It's never been this busy, and I don't see anyone that I recognise.

I pour myself half a glass of rum, fill the rest up with coke, and neck it. The music is so loud, louder than usual, blasting out of speakers in all the rooms. I pour myself another drink.

An hour later I'm slumped on the futon in the big lounge, with a long-haired guy I don't know. He's been talking to me about the waves in Australia for thirty minutes. It's so boring, but then I'm SO drunk. The music beats through my body, and my ears are ringing. I still haven't seen anyone I know. I flick at the beads on my bracelet, sinking further into the shadows in the corner of the room. I can't see anything beyond the forest of legs in front of me. I yawn. I should go home.

"Am I boring you?" he says.

"Yes," I say.

He puts his drink on the floor and starts kissing me, and it hurts. His tongue stabs into my mouth, like he wants to cut me. He smells of beer, and damp, and sweat, and metal, and garlic. He tastes disgusting. I try to wriggle out from underneath him, but he grabs the flesh at the top of my arms and moves himself on top of me. Nobody can see I'm trying to stop him.

"Get off," I say, squirming my head, trying to push him away. I feel sick.

His thigh is pinning my legs down. He holds my wrists with one of his hands above my head and digs his fingers into my cheeks with the other.

"You're a fucking prick tease," he says, shoving his tongue in my mouth again. He's so heavy, it feels like I'm belted down. I can't get his tongue out of my mouth. His hair is in my eyes, and I can't see anything. His fingers are digging harder into my cheeks. I'm laying flat on the futon. He's laying directly on top of me, pinning me down, one of his knees is between my legs.

Nobody can hear me shouting over the music. There are people everywhere. I can see their bare feet on the floorboards beside me. This is going to happen and there are people everywhere.

"GET OFF ME!" I scream in his face.

"Shut up, you stupid bitch," he says, covering my mouth with his cheek, trying to undo my jeans.

And then, suddenly, I'm free. I scramble to my feet, coughing the taste of him from my mouth.

"Get the fuck away from her," Aunt Vita screams in his face.

Byron has him in a headlock.

"Who's this, your fucking mother?" he says. His face is red, his mouth covered in his own phlegm. He spits on the floor.

"Deal with that," she says to Byron, as he drags him away.

"What are you doing here?" she says, incredulous.

We are standing in the hallway, as far from the music as we can get, but it's still hard to hear.

"What are YOU doing here?" I say, closing my eyes, but everything spins.

Byron walks towards us, nodding at Aunt Vita. They stand in front of me like Batman and Robin.

"Sober up, you're coming home," Aunt Vita says, grabbing my hand, but I throw it off.

"I don't need you to look after me. I look after myself!" I can hear myself slurring.

"Oh, clearly," she shouts, gesturing at the sofa.

"Vita, I've got this, tonight." Byron reaches out and puts his hand on her arm gently.

She looks from me to him and throws her hands in the air. "This wasn't the deal!" she says to us both, and storms off.

"So, you know each other," I slur at Byron. I'm propped on a beanbag on the deck.

"Drink your water," he says.

"Nobody ever tells me the truth anyway," I say.

"Diana, why are you so drunk?"

I laugh, false and dramatic, and it makes me cough. I feel a sliver of sick shoot up my throat and I cover my mouth. I swallow it back down and swig my water.

"Everything is shit. Literally everything is the shittest it's ever been," I say.

The water gurgles around my tummy, and it hurts. My muscles convulse. I gag. The first, full mouthful of sick explodes from my stomach into my mouth.

"Damn, I'll get a bucket," Byron says, running off.

The sick is oozing out between my fingers, and I run into the garden. I throw up over a bush. I feel weak, and my head rushes.

Tears are streaming down my face at the exhaustion, as my stomach muscles convulse again, and more sick rushes up and out of me. I wipe my eyes, and my mouth. I look through into the next garden.

The figure in the bird mask is standing by the gate, watching me.

"You aren't even real, I'm drunk," I say, but he shakes his head and walks around the side of the house. I slump to the ground.

I wake up briefly, as I'm picked up and carried away in the dark.

5

I'm lying in a comfortable bed, under a duvet. I feel for my clothes. They aren't mine. I'm wearing a T-shirt I don't recognise, and a pair of men's pajama trousers. I sit up and it's like arrows are being fired into my brain. I clutch my head and try to focus.

Byron is in the corner on a huge beanbag, still in his clothes from last night. Three wetsuits hang on hooks in the corner.

"Good morning," he says rubbing his eyes, yawning. "How's the head?"

"Really bad. What happened?"

"Rum happened, mostly. You got drunk again, Diana."

"But how did I get here?" I gesture at the bed, and the clothes that aren't mine.

"You passed out in the garden. Your clothes were covered in puke, so I got Michelle to change you. Then we put you to bed."

I shake my head, and it hurts. I remember getting to the party and pouring myself drinks.

"Wait, was my aunt here?" I say, wide-eyed.

"Briefly."

"But, how? Why?"

Bryon makes a *beats me* face.

I look at my hands. They are filthy. The dirt under my nails has stuck.

There are half full glasses of alcohol everywhere. Byron cleans and clears an area of the kitchen counter, grabbing bags of green leaves and an avocado from the cupboard, as I curl up on the wooden bench and close my eyes. A terrible noise threatens to explode my brain. I open my eyes to see him pressing down on a food blender. He pours the mixture into a pint glass and cracks a raw egg in the middle.

"Drink this," he says, passing it to me. "You'll feel better."

I down it, no gagging.

~

Felix is SO angry. I check my watch: it's 9.45am.

"What time do you call this?" he seethes, storming past me with three plates.

"I'm so sorry, Felix. Isn't Gloria here?" I look around desperately. I listen for the sounds of her, but there is nothing.

"No, she bloody isn't. Not a bloody word from either of you. I'm not a charity ya' know! There are other people that want these jobs."

"I'm so sorry, Felix. I'm here now."

I shove my stuff under the counter, plug my phone in to the wall, and deal with the immediate, angry orders and cups of tea.

After twenty minutes everyone seems happier, and my phone is alive again. I bang in the message 'WHERE ARE YOU?!!!!'.

As soon as I can I run to the new library. It smells of paint and new carpets. The main room has doubled in size, and the bookshelves are all arranged around the sides instead of snaking through the middle.

Richard and the library manager, a tanned old lady with glasses and orange lipstick, are loading books back onto the shelves.

"Hey," I whisper, "I need to talk to you."

"What's going on?" he says, putting a stack of self-help books down.

"Gloria is missing," I say. "She didn't come to work, and she won't reply to any of my messages,"

"That doesn't mean she's missing. She's probably at home."

"No, I mean she hasn't replied to me for a whole day, not even yesterday, and I went to the flat and it was deserted. And she didn't even call Felix this morning, to say she wasn't coming in. Something is wrong Richard, I know it."

When we ring the doorbell at the flat, I hear movement inside. Nanna Gloria shuffles slowly towards the front door as I tap my foot impatiently.

"Oh, I thought you were Gloria," she says, turning, shuffling back to the lounge.

"Haven't you seen her today, Nanna Gloria?" I say, poking my head around Gloria's bedroom door. The bed isn't made. The duvet is in the same position that it was two days ago. I can't see her boots. I can't see her phone.

"No, dear. She'll be home soon I expect. You can wait in her room if you'd like."

She positions herself in front of her armchair and drops back into it with a small thud.

"What are we looking for?" Richard says.

"I don't know. A photo maybe? Her phone? I want to know who she was seeing."

Richard starts pulling the bed away from the wall.

"No, she's not Julie," I say, rolling my eyes. "Just check the drawers and stuff."

I find it straightaway in a drawer, stuffed behind bikinis.

"This isn't her phone," I say. It's a small, silver iPhone, brand new, not even in a case. I tap in her usual password 'D1R0SS'. There's no photo, just a blue screen. WhatsApp is all she's downloaded, and all the messages are from one unsaved number. No name, no kisses.

Tonight. 8pm. beach.

Tonight. 10pm. Tesco's carpark.

Tomorrow. 11pm. path.

"Do we call the number?" I say.

"Check the photos," Richard says.

6

J osh Beltrome's face stares out at us from Gloria's secret phone. He looks different. A bit less of an asshole, if that's even possible. There is a selfie of the two of them together, kissing, as Gloria holds the phone at arm's length.

I want to slap his face away from hers. I swipe and a huge, naked, erect, penis fills the screen. I practically drop the phone.

Richard and I both look away, and his cheeks go FULL tomato. We sit down next to each other on the bed.

"We don't need to call the number, then," I say.

"We don't know for certain he's the reason she's missing," Richard says. "We don't know for certain she *is* missing."

"Richard, I have to tell you something, but you have to swear you won't tell anyone."

He nods seriously. I hear Nanna Gloria shuffling into the kitchen outside.

"Gloria is pregnant," I whisper.

He sighs heavily. "So was Julie," he says.

"How do you know, from the letters?" I say, but he shakes his head.

"She told me," he says, digging his nails into his palm.

I pull his fingers away. I've seen too much blood recently.

"I don't understand. Why would she tell *you* that?"

He takes a deep breath. "Because it was my baby," Richard says quietly.

What the ACTUAL FUCK?

7

I message Aunt Vita. 'Are you coming to the shop?'

The reply comes instantly. 'In an hour'. She's still mad, of course.

"So?" I say to Richard, as we pull up outside.

"So," he says, "we wait."

It's what we've agreed. We'll tell Vita everything about Ralph, and Julie, and Gloria and she'll know what to do.

Richard unlocks the shop and goes inside. He hasn't explained anything about Julie and the baby, and I'm starting to wonder if I even heard him right.

I glance over at Breakers. Audrey, Virginia, and Josh are walking out. I'm running before I know I'm running.

"I know!" I shout at Josh.

"Oh fuck, Pound Shop, what now?" Audrey says. "Can't you leave us alone?"

"Shall I tell everyone?" I shout at him as he walks off down the street. I pull at his arm and he spins around, glaring at me.

The back of his hand raises, and he holds it like it's on a spring, like it could fly towards my face at any moment, but I'm not scared, even if I should be.

I step forwards and get in his face. "I know *everything*," I whisper. "Do you even know everything, Josh?"

Someone puts their hand over my mouth and lifts me in the air. I kick and scream as he carries me away.

Jamie dumps me on the bench outside of Two Scoops.

"Never touch me again without my permission," I say. "I'm not your property. Stop carrying me around."

"Go back to London, Diana, and leave us alone," he says, and starts to walk away.

"Gloria is missing, and so is Julie Peters," I shout at the back of his head.

His fists clench by his sides, but he doesn't turn around.

"You're so scared, you're pathetic," I say.

"I didn't even like you, Diana, okay? I just thought you'd be easy." But he won't look at me. I can feel my lip trembling, but I'm not going to cry. "I don't believe you," I say quietly.

"Believe what you want. Just leave, before something happens that I can't stop."

"Like what, Jamie? What's going to happen to me? What does your dad do to people?"

Something hardens his face. "Just go, Diana, before you really get hurt."

"I'm already hurt," I whisper, as he walks away.

I wipe my eyes as Aunt Vita walks in the shop. Richard bolts the front door behind her.

"What's going on?" she says, looking between us, alarmed.

"Gloria is missing," I say.

"What? When did you last see her?"

"Two days ago. We arranged to meet yesterday, and she didn't show up. She's not answering any of my messages, she didn't come to work, and Nanna Gloria hasn't seen her either."

"We found a phone in her bedroom," Richard says.

I put it on the counter in front of her. She eyes it with suspicion.

"Okay," is all she says.

"Gloria was dating Josh Beltrome. So was Julie Peters. Now, they are both missing."

"Shit," she says, narrowing her eyes.

"And they were both pregnant," Richard says.

"Shit," she says again, leaning against the counter, covering her face with her hands.

"Do you know where Ralph is?" Richard says.

She shakes her head. "Susan is trying to find out. He's disappeared from the system. It's all very…odd."

"Won't Mr. Srao tell us, if you ask him?" I say.

"Mr. Srao was arrested again this morning," she says.

"No," Richard says, turning pale.

"His mother is in hospital, and the twins have been taken into care."

I feel like I'm hanging in the air, a foot from the ground.

"What's happening, Vita?" Richard asks. "This can't all be coincidence."

"I don't know," Aunt Vita says. "But you are right - something feels *very* wrong. Have you reported Gloria missing?"

"The local police are corrupt. They are being paid by Hugo Beltrome," I say. "And he's still here, in town."

"Okay," my aunt says. "Will you two please stay here, together, and keep the door bolted. I need to speak to someone."

"Can't I come with you?" I ask. I want to be with her. I want to do something.

"I can't bring you with me this time, darling, but I promise I'll tell you everything later. Please just stay together, okay?"

We nod, and she rushes off, without a backwards glance.

"It all leads back to Thetis, doesn't it?" I say, half an hour later.

We are leaning on the counter. It's the first thing either of us have said since Aunt Vita left. Richard nods.

"We can't just stand here, Richard. They could be hurting them."

He looks so sad. He hasn't told anybody else. He could have been a father.

"We aren't powerless," I say. "Why aren't we doing something?"

"We can't just knock on the door at Thetis and demand to know what they've done," he says.

I bite my lip and think, and the fog in my brain clears.

"What day is it?" I say.

"Thursday," Richard says. "Why?"

8

I find the dress I wore to the refuge party hanging up in my aunt's bedroom. I throw Howard a treat and slam the door behind me.

I text Aunt Vita. 'With Richard, he had to meet his granddad, he'll walk me home xx'.

I hover behind the library scaffolding in the square. I've never felt this nervous, or this sick. I gulp it down, again and again. Not today. The monster car pulls up dead on 6pm, and I sprint over and jump in before anyone sees.

The Mayan watches me in the mirror as we drive out of town, towards the cliffs. The sun is in front of us, low and hot and wide, filling the sky. It's the same yellow as his eyes. We take a sharp right, along a long tree-lined driveway, and I fall sideways on the seat.

"Okay?" he says, as I sit up.

I ignore him.

"You look so well, Diana," he says. "This sea air suits you. You should have done this long ago."

I don't answer.

The car growls quietly as we wait for the Thetis gates to open, and The Mayan whistles a nursery rhyme.

The floor is white marble. A huge chandelier hangs above me, glass daggers pointing at my head. Old blue vases of white flowers sit elegantly on dark tables, perfectly spaced along a vast pale wall. Gold framed mirrors have the same scratchy glass as the one in Aunt Vita's bedroom. A flight of stairs leads up to the left. Photos of old white men in slim, silver frames hang in cliques. It's the most beautiful room I've ever seen, and I hate it.

A door opens down the hall and a tall man walks out, staring at his phone, heading straight towards me. He doesn't even realise I'm standing here.

I cough, and he looks up. I *know* him.

He turns and disappears through the same space as The Mayan.

"Diana," Hugo Beltrome says behind me.

I jump, and spin around.

He holds out his hand for me to shake, and envelopes my fingers, squeezing too tightly. "I'm so glad you came. Welcome to Thetis."

～

We are alone in a panelled room with blood-red sofas and thousands of books, in the ruins of the old house. We walked up four flights of stairs and along a passageway made completely of glass, connected to an old stone wall. I cradle a tumbler of elderflower cordial that I don't trust.

Hugo Beltrome pours himself a glass of sherry. "What do you think of the school?" he says.

I am sitting at one end of a long sofa. He sits at the other and crosses his legs.

"It's big," I say.

He leans back, sips his drink, and smiles. "I believe that every child has a gift, Diana. It is the duty of their parents and educators to find it, to allow them to be the best versions of themselves. Then, they will be at their happiest, their healthiest, and their most successful. In this way they make the best contribution to society they can."

"You believe that every *male* child has a gift," I say, correcting him.

He smiles as if I don't understand something vital. "Well, women are born with the greatest gift already, Diana. Us men have to work a little harder to find ours."

"I must have missed all the pictures of women giving birth in the hall downstairs," I mumble. He ignores that, brushing an imaginary speck of dust from his trousers. That's what he does with anything he doesn't like.

"Diana, like it or not, you are at a crossroads, and you have a simple choice to make about the shape of your life from today onwards. As we grow older, we are often faced with difficult decisions. The trick is to act without emotion, based on the facts. I understand that you may want to cling to the safety of what you've known before, even if it actually wasn't comfortable: your broken, dangerous little house, your challenging school environment, the constant financial struggles. There is safety in what we know, even if it isn't enjoyable. But, Diana, you are an adult now and I am presenting you with another option. It will mean facing up to some difficult and perhaps even painful truths about the world, while acknowledging that the people that have helped you thus far may not be the right people to guide you through the next stages of your life."

"You're saying I should ditch my dad?"

"I'm saying you have a choice, Diana, and the decision you make, if you are brave, may bring you a level of happiness that you've never known."

"I don't understand," I say. "Why me? I know I'm clever, but there are lots of clever kids. Plus, I'm a girl, and you hate girls."

"I do not *hate* girls, and you aren't just clever, Diana. You are exceptional. It's not the time or place to fully explain it to you today, but you will come to see that we are inextricably linked. I cannot impress upon you just how important you are to me. You have a gift, and now you have a choice. It may prove difficult, but history is governed by people who made difficult choices."

"Like Hitler?"

Hugo rolls his black eyes. "No, Diana, not like Hitler. That's beneath you. But our leaders, our brilliant minds, the names that litter the history books with their good deeds and their progress, they actively chose their path. They weren't passive. They made fundamental decisions at important points, just like this, to prioritise their success over their personal comfort."

"Aunt Vita says that history books are unrepresentative and subjective. They just tell the stories of the most powerful, who are usually white and male, and their sanitised versions of what they did to win."

Hugo smiles and rolls his eyes again, at Aunt Vita, and everybody that isn't him. "Well, your Aunt Vita says a lot of things. Perhaps some new influences will do you good, Diana."

"So, you're saying if I join your school, I can change the world?"

"Perhaps. But what I do know for certain is that if you attend my schools you become part of my family, which means you have my protection. The great secret, Diana, is that life is only hard for some people, but then I think you already know that. All your nasty little schoolmates and their bullying ways. You are the brightest of them all so shouldn't you be treated better? Why does their wealth give them status, but your intelligence doesn't? That isn't fair, but it *is* life. I know that you know what it means to feel powerless, but now you have a choice. I am giving you that choice. You don't have to be a victim of circumstances anymore."

"I don't want to be a victim," I say, and it's the truth.

How wonderful must it be to feel safe? To know that your life is going to be okay, that you'll have money, that trouble won't find you, that you'll be cocooned from the challenges of the everyday. To exist above it all on a cloud of wealth and protection.

I think of Aunt Vita, and her daily slog just to help everyone else get by, running around trying to save the word, and right all the wrongs, and soften the blow of all the problems that beset people, while her own life is a shambles, and her garden gate keeps falling over, and her roof leaks, and she has her crazy conversations with the ocean. But still, I think she's happy.

I look at Hugo Beltrome, smirking at me from his expensive cloud. Does he seem happy?

He sees me looking at him, and smiles. "What are you thinking Diana?"

"It's certainly a very appealing offer, Mr. Beltrome. It would be nice to feel...protected. I assume The Mayan does that for you, too?"

"Oh, that silly nickname the boys use is so sinister. Juan is an old friend and a trusted colleague."

"And a cleaner?" I say.

He looks at me quizzically, and a shot of fear runs down my spine.

"This is the biggest choice you may ever make Diana. I'd take it very seriously if I were you."

"Can I ask you a question first please, Mr. Beltrome?"

"Of course." He puts down his sherry and gives me his full black-eyed attention.

"What happens to the mothers of your children?"

He coughs. Once. "I have full custody of my children, Diana. Their mothers were happy with the legal arrangements we came to."

"But you have, like, twenty children just here at Thetis. Where are all their mothers?"

"The boys have everything they need here, Diana. I can't speak to the location of women who are no longer in my life."

"So, they just went away? Without their babies?"

He nods.

"But why would they do that? Just leave them and go and...oh, shiiiiiiit," I say.

Something vital lands in my brain, like a block falling in to place. I can't believe I didn't see it until now.

"You grew an army," I say, incredulous.

I've always done the voluntary reading of course. I read The Art of War last Christmas, for history. My brain locks on the mind-map of my revision notes.

"Regard your soldiers as your children and they will follow you into the deepest valleys," I recite from memory. "Look on them as your own beloved sons, and they will stand by you even unto death."

"Diana, I applaud your knowledge, but not your reasoning. You are being overly dramatic, as teenage girls are wont to do. I simply negotiated custody of my children. I am their father, after all."

"You didn't care about their mothers at all, you just wanted another loyal body to work for you, to make you money. But what about the mothers who didn't want to give you their babies?" I ask. "There must have been at least one who wouldn't leave without a fight?"

He flicks imaginary specks from his trousers. I swear he smirks.

"What happened to them, Mr. Beltrome?" I say again.

"Be careful, Diana," is all he says. He sips his sherry, and I know Gloria is in terrible danger.

The view through the window in Hugo's study is spectacular, like a painting. A big, round sun lingers above a still, blue ocean. Clusters of the purple flowering Lattering bushes edge a perfectly manicured lawn. White roses cling to a high gated wall. I think I'm in shock.

"Also, where are their sisters?" I whisper.

Hugo Beltrome gives a bored sigh, and re-crosses his legs.

"This conversation isn't productive, Diana, and you are being ridiculous. This isn't a horror story. Your imagination has clearly been allowed to run riot for too long."

"But I'd like to know," I say, "if I'm going to join your school, your family. If I'm so important. Have you killed them all? Are they all dead?"

He laughs then, like I'm a joke. "Diana, of course not. I'm not a monster. Think of it this way...have you heard of Arthur Schopenhauer?"

I shake my head.

"He was a German philosopher. He said that fundamental truth passes through three stages. First, it is ridiculed. Then, it is violently opposed. Finally, it is accepted as being self-evident. You can laugh at it, or oppose it, but that doesn't mean what I believe won't eventually come to be seen as the truth. Feminism has fundamentally harmed society, Diana. It is confusing and unnatural. It has created sad, rageful, suicidal societies. You just haven't realised it yet."

"But where are all the girls?" I say.

"Diana, you aren't listening to me. There are whole villages in India where no girls are ever born. There are plenty of steps you can take to control life's outcomes, if you have the resources and the requirement."

"But what if it's too late, by the time you find out? Or they make a mistake with the scans? They say that happens all the time. People paint their nursery pink and then they have a boy. What happens then?"

"Diana, your mind is running away with itself to some fanciful places."

"Okay, if you won't tell me that, will you tell me this? I'm a girl. Why do you even want me here?"

"I told you, Diana. Because you are special." He leans over and passes me a small white card. It has a phone number on it, in gold type, but nothing else. "This is my personal number, Diana. Only my family have it. And now I am giving it to you."

"You keep saying that, that I'm special. Why?"

He opens his mouth to speak, but a knock on the door startles us both.

"Come in," Hugo says, but he is irritated.

"What is it, Ford?" Hugo says.

I *know* him.

He passes Hugo a note, and his expression changes. He's furious.

"Please excuse me for a few moments, Diana. We are having a small gathering tonight, and I need to speak to one of my guests."

He nods at Ford and walks out. The tall man stands uncomfortably in front of the door.

I know his face. I know that name. Ford. Somebody has said that name to me recently. I've read that name. More blocks land and fit together in my brain at once....

The noise was at the hospital, as he stood outside my dad's door, after his operation. He was chewing gum. He's always chewing gum. He was younger then. And 'Inspector Ford' is written in spiders on the back of the business card Mrs. Campbell gave me, after Julie disappeared. "Inspector Ford told me this morning," Mr. Srao shouted at us on the steps of his house.

"I just got my period," I say standing up. "If I don't go now there will be blood everywhere."

Ford coughs so hard he swallows his gum. I hope he chokes on it.

"I don't want it to drip all over the white floor," I say, as Ford walks ahead of me. He's practically gagging.

"It's at the far end on the right," he says, stopping, leaning against the wall, refusing to look at me as I push my skirt between my legs for maximum effect. He pulls out his phone and starts poking it angrily.

I duck around the corner, and the bathroom door swings shut on its own.

I slip off my shoes, holding them in my hands like weapons, and tiptoe along the corridor as quickly as I can. The stone walls become glass, and the floor beneath me is completely clear. The courtyard is thirty feet below me.

The Mayan stalks across it urgently. It reminds me of visiting the aquarium with my dad when I was little. You had to walk across glass to get to the main tunnels. Fish danced over our heads as a giant shark appeared beneath us, eyeing me up like breakfast. I knew the shark couldn't *really* eat me, but I wouldn't have been surprised if he'd snapped through that glass and swallowed me whole.

Just because you know something is true, it doesn't mean you believe it.

I turn left at the end of the glass corridor and run down the first flight of stairs. There are voices coming up the stairs. I flatten my back up against the wall behind a heavy curtain and turn my feet sideways on; ballet position number one.

"Fuck, I'm hungry. Dinner was shit. We should fire the fucking cook," Josh says, kicking every step before him.

I hold my breath. My heart is beating too loud, too hard, too fast.

When all I can hear again is the sound of my heart banging in my chest, I poke my head out. I run down the stairs, two at a time, and swerve around the corner.

I crash straight into someone's chest and freeze as he grabs me by the arms and whispers, "What are you doing here, Diana?"

9

"I'm leaving," I say, shrugging him off.

"But why are you here?" Jamie says, looking around like we are being watched.

"Your dad invited me. He wants me to go to your school."

Jamie shakes his head, horrified. "No, Diana. You can't. You have to leave."

"Don't worry, I'm going," I say. "Which way is it?"

"I'll show you."

Jamie leads me along a corridor, checking before each doorway, stopping at the end, before we turn towards a flight of stairs that look familiar.

"It's down there, two lefts and a right. I'm sorry, I didn't ask if I could touch you," he says.

He's been leading me by the hand. He drops it like it's hot.

"Aren't you going to show me the way out?" I ask.

"I can't. There are cameras."

I stare at his beautiful, frightened face. "What happens here?" I say.

Jamie opens his mouth to speak, but a soft, low whistle replies, a twisted version of a nursery rhyme. He pushes me through a doorway on the left, and around a corner.

"Go down there," he says, pointing to a dark flight of stairs. "Then keep turning right, until you get to a big, green door. It leads to the storeroom and you can get out onto the lawn through the service gate, but don't go across the grass. It has sensors and they'll go off."

The whistle is getting closer.

"I'll distract him," Jamie says. "Now go."

I run right, and right again, but there is no green door, just dark corridors leading to even darker rooms. It feels like I'm going further and further into the pit of the old building. I try not to think about dungeons, and chains on blood spattered walls. I try not to think about the fact that Jamie might have lied.

I run down a thin line of stairs with no bannister, into a small den filled with bean bags, and a massive TV on the wall. I stop suddenly on the bottom step. Something is wrong. I'm not alone.

"Hello," a voice says from the shadows. "Can I help you?"

A young boy stands up from a bean bag in the corner. He must be eleven or twelve. He looks familiar, but not exactly like Jamie. He's playing a game on his phone.

My heart is banging in my chest and I'm struggling to control my adrenaline.

"I'm just trying to find the way out," I say, as casually as I can.

"Oh, it's through here, I'll show you," he says, smiling, taking my hand.

"Are you having a baby?" he says. His fingers are locked in mine as if we are safely crossing the road.

"No. But a friend of mine is. She has pink and brown hair and brown skin, and she's very beautiful. Have you met her?"

"Yes, I saw her yesterday, at the top of the house," he says, and I have to stop myself crying out. "She has a bit of her hair missing, like a cat who's had an operation. They are waiting for Doctor Cole to come and see her. They don't think I listen, but I do," he says.

"Is she okay?" I say, trembling.

He shrugs. "She was shouting for a while. No crying though. Sometimes they cry."

"I really need to give her a message. Do you know where she is now?"

"No," he says, shaking his head, leading me around a corner to a big, green door.

"She's not still at the top of the house?" I say, a little desperately.

He shakes his head. He's sweet. He doesn't know this is a house of horror. "I haven't seen her today," he says. "Maybe The Mayan took her for a walk?"

I stand with one hand on the door. "What's your name?" I say, as a new set of voices begins to descend above us.

I pull on the handle and the old door creaks open. There is a store room on the other side, packed full of boxes, and bottles, and brooms.

"Gulliver Beltrome," he says.

He's so innocent. "What's yours?"

"Diana."

His expression changes. The voices are near. I should run. I can't rescue him too.

"Why are you sad?" I say, not running.

"My mum knows somebody called Diana," he says. "She talks about her a lot."

His eyes are the same colour as mine.

I take a step into the storeroom.

"It is funny though," he says, breaking into a big, silly wide-mouthed smile, just like Aunt Vita.

"What is?" I say.

"You look just like her. My mum." He laughs, but my heart has stopped.

"What's your mum's name, Gulliver?" I ask. *Please* don't say it.

"Lana Beltrome, of course," he says. "Bye, Diana, it was nice to meet you."

He closes the green door in my face.

BEFORE

J uan is concerned. *She refuses to eat, and without food she has no sedatives, and without sedatives, she is not calm. She just keeps muttering the girl's name, over and over: Diana, Diana. Diana.*

It has been the same every morning for a month, since he gave her the photos of Diana on her sixteenth birthday. Diana sat behind the house, on her mother's bench. It was the perfect shot, he thought, she looked so beautiful. But now he understands his mistake. She did look beautiful, but she was sad, and alone, and something fundamental in Lana has shifted. She wants to see her daughter again. She thinks she needs to save her.

"What do we even know about the girl?" Hugo asks him.

"Diana was sixteen last month. It wouldn't be kidnapping any longer."

"And what of Tom, and his investigation?"

"I mean, he knows some things, mainly about the Hunt, but nothing anyone would take seriously. He would be easy to take care of."

"What are you thinking, my friend?"

"Perhaps we tell him we have some information about you. We arrange to meet and then, perhaps, remove him from the equation."

"And the child?"

"Diana would go to Vita, I believe."

"In Lattering you mean?"

Juan nods and Hugo smiles.

"Oh, then it would be simple, wouldn't it? Get Tom out of the picture – mental health or something, best not to do anything too final at first, to risk upsetting the child – and then convince Diana to come and look at the school. What alternative would there be for her in Lattering? And then, when she's settled, and one of us, we gradually reintroduce the idea that her mother has been away, but now... She'll be so happy she's alive, I can't imagine she'll even question it. And so, Diana will be my gift to Lana, and Gulliver, Tom will fade from her memory and at that point we make his situation more final. Yes, that's perfect. Let us begin Juan, it feels very straightforward, no?"

Juan nods and turns to leave.

"And what of Vita?" he asks at the door. "If she tries to stop Diana coming to Thetis?"

Hugo sits back down at his desk and answers without even looking up from his notes, "Women who live alone choke all the time."

~

*J*uan stands in the corner of the sitting room watching Lana at the piano. She presses the same key over and over, a repetitive, dull, low thud. With every note she whispers the same name. She needs her medication.

He loves her more than Hugo, now.

Back at his computer, he flicks on the camera in the kitchen. Diana is having breakfast alone, revising as usual. She works harder than any Thetis boy. Her hair is down this morning. She's washed it. She looks just like her mother. He hates that uniform, he always has. There is so much he will teach her. He will be the father she deserves. She will be the daughter he lost.

He flicks to the CCTV camera at the top of Beach Road. Somebody has dumped a bag of clothes outside the refuge shop overnight. Half of the contents have already fallen out onto the pavement. He sighs, because money never cleans up its own mess.

Vita hurries out of Seagulls and walks towards the shop. That's the other thing of course. Vita doesn't live alone anymore. She's been married for a year. A carbon monoxide leak will be cleanest. He'll have to kill them both.

Juan sits down with a pen and paper, to compose a letter.

Dear Mr. Lind,
I have valuable information about the illegal practices of Hugo Beltrome, and the disappearance of your wife. If you want to know more, meet me at the offices of Blair, Dixon, Garvey and Law, on Lincolns Inn Fields, tomorrow at 8am. Come alone, and make arrangements to be gone for a short while. There is much to show you, not all of it in London. You do not know if you can trust me, but do you have a choice?
A Friend

PART IX

1

I don't know *how* Byron knew I would fall from the bottom of the secret path at that moment in to the freezing water, or that I would be exhausted, and crying, and need him to carry me out of the ocean. But he was just standing there, waiting.

At the big kitchen table at Mandalay, Richard and I take it in turns to tell Byron everything.

"So where does Hugo think you are now?" Richard says seriously, holding a mug of Byron's tea, not drinking it.

"I messaged him on his private number. I said I had to leave because I had a personal emergency."

"Will he believe you?" Byron says.

"He'll have to. I told him I needed time to think about going to his school."

"But why would Hugo Beltrome do what *you* say?" Richard says.

I didn't know the answer before. I think I do now, but I'm not ready to share that information yet. I'm not even ready to think about it yet. So I ignore it.

"Julie Peters was pregnant," I say to Byron, and he nods as if he already knew.

"So is Gloria, and she's in there, or she was yesterday at least. In the room where they 'keep the girls'. They are waiting for the doctor to come and see her."

Every time I remember this isn't a dream I want to scream.

"How do you know she's there?" Byron says.

"A kid told me. He'd seen her. Hugo gets women pregnant and then pays their mothers to go away. Now Josh is doing it too. Like father, like son."

"And mothers really just leave their babies?" Richard says, incredulous.

"I don't think they have any choice. I think he picks women nobody cares about. Look at Julie. Look at Gloria. They had no parents close by, no teachers wondering why they've missed class. No money. I guess he thought nobody would even notice they were missing if they refused to go along with his plan."

"When is Gloria's baby due?" Byron says.

"We don't know, and Byron, we don't know the sex either."

"So?" Richard asks.

"So, Hugo wouldn't tell me what happens to the girls."

"What do we do now?" Richard says.

"We go back for Gloria," I say. "They won't be expecting us."

The idea terrifies me but so does the thought chipping away at my brain. I left Gloria in there. She would never do that to me. There is something else I feel, too. A rage is creeping around inside me like a poison, mixing with my blood, coursing up and down my spine, stabbing at my heart. Even when The Debs were at their worst, I *never* felt like this. I want to run at him screaming, and tear him open, and puncture his lungs. I want him to physically experience my hatred.

I close my eyes and clear my mind until it's white, and hot, and certain, and send a promise out into the universe so that Hugo will hear it, in the symphony of the trees and the crashing of the waves. I am coming for you, Hugo Beltrome. I will go to war for Gloria.

2

"There's no way into Thetis though," Richard says. He looks serious and determined.

"There's a path," Byron and I say at the same time.

"Tell Vita I'm here with you," I say to Byron, and he nods. "How do you know her?" I ask.

'My dad used to work for Vita when she was a barrister. Now he's too old and I do it, when she needs me."

"Do what?" Richard says, but I already know. I take off the amber bracelet on my wrist and place it on the table between us.

"It's a tracker, isn't it?" I say. "You've known where I am the whole time I've had it on."

Byron nods.

"You're a private investigator?" Richard says, his eyes wide.

Byron nods again.

"Why are you spying on me?" I say to Byron. "Am I in danger?"

"I wasn't brought here to spy on you, Diana. Vita asked me to investigate Hugo, and then he showed up in Lattering, just as you arrived, so then I had to look out for you, too."

"Because of my mother's letter," I say, and Byron nods, just as the clock on the wall strikes 8pm.

We all turn to face it.

"So, are we going back to Thetis tonight?" Richard says.

We look at each other, waiting for somebody else to decide.

"Let's go," I say.

～

We lie flat on the ground twenty feet from the Thetis courtyard. Flaming torches are spaced every few feet. It's all shadows and fire, and it's eerie as fucking hell.

"What's going on?" I say to Byron, but he shakes his head.

"I haven't seen anything like this before."

Richard lies next to me, the heat from his body keeping me warm. I feel like I'll never want to sleep again.

Tall, grey, garden doors open and Hugo Beltrome walks out, followed by Josh. It's weird that they don't know I can see them. It makes me feel powerful. They are both wearing long purple robes, like priests at Easter. They walk around the square, stopping directly in front of us, just beyond the bushes. Their faces are framed by the gaps in the branches. Josh is taller than his father now, just an inch. I wonder how that makes them both feel.

"This girl and her baby are utterly unsuitable," Hugo says coldly to his son. "Juan will have to take care of this now. There is more important work for Juan to be doing, but now he must clear up your mess."

"What about Doctor Cole?" Josh says quietly.

"It's too late for that. Your mistakes have repercussions. Do you understand that, Josh?"

His son studies his shoes, saying nothing. His arms hang weakly by his sides like a little boy. Hugo slaps him around the face, and Josh looks up.

"And this business with the Srao boy, too. What was that?"

I feel Richard stiffen beside me. Now we'll *really* know.

"Answer me," Hugo demands quietly.

"I thought you *wanted* me to be like you," Josh says.

Hugo slaps him across the face, but *really* hard this time. "Not like this!"

"But he was threatening to expose the family."

"Then you should have brought it to me." Hugo sighs, and grasps his son's chin gently, lifting his head up to face him.

Josh looks like a boy, desperate for his father's forgiveness, and Hugo's face softens.

"It's partly my fault, Josh," Hugo says softly. "Your mother was incredibly stupid. You were a terrible mistake."

Hugo turns and walks away, into the centre of the courtyard.

Josh stands there rubbing the skin on his cheek where his father slapped him. I almost feel sorry for him. Then he straightens his back and raises his chin, and he looks like himself again. He strides back inside and I remember he's stolen my best friend, and her life is in danger, and he left Ralph for dead. Even if his dad has made him a monster, he's still a monster.

The Thetis students begin walking out in single file through the grey doors, a procession of scary looking altar boys, each carrying a candle. Josh is first in line, followed by Jamie, and then Gulliver. There must be at least twenty of them.

The Mayan loiters on the other side of the square, almost hidden in the shadows. He keeps scanning the darkness, slowly turning his head, like a searchlight over a prison.

The boys stop and stand in designated spots, forming a ring around their father. The coughs and shuffles subside, and silence reigns.

"Famulus usque ad mortem," Hugo says loudly, like a bad Shakespearian actor.

"Famulus usque ad mortem," the boys repeat.

"Fidelitas usque ad mortem," Hugo shouts.

"Fidelitas usque ad mortem," the boys say.

"What is that, Latin?" Byron whispers.

I nod, and Richard and I translate simultaneously, "Family until death, loyalty until death."

3

I understand about half of what's being said as they chant like some freak-show congregation, and their father stands before them, absorbing their fear like electricity, like he's literally powering up.

I get a strange flashback. I'm tucked under the arm of my dad on our battered sofa, with a cup of tea and a cheese sandwich for lunch, watching black and white thrillers on a rainy Sunday afternoon. I'm warm and safe and I feel so grateful. Monsters aren't born, they are made. He's ruining their lives.

"How are we going to get inside without being seen?" Richard asks.

I glance over at The Mayan. His head has stopped moving, and he's looking in our direction. My thighs start shaking. We are twenty feet behind the bushes, lying on the ground, all together. Why am I trembling? He isn't God. He can't possibly see through the bushes. He begins walking slowly around the square, towards us...

"Bryon, I've got a bad feeling," Richard whispers.

"Me too," Byron says. "Let's go."

"But we can't just leave Gloria in there," I say desperately.

"We've got no choice," Byron says. "We'll come back for her, with a better plan, but now we have to go."

He drags me up off the ground as The Mayan begins to run.

The darkness is everywhere. I'm in front, jumping over bushes and tree roots. Byron is behind me, muttering for me to watch my step. Richard follows at the back. Something thumps the ground and I spin around. Richard is on the floor, ten metres behind us, holding his knee.

"Keep going, but watch out for the cliff," Byron whispers.

I run twenty metres and duck behind a tree. I peer around just as the torch beams hits the spot where our bodies flattened the grass.

Byron is supporting Richard back down the path, his arm draped over his shoulder. He throws Richard behind a tree as the torch pans up. I blink as my eyes adjust to the light. Byron is jogging towards The Mayan, waving. What is he doing?

"You are trespassing on private property my friend," The Mayan calls out, walking forwards, shining the light in Byron's eyes. Is one of them going to stop moving, or will there be a head-on collision?

I see the shape of Richard, pressed behind the tree, unmoving.

"I was just out for a walk, friend," Byron says. I can hear him smiling.

"Then you must be very lost. There is nothing up here for you to see."

They stop, right in front of each other. Byron is at least a foot taller, and his back is twice as wide. You'd pick him in a fight, usually...

"Yeah I'm crazy lost man! Which way is the sea again?"

The Mayan points directly over the cliff, and Byron laughs.

"Okay, thanks. I'll head back down then." Byron turns and starts to walk away.

"Maybe I'll see you again, friend?" The Mayan shouts out, unmoving.

Byron walks past the tree where Richard is hiding, as The

Mayan watches. Byron walks past me, winking. I stay where I am, hidden from sight.

Finally, The Mayan turns and walks quickly away, his flashlight pointing back towards the house.

Byron doubles back and drops down next to me. He puts his finger to his lips. We sit in black silence for another ten minutes. Finally, he nods, and I cup my hands to my mouth. It is my best impression of Ralph's bird noise. We hear movement, and Richard limps over. Bryon supports him as we trek slowly back down the path to the ocean.

4

We sit in a line on the porch outside Mandalay in various stages of shock, like three wet, wise monkeys.

Byron's phone buzzes.

"Vita wants to know where you are," he says, as my phone buzzes too.

I type 'Sorry it's late. Richard is walking me home now xx'.

Richard pushes himself gingerly to his feet, trying to bear his weight on his leg. He winces, then does it again, and again, until the pain fades.

"No man, I'll take her," Byron says, but Richard shakes his head.

"We should go back at dawn, and split up," I say to Byron, as he stares out at the ocean.

"Yeah maybe. I need to think," he says. "I'm going for a surf."

It has just started to rain.

"In that?" I say.

The waves look big and angry, like an army advancing towards the beach.

"That's thinking weather," he says.

"I'm sorry, Diana," Richard says, as we stand outside Shalimar.

"For what?" I say.

"For falling over. For nearly getting us caught."

"Don't be stupid, it was pitch black," I say. My legs feel like dead weights. I'm exhausted. "And stop being sorry for everything. You haven't done anything wrong. None of this is your fault. You're…" I don't finish because I don't want to say it. You're different now. I can see you, now. You're six feet tall but I didn't really see you before.

"She'll be alright, you know?" Richard says. "Gloria is stronger than anybody I've ever met, and not because she was broken and put back together. She was just made that way."

He's trying to make me feel better, but the truth is he *can't* know that. I need to put my body in between Gloria and Hugo. I need him to go through me to get to her.

"Richard, can I ask you a question?" I say.

He doesn't nod, but he doesn't shake his head either.

"What happened with Julie?"

He shrugs, like he doesn't even know. His eyes are grey. "She used to come into the library when she first moved here, twice a week, and borrow all these thrillers, like Dan Brown and stuff. She was always late returning them, but I'd let her off the fines. We started talking, and one day she asked me out, but she didn't want anyone to know."

"That's shit," I say, and he actually smiles.

"It wasn't *that* shit."

Gross. I don't want to know. Except I think I do, suddenly.

"Keeping it from Ralph was a pain. He'd seen her around, and was already obsessed with her, because she was the same height as him."

We smile in spite of everything. It's nice to think of Ralph as himself, and not silent in a hospital bed, riddled with tubes, almost dead.

"So, then what happened?" I say.

"Then she started getting sick in the mornings."

"You'd had sex?" I ask, as if that needs confirming.

He nods. I feel something akin to a shooting pain, somewhere in my chest.

"It was almost all we did, really. She thought that was the only reason I liked her."

I look at my shoes. I've never thought of Richard like that, and now it's all I can picture. The height of him, how much he must weigh, how his face would look if it was that close to mine.

It changes the fact that he kissed me. It makes the kiss seem different. Older. I wish I could remember it properly.

"She was drinking, and someone – I presume Josh – had started dealing her coke. I told her to stop and take a test, but she said I was crazy, and that I just wanted to tell everybody about us. So she ended it. Then I guess she started seeing Josh."

"Did you follow her?" I say.

"No. I tried to talk to her a few times. I wanted to know if she was still pregnant, but she wouldn't talk to me. Then Ralph started telling me what she was doing, without even knowing about us."

"Will you come in and see Vita?" I say, but he shakes his head.

"I need to get home." He gestures at his knee and rolls his eyes.

"See you tomorrow, then." He stares at me, a fraction too long, and I think Richard is going to say something else, but he doesn't. He turns and limps away, and I watch him go.

Aunt Vita is asleep on the sofa, with Howard on her belly and her face pressed into a cushion. Her glasses are squished and close to snapping. She's wearing denim shorts and goosebumps have popped up all over her legs.

I turn off all the lights apart from one lamp in the corner. She mutters in her sleep, and I drop a blanket over her legs.

I clear up the newspapers lying around her and run myself a glass of water, bolting the kitchen door, moving on auto-pilot, as the patter of raindrops on the kitchen window suddenly turns to hammering hail.

Outside the bushes thrash violently against the fence, and I watch the Shalimar sign uproot and smash into the gate. The wind whistles through the space at the bottom of the door as thunder cracks the sky in half. Lightning illuminates the garden like fireworks, and Howard whimpers in his sleep.

I'm exhausted, but I can't sleep. My mind is racing. I hear a police siren in the distance. I stare up at the neon stars on my ceiling.

I feel like the biggest fucking hypocrite but desperate times, desperate measures, and I need help. I take a deep breath, and whisper the words in the dark.

"Hey God-not-God. It's Diana Lind. You don't know me because, well, I don't normally think you exist, so I know I have absolutely no right to ask but I really need you to do something, please. I need you to look after Ralph, and absolutely keep him alive. And I need you to find Gloria and throw, like, a protective invisible God cloak over her, like that Harry Potter one maybe, and keep her safe until I can get to her. I need you to tell her I'm coming. And I need you to tell her something for me: I'm so sorry. She was right from the start. I was so caught up with my own shit, because I was the poor one, the not-pretty one, the not-thin-enough one. The bullied one. The one without a mum. The one with a sad dad. I was the one who didn't have anyone else - no aunties who aren't really my aunties, no village that raised me. I was so caught up with how shit I thought I had it that I didn't stop and look around. I thought I was unlucky, but I'm so lucky. Look at how lucky I am. And I know I just needed to turn my head to see. I just needed to *want* to look. But I promise I'll never look away again. Because I realise that Gloria had to change my life for me to really value hers. So, I guess what I'm really saying is, just stay alive for me Gloria, just for one more night, and then I'll tell you in person that you were right about me, and about everything. Because I promise you I'm coming for you."

I take a deep breath. How do you even end a prayer?

"So... if you could do that, kind of asap, that would be great. And, you know, thanks very much for your time and consideration in advance. Amen?"

When sleep finally comes, it's nightmares. I bolt upright at 5am. Aunt Vita is asleep in the corner of my room, holding a baseball bat.

5

The sand is littered with wood and seaweed and debris. Beach umbrellas are scattered randomly across the dunes like bodies.

Aunt Vita walks beside me on the path towards Mandalay. Howard scuttles ahead of us on a short lead. I fiddle with the beads on my wrist.

"Aunt Vita, I know about Byron," I say. "What was in the letter you took from my house?"

She pushes the gate at Mandalay and it falls off its hinge. Two surfboards have been blown into the middle of the path, so we step over them.

"Your mother left your dad a note, just before she died. He told me about it the day before he was arrested."

"And?"

"And it said that she was being threatened by Hugo. She was trying to protect you, when she did what she did. She thought it meant he would leave you alone."

"She'd had an affair with him," I say.

Aunt Vita sighs heavily. "Yes. Very briefly. She and your father were having trouble that summer... Tom was no saint and..."

I shake my head. I don't want to hear the sordid details of my parents' sex lives.

"But why did my dad show you the letter now, after all this time?"

"Because he got another letter, the day before he was arrested, telling him somebody had information about Hugo. That's what he's been doing for the last ten years, trying to work out how to catch him in the act. Trying to show the world what a terrible man he is. I'm sorry I didn't tell you before."

"It's okay, I understand. And I haven't told you everything either. I met a Thetis boy yesterday, younger than me. His name is Gulliver, and he's Hugo's son. He said I look like his mother, and that she talks about somebody called Diana all the time and... her name is Lana."

Aunt Vita grabs for my hand to steady herself, as her eyes flood with tears and she sobs loudly, once, like she needs to gasp in air just to stay alive. "I knew it," she whispers. "I knew she was still out there somewhere. I felt it."

The front door to Mandalay opens behind her, and a policewoman walks out, shaking hands with one of the surfers I know. He follows the policewoman down the steps. She nods as she walks past us.

"Hey, what's going on?" I say to him.

He looks disturbed. "Byron didn't come back from his surf last night," he says.

"He went out in the storm?" Aunt Vita says.

"He said it was thinking weather," I say. "Is his board missing?"

He shrugs and nods at the same time.

"I'm calling Susan at the hospital," Aunt Vita says. "Maybe he went around the cliffs and ended up in one of the other towns, or..."

Aunt Vita walks away and starts talking on her phone in her loud whisper.

Howard is playing at my feet, getting his lead caught around my legs. I walk him back out to the path and over to the beach. He jumps at the sensation of sand, four paws in the air at once.

It's almost deserted. The ocean is flat like a table now. There is something moving in the water though...a solitary, dark figure trudging out of the waves, dragging a board behind him.

I scoop up Howard. I'm running but my flip-flops sink into the sand, the ground literally shifting beneath me as if some invisible force is dragging me down. I stop. I can't move. Howard barks angrily, and I clutch him to my chest.

"Good morning, Diana," The Mayan shouts, emerging from the water. He strolls up the beach, his long hair dripping, his black trousers and shirt stuck to his body, carrying a surfboard under his arm.

Byron's board.

"Rough night for a swim," he says, winking, walking away.

BEFORE

He follows her home, always fifty paces behind, using the shadow of expensive London walls and the shade of overhanging cherry trees to his advantage.

When he occasionally crosses the road, discreetly slotting in behind dog walkers or mums, it is more for professional pride than necessity, because she never looks up. She stares at other people's lives on her phone. She seems so sad.

He wishes he could walk beside her and tell her everything is going to be okay. She will have her mother back soon. She will have a new school, and a new life, and the bullies, and the anxiety, will be fragments of an ugly past. Nothing and nobody will hurt her again.

He wishes he could tell her that memories shift around like sand in your mind. That even the grains of unbearable pain eventually fall to the bottom, and the sunlight, and the smiles, and the laughter, rise to the top and protect you from the underneath. He wishes he could tell her that he will make it his job to look after her, no matter what.

He slips into the kitchen and sits down at the table, peeling himself a banana from the bowl, waiting for the footsteps above him to stop. He runs himself a glass of water and checks his watch.

In her room he steps over the floorboard that began to creak again last week. Diana is asleep on the bed, exhausted.

Juan presses the handkerchief gently over her mouth, only five seconds. A little extra help to sleep till morning, princess. Soon you will be in Lattering, and everything will change.

PART X

1

A soft tapping at the kitchen door makes us all jump. Vita nods at Richard who gets up to open it.

Susan is standing on the doorstep dressed in pristine white doctors' scrubs. She looks like the lead in a soap opera. She sits down next to Aunt Vita at the table and takes a casual swig of cold coffee from her Hillary Clinton mug.

It irritates me. I don't know why. I look around at the four of us sitting here, scared, unsure, pale. So white. I wouldn't have even noticed before. The world treats people differently.

"Is there any news?" I ask Susan.

"Ralph's medical records disappeared from our system overnight," she says sadly. "I was hoping Byron might know something."

"You know Byron is a private investigator?" I say, irritated again.

"Susan knows everything, Diana," Aunt Vita says.

"Why?" I say.

"Because she's your wife," Richard says to Vita, sitting down next to me.

I look at their hands on the table. Aunt Vita's fingers are twisted through Susan's.

"I wanted us to get to know each other first," Aunt Vita says quietly.

"I knew you had someone. It's totally cool." I shrug. Am I cool? They are both wearing the same silver band on their wedding finger, with a tiny diamond in the middle. Of course they are married.

My phone buzzes on the table, and Aunt Vita literally jumps. I read the message aloud. "Diana. There is a school gathering tonight at the house. Please join us."

I stand up.

"Where are you going?" Aunt Vita says, confused.

"To get ready."

"For what?" she says, being deliberately dense.

"I'm obviously going."

"You aren't going anywhere," Aunt Vita says, kicking back her chair, pushing herself up with her balled fists on the table.

"Gloria is in there, and maybe Byron now too, and maybe even Ralph. I'll wear my bracelet, you can track me the whole time." I shrug like it's ordinary to have secret spy gadgets lying around, and I'm invincible.

"Do you think this is a game, Diana?" Aunt Vita shouts. "You can't just walk in there on your own. We don't even know how that damn bracelet works, Byron isn't here!" Her voice has reached dog whistle levels.

Susan places her hand gently on Aunt Vita's arm and I see her visibly relax, like hypnotherapy or something.

"Richard can figure out how it works," I say, but he shakes his head.

"I don't have any of Byron's stuff. I'll have to take it apart, and then it might not work when I put it back together."

"So, you can't go," Aunt Vita says, triumphant, folding her arms, like she's won.

"Although there is another way...," Richard says.

We all turn to look at him at the same time.

❧

346

"It's just basic Sonar and Bluetooth, it's not dangerous," Richard says, like we all know how simple that is.

Aunt Vita looks from me to Susan to Richard, and back to me, like a cat following a laser around the walls.

"You are going to sew a microchip into my skin?" I say.

"Officially it's a sensor, but yes," Richard says.

"And then what happens?"

"Then, if I'm within about 500 metres of you, it will work like a compass. It will start to throb, and the closer you get to me, the more powerful the sensation. Hotter, colder, but as sensations, so stronger, or weaker," Richard says. "It will lead you to me."

"It must be dangerous," Aunt Vita says, but her wife shakes her head.

"It will be no worse than having your ears pierced, or a tattoo," Susan says calmly. "I can use a local anaesthetic if you need it, Diana?"

"Won't it be noticeable? Won't Hugo see it?" Aunt Vita says.

"They are seriously tiny," Richard says. "But you can cover it with a plaster if you want?"

"And as long as you keep the wound clean and dry, it should be fine, the same as any wound," Susan says.

Aunt Vita bites her lip and shakes her head.

"We need more time, more planning," she says.

"We don't have time, Aunt Vita!" I shout. "Gloria is in there, but she might not be tomorrow, or even tonight. We don't know what he does with the girls! We have to try something. Someone just needs to distract The Mayan, somehow. The rest are a bunch of kids in fancy dress."

"What if Inspector Ford is there?" Richard says.

"I don't know. I just know we have to try."

"Okay," Aunt Vita says, nodding, "but I'm coming with you."

I roll my eyes. Ridiculous idea. "Hugo won't let you in, Aunt Vita."

"Okay, I'll hide, and you can let me in when you get there," she says, like that's easy.

"I mean, I can try, if you get to the store room and he lets me out of his sight."

It won't work. She's going to spend two hours squatting in the bushes.

"I'll come with you," Richard says to Aunt Vita.

"I'll get my hospital bag from the truck," Susan says, opening the back door.

~

One of my hands is flat, splayed out on the table, as the tip of Susan's scalpel hovers above it. I squeeze Aunt Vita's fingers with my other hand. My skin looks so…intact.

"Are you sure you don't want a local anaesthetic?" Susan asks.

"No, I need to be able to feel."

"Shout something out if it hurts, okay?" she says, smiling.

I take a deep breath, and the knife cuts into my hand. The flesh parts cleanly, and my blood rushes out. I take deep breaths, the way I think pregnant women must do when they are about to give birth.

Susan picks up a tiny piece of metal with a pair of long surgical tweezers. "Ready?" she asks.

She presses the metal into the cut.

I squeeze Aunt Vita's fingers so hard she cries out.

~

"What do we do if we find them?" Richard says, inspecting the stitches in my hand over the kitchen sink.

Sunlight pours through the window. There are daffodils in a vase. Life is still life, but it's different.

"*When* we find them," I say, looking up at him. "We'll get them out of there, somehow."

"Do you think he'd hurt you?" Richard says. He hasn't let go of my hand.

I shake my head. Not if Lana really is alive.

348

"Do you think he'd hurt me?" Richard says. He *still* hasn't let go of my hand, and I haven't tried to make him.

I don't answer. He gulps, and nods. "Yeah, I think so too."

2

I look over at Hugo as he sips his sherry. I want to fly at him from this end of the sofa, and wrap my fingers around his throat, and squeeze, and scream, WHERE IS SHE? Instead I say, "I've had some time to think about it, and I would be very grateful to accept your invitation, and come to live and study at Thetis next term."

Hugo smiles as if he knew it all along, of course, because nobody ever says no to him.

"It will relieve the pressure on my dad. I don't want him to worry about me. And it's an amazing opportunity."

I swallow, and it tastes like bile.

"I think you will be *very* happy here, Diana," Hugo says. He thinks he's so impressive, but it's all just paper.

"Like family," I say, and he beams.

"Good. Then you are ready."

Every Thetis boy I've seen is in the big, beautiful room that opens onto the garden. Jaws literally drop open as we walk in. I'm an intruder. I'm a *girl*. They look to their father for an explanation, confused. But he's not their dad, he's their owner.

Jamie is standing in the corner on his own. When he sees me his face freezes. Josh turns around as the room falls silent. His face goes red, and his mouth starts twitching like a dog about to maul a child. I smile sweetly.

A really old woman is sitting in the corner, holding a baby that's long, and anxious, and crying. I know straight away that's Richard's son.

"I have some news," Hugo says. "Diana is joining Thetis next term. She is important to me, and you will make her feel welcome. There will be no questions."

Hugo walks out through the doors as a random kid hands me a set of robes and a candle.

"Thanks," I say. The material grazes the stitches in my hand as I pull it on, and I swallow a cry.

I can feel Jamie staring. Josh glares and I mouth 'fuck you'. I think his head might explode.

"Fall in," he shouts angrily, and the boys assemble behind him.

I take a place somewhere near the back.

Jamie walks down the line, lighting everybody's candle. "Why?" he whispers through gritted teeth, as he holds out the match.

"You know why," I whisper back.

Josh leads us out in single file. The smell of lavender and lemons overwhelms me. I never knew something so beautiful could be so ugly. The ocean lies before us, sparkling in the dying rays of this terrible day's sun. If this is the last view I see, at least there's no filter required.

I tuck myself behind one of the other boys. Kent? Craig? Ken? It doesn't matter, they are all the same.

I spot The Mayan standing on the other side of the courtyard, his yellow eyes boring into me like lasers. A hungry looking German Shepherd twists on a lead around his feet.

Hugo stands in the middle of it all. His face is even uglier in the dusk, as if you can see what he's *really* thinking. There is a structure behind him that wasn't there last night. It's ten feet high, an upright plank of wood with an arm jutting out at the top, and a large box beside it.

"This is my final night in Lattering," Hugo says. "Lessons will begin again soon. Things must return to normal. This summer has been too eventful. There is an enemy among us."

Hugo Beltrome stares straight at me. He picks up one end of the long, thick rope lying at his feet. The other end is wrapped around a metal pole that has been sunk into the ground, in the middle of the courtyard. He steps back and, with a practised swing, throws the rope over the top of the wooden arm. It lands heavily, and everybody stares as a noose swings and settles in the air.

The sensor in my hand starts to throb. The younger boys glance anxiously at each other.

"Someone has been spying on us."

Adrenalin and fear make the nerves in my neck spasm. I gag, for the first time in forever. I look over at The Mayan, but he has disappeared. My heart is banging in my chest. Have I read this totally wrong? Would Hugo hurt me? Should I run? But which way? Forwards and straight over the side of the cliff? I take a tentative step backwards, towards the house, but a line of Kens and Craigs are in my way.

I scan the crowd desperately for Jamie. He wouldn't let this happen, would he? But when I finally spot him, he isn't even looking at me. He is staring, horrified, at something over my shoulder. Against my better judgement, I turn around.

The Mayan leads a broken Byron into the centre of the courtyard. His eyes are half-closed, and his head is lolling around on his neck like one of those toy dogs staring out from the back of a car. His cheeks are badly swollen. His left arm hangs weakly at his side like it's fractured in ten different places, and fresh blood seeps through the bandage on his stomach.

I have to stop myself from screaming. My hand starts to throb thick, dull pulses of pain as my body tries to expel the foreign object lurking beneath my skin.

I look back over at Jamie, but he is staring at the ground in front of him, with his hand over his mouth. I think he might even be crying, and I want to scream.

What the fuck happens here?

Josh is grinning like a psycho as The Mayan props Byron

against the gallows, holding him upright with his shoulder, retrieving a short length of rope from his back pocket. Byron's wrists are bound behind his back. His left arm is clearly smashed to bits. One of the younger boys is whimpering loudly. He must only be eight or nine. Hugo walks towards him and I think he might hug him, or place a comforting arm on his shoulder, but he slaps him, hard, around the face. The whimpering stops, and the boy stands up straight. Silent tears spill down his cheeks.

Something bright shines directly in my eyes. Instinctively, I twitch it away, but then it happens again. I follow the direction of the light to the trees at the top of the cliff.

The Mayan looks up at the pale sea of Thetis heads, all suddenly twitching in front of him as tiny laser beams attack their eyes.

The German Shepherd is splayed on the ground licking its balls, tied to a post by the garden doors, but it starts going nuts, straining desperately at its lead to escape, barking and growling and frothing at the mouth.

I know why. This was Susan's plan. Mariam and Tony and Susan, and Helen as the getaway driver, with their army of brains and utensils. Aunt Vita's gang of unlikely heroes have scaled the path and are hiding in the bushes with their tiny doctors' torches and their mirrors, blowing furiously on dog whistles.

The Mayan lets go of Byron like a hot rock and sprints for the trees.

3

Byron manages to stay on his feet for a couple of seconds before collapsing like his bones have melted. The patches of white on his bandage turn red with fresh blood.

Jamie pukes saliva in the corner.

"Get something," Hugo shouts, and a wooden chair is dragged into the middle of the courtyard by one of the boys.

Jamie lifts and drops Byron on to the seat. Byron's broken arm is twisted at an unspeakable angle, like nothing in nature. His head hangs heavily forwards, and Jamie desperately tries to keep it upright, as the buzzer at the front gate begins to go off. With the dogs still yelling the noise is overwhelming, a symphony of chaos and fear.

Everyone turns to face the gates as I spot Aunt Vita and Richard sprint along the side of the bushes, towards the back of the house. One of the dogs sees them too and goes crazy, but he was already going crazy, so nobody even notices. I point desperately at Byron, and the noose above his head, and raise my hands in despair, but Aunt Vita points urgently at the house.

"Nothing happens until I get back," Hugo shouts at everyone, striding furiously towards the gates. "Josh, come with me! Jamie, you're in charge."

Hugo and Josh peel off their robes as they go. The dog stops barking. The youngest boy openly whimpers, and Byron moans.

"What should we do, Jamie?" one of the children asks. He sounds so innocent.

Jamie walks into the middle of the circle. "Let's close our eyes, bow our heads, and recite the mantra," Jamie says.

Everybody lowers their head except me, and Jamie. He nods at me, and I slip quietly away.

Richard and Aunt Vita are crouching on the other side of the storeroom door.

"Can I have that?" Richard asks.

I yank the robe off and feel an emotional weight lift too. Wearing it made me one of them.

"Byron is in the courtyard. He's been beaten, and drugged. The weirdos are chanting."

"Is your hand okay?" Richard says, reaching for my palm. The skin around the plaster is red and angry. It's itchy and throbbing like hell.

"It's fine," I say.

He raises his arm and points to a plaster on the right side of his hand.

"You've done it too? Then who has the tracker?" I say. I wanted it to be him.

"Susan," Aunt Vita says.

Richard pulls on the robe. It doesn't even reach his ankles, but he lifts up the hood and he could be Josh.

"Be careful," I say.

"Of course." He runs off towards the back of the house.

"Should we go with him?" I say to Aunt Vita.

She stares after him sadly but shakes her head. "No. Richard will find a way, but tonight will change everything. We have to get Gloria out."

We run up four flights of stone stairs, briefly checking every classroom, communal study, and lounge. We scale another set of stairs and find ourselves in a long, white corridor with a series of rooms on either side. We try the first door, and it's unlocked. Two single beds sit neatly against each wall, beside a pair of matching desks. There are football posters on the wall. The rest of the rooms are versions of the same.

We climb more stairs that lead to another corridor with half as many doors. We try the first one. It's bigger, with only one bed and one desk. In the middle of the wall is a huge picture of a naked, blonde woman with no body hair. She has a dog leash around her neck. The room *stinks* of Josh.

At the end of the corridor two more flights of stairs lead in different directions.

"Which way now?" Aunt Vita says desperately.

We are running out of time. I look down at my hands; they are shaking violently. This can't be it. She has to be here. Screw it.

"Gloria," I half shout. It echoes down the empty corridor.

Aunt Vita looks alarmed.

"We have to!" I say.

"Gloria," I shout louder.

"Gloria," Aunt Vita shouts.

We stop and listen. Nothing.

"GLORIA!" I shout, at the absolute top of my lungs, tears spilling out of my eyes.

Then I hear it.

4

I've never run anywhere so fast. I fall up the top of the stairs into a lonely attic corridor. At the end, all on its own, is a small white door.

"Gloria?" I shout, running. I twist the doorknob, but my fingers are sweaty, and slippery, and keep sliding off. I hear shuffling behind the door.

"Gloria, are you in there?" I whisper at the door.

The reply is faint. "Diana?"

"Yes, it's me, I'm here to get you out."

"The door is locked," Gloria says. "The Spanish dude has the key."

She sounds so sleepy.

"What do we do?" I say to Aunt Vita.

She is standing behind me, sizing up the door. She presses her hand and her ear to the wood.

"Gloria, darling, it's Vita. Can you hear me? Stand back, darling, okay?"

We hear more shuffling on the other side.

"Ready?" Aunt Vita says.

"Yeah," Gloria says.

Aunt Vita looks at me. "Let's do this," she says.

We both start kicking the door, as hard as we can, as if we rehearsed it. I feel like it's going to break my leg, but I can't stop. I picture Gloria trapped on the other side. I picture my dad, locked up somewhere. I picture Hugo Beltrome's face and I kick, and I kick, as hard as I can. The door starts to splinter, and suddenly I see her again.

Tears are running down her cheeks. One of her eyes is half closed, and black and yellow with bruises. Her hair is long and straight, clean and un-styled. She is wearing a plain, white nightshirt, like a surgical gown. She looks like a child. A pregnant child.

I climb through the small hole in the door, catching my dress on the splinters and yanking it free, ripping holes in the material.

"Hi," she says, clutching my hand.

"Have they hurt you?" I say. If I could pick her up I would. Instead I stroke the tears away from the bruises on her face.

"I'm okay," she says, but it's clearly a lie.

"Can you walk?" I say.

She nods, as Aunt Vita launches at the wood with an angry kick, and the right side of the door falls on the floor.

"That's done it," she says, panting, her hands on her hips.

Aunt Vita holds Gloria's arm on her right side, and I do the same on her left. Her bump is in front of us. There is an actual baby in there.

"I'm sorry," she keeps saying, as she trips and stumbles, and her legs collapse beneath her.

"Shush," I say. "It's fine."

We reach the first floor as a chorus of young voices floods inside on the floor below us.

"Shit," Aunt Vita says. "What's going on?"

I run to the window and look down at the garden. Byron is still slumped on the chair in the middle of the courtyard, his head hanging forwards. A solitary robed figure kneels behind him. Everybody else has disappeared. The hooded figure stands and throws the rope that was tying Byron's wrists on the floor. He hooks Byron's good arm over his shoulder, and pulls him up, taking his weight on his side. The hood falls away from his head. It's Richard. But as he starts to lift and drag Byron slowly across the courtyard, another tall figure appears in front of him. Richard is concentrating so hard on keeping Byron upright he doesn't even notice.

I bang on the window with my palm. I need him to hear me. Look up, Richard. LOOK UP, RICHARD!

"No!" I shout as the hooded figure grabs Byron, but they begin to carry him across the courtyard, together, and his hood falls away. It's Jamie.

"What is going on?" I hear Hugo booming from downstairs. "Where is Juan? Why have you all come back inside?"

"Jamie told us to wait in the library." I hear Gulliver say.

"Diana, we have to go," Aunt Vita says at my side.

I spot the narrow staircase at the end of the corridor.

We burst out into the courtyard, as Jamie runs towards us.

"The Mayan has gone to the front gates with the dogs, but he'll realise pretty quickly and lock the place down. Josh and dad are searching the house. Richard has Byron on the cliff path. Go that way."

Aunt Vita is staring at the gallows in the middle of the courtyard. Byron's blood is red on the paving. She's gone completely pale.

"There is evil here," she says to Jamie, "and you don't have to be a part of it."

"I've got nowhere else to go," he says.

"Thank you, for your help," I say to him.

"Don't," he says, and walks away, back into his house.

5

The path is too narrow for all three of us to descend at once, so we take it in turns to support Gloria. She is woozy and groaning, clutching her belly, occasionally crying out, as the dark settles in around us.

"My hand has stopped throbbing," I say to Aunt Vita, as we reach the bottom of the steps.

"I need to tell Susan where we are," she says, grabbing for her phone.

Vita jumps into the water at the bottom of the path. It is only waist deep.

I stand behind Gloria and help lower her down until she is sitting on the rock. Her gown is open at the back, and I can see the goosebumps on her naked shoulders, and the tiny rainbow tattoo where her bum meets her back.

I sit behind her, with my legs on either side, and we belly flop into the water together.

We wade towards the beach. Richard is ahead of us, moving really slowly, dragging Byron along the sand as his legs lag behind him. Richard stumbles, and the full weight of Byron falls on top of him. Pushing himself to his feet, he hoists Bryon's body up again. He is exhausted.

"Go and help him," I say to Aunt Vita. "Get Byron to the truck, then come back for us."

"Are you sure?" she says.

"Aunt Vita - go. We are right behind you. I can support Gloria; the water isn't even deep. Go and help them."

"Okay, I'll be right back," she says, and sprint-splashes off, her knees high, trying to outwit the water.

My hand starts to throb violently and I cry out, in pain and relief, as Susan's truck swings into view in the distance.

It screeches to a halt just before the dunes. Vita catches up with Richard and together they carry Byron along the beach like a torturous three-legged race. Anthony and Susan jump out of the van and run towards them in slow motion across the dunes, their legs sinking into hills of soft sand.

Gloria stumbles next to me and falls face first into the water, moaning, clutching her stomach.

I pull her up and lock my arm around her waist.

"I'm so tired Lady Diana," she says, her eyes closing, the weight of her relaxing back onto me.

"Can you keep walking?" I say, struggling to stay upright, but she just moans.

"It's okay, we can just wait for them here. They'll come back. We'll just stay here in the water, and you can float, pregnant women do that."

I lower her gently back into the water and lock my hands under her back and crouch down, allowing the ocean to take some of my weight, too. I rest my head next to her shoulder, and whisper Diana Ross in her ear. She smiles, but tears stream down her face.

"Just wait," I say. "They'll be back for us soon. Just hold on."

Then I hear the whistle. I look towards the beach. The truck is too far. Richard and Vita run Byron towards Anthony and Susan, but they don't seem to be getting any closer. The dogs start barking. I look back at the cliffs. Flashes of his head appear between the bushes and the trees, bouncing down the steps, three at a time, like a hurdler, fearless, indifferent to the sheer drop to his left.

I look back at the truck. Richard and Vita are still carrying Byron towards the dunes. They can't see The Mayan coming down the cliff. They can't see me waving. We won't make it to the beach on our own. He's faster than us, and he's coming.

I peel off my cardigan and throw it as far as I can, into the waves. I've read about tracker dogs; you have to confuse them. Clothes are the best diversion, even if they are soaking wet.

With my dress stuck to my body and the wet, heavy mass of my hair pushed back from my face, I gently pull floating Gloria back out into the ocean, against the heave of warm waves. I have a plan. It's a terrible one, but it's a plan. I'm heading for the caves.

6

The biggest cave opening is high up. This is the one I've seen kids jumping from during the day, boys scrambling up and sitting on the edge, dangling their feet into the water below. Teenage couples disappear inside, and emerge, dishevelled but smiling, twenty minutes later. It's still above the water line, which would be okay if we could both push ourselves up and in, but Gloria isn't responding at all. Waves are breaking against the rocks and the foam splashes up and inside, but as the water recedes I see the ledge below the opening. If I can get us both onto that, if I pull and a big wave pushes us, we could both fall into the cave.

I hear a whistle on the beach behind me. I'm on my toes now, the sand beneath my feet falling away. I can see The Mayan on the beach, searching the dunes. The van has disappeared. We are on our own. So it's drown, surrender, or this.

I guide Gloria's floating form relatively easily onto the ledge and push myself up. I position myself behind her, my legs on either side of her body, the back of her head against my belly, my hands in her armpits, and I wait. One big wave and we'll be into the cave, as long as it's not *too* big, because then we'll just smash into the rocks and die.

I see it forming, twenty metres away. It starts to pick up speed, a wall of water approaching.

I whisper into Gloria's ear, "Okay, don't be scared. It's just water, and we are going to float backwards. We are just going to float."

She has no idea what I'm saying. I hold my breath as the wave breaks...

My head immediately goes under. The foam floods into my mouth and the salt stings my eyes, as I push Gloria's head up with my chest, and hold on under her arms, and pull her with me.

We land with a thud inside the cave. Three inches of water beneath me don't soften the fall. The weight of Gloria is on me, belly up, but I can breathe. I gasp the air around me and it smells terrible, of seaweed, and damp, and rot.

Unknown nature stuff is dripping down slimy walls. There is a ledge at the back of the cave, just big enough for us to sit on. I brush two Coke cans and an empty Pommes Bear wrapper into the water with disgust, as if littering is the worst thing I've seen today.

I peel off my dress and lay Gloria's naked back against my skin. That's what they tell you to do, to share body warmth, to stay alive. She is shivering, and I drape my wet dress across her front like a blanket, in case it helps, but I put my hands flat on her belly, to share any heat I can with the baby. The sunlight doesn't make it in here.

I can't hear the dogs anymore, or The Mayan's whistle, just the ocean as it breaks against the cliffs, and the sound of my own breathing. The water rises slowly around us, and I try not to fall asleep. I only realise my hand isn't throbbing anymore when the baby wriggles beneath it. I hold my breath and wait for it to move again. It shifts, and kicks, and settles.

Aunt Vita and Richard will be out there, searching for us in the darkness, but this is up to me now. If I can keep the three of us alive tonight that will always be enough for me, I'll never ask for anything else. That will be all that matters, forever.

BEFORE

W e went to the beach to escape. Vita found the house and insisted on paying for it, even though she'd only come down on the weekends because of her case. I sent Tom the address and told him to come for odd days if he wanted. He said he was sorry, again, over and over. I'm sorry, Lana, I'm sorry. I didn't need to hear it again. I just needed to decide if sorry was enough.

On our tenth day in Lattering I met a man at the beach. He was sad and lonely, and I knew how that felt, so I offered to cook him dinner. Vita always said I was naive, but then lawyers don't trust anyone. Truthfully, I just wanted to hear somebody else's problems for a night. He said his life felt pointless, and terrible, and he was about to end it, but then he met me. He called me Thetis, his Goddess of Water. I'd saved him.

Vita arrived from London the following evening. She was so angry with Tom about the affair, angrier than me, I think. It didn't take much for her to convince me to go to dinner with Hugo. He was so charming, and polite, and manners matter. Standing outside our house at the end of the evening, he told me he was in love with me.

I only went to the house to tell him I couldn't see him again, that he couldn't possibly love me because he didn't even know me. He said he understood, and asked me to stay for dinner, no hard feelings. He was confident, less lost. I drank too much wine, a combination of nerves and relief, so when he kissed me, in the candlelit ballroom of Poseidon, I kissed him back. I was drunk, and he was so handsome, and I wanted to be selfish. Tom had only thought of himself when he'd slept with that woman. She had only thought of herself when she slept with my husband. Why did other people get to forget who they were for a night, and not me?

I woke up in Hugo's bed, and he asked me to marry him. I told him I was sorry, but I'd made a terrible mistake. His driver smoked a cigarette that smelt like Christmas, and whistled nursery rhymes all the way back to Brizo.

Tom arrived the next morning. I watched him playing with Diana. As they ran from the waves and buried each other in the sand, I knew I still loved him. We all make mistakes. Vita was livid, of course, crying with rage when I told her we'd go back to London with Tom the following weekend. She refused to leave Brizo until the end of the summer, as originally planned.

I didn't see Hugo again in that final week in Lattering, but Diana and I seemed to bump into his driver everywhere. He was always there when I looked up, reading his newspaper or leaning on his car. He'd blow Diana a kiss and she'd wave. Then Tom drove down on Saturday, and we left the beach as a family.

By the middle of August, I was being sick every morning. I took a test, but I already knew. I was pregnant, and it could only be Hugo's. I travelled back to Lattering with Diana on a Thursday. Vita cried and apologized for her previous behaviour. She confessed to me that she had fallen in love with a colleague, but that it was complicated, and it was making her angry and sad.

I put Diana to bed and asked Vita to stay with her for an hour. I'd written Hugo a letter. I was going to leave it with a servant, like a coward, but Hugo answered the door to Poseidon himself.

He told me he would never allow another man to raise his child. I must divorce Tom and marry him. I ran from the house, back to Brizo, and Vita.

She was terrified at first. I was hysterical, and she was certain I'd been attacked. That turned to fury as I refused to tell her what had happened. I couldn't bring myself to admit it, even to her. She packed her bag in a rage and stormed back to London. That night I crept into Diana's room and curled up behind her on the bed, watching her chest rise and fall, listening to the sounds of her sleeping. I couldn't stop crying, eventually crawling into the big bed on my own so as not to wake her. The following morning, she was gone.

I was scrambling around the house, screaming her name, when there was a knock on the door. It was Hugo's driver. Diana was still snug in her pajamas, asleep in his arms. Tucked inside her pocket was a photo of Vita, asleep in her bedroom in London, a copy of that morning's newspaper resting on the pillow behind her head. My phone rang.

"Answer it, Lana," the driver said. It was Tom. He had been arrested. The phone went dead.

"Mr. Beltrome would like to speak to you," the driver said. My phone rang again. I clutched Diana to my chest as I answered.

"The police can't help you now," Hugo said.

I began to sob, as Diana wriggled in my arms.

"Don't cry, Lana, it won't help," he said. "I'm not interested in hurting anyone. I just want you, and my baby of course."

Suddenly everything seemed clear.

"Will you give me your word, Hugo, that you won't hurt them, if I leave them?"

"Of course. I don't care about them. You have my word. I only want you."

"You swear it? You will leave Diana, and Tom, and Vita alone, if I leave?"

"I swear, Lana. I'm not a monster. I just want what's mine."

Tom was released without charge and drove straight to Lattering.

I took forever putting Diana to bed that night. We played our spider game, my two fingers running up her tummy and bouncing off her nose.

Tom was exhausted. I kissed him goodnight, telling him I'd clear up the kitchen before coming to bed, and that we'd leave in the morning. I left my letter on the table.

There had been a storm, and I remember the first big wave as it hit me. My ears blocked, and I tried not to fight it. The water was full of driftwood and sand. I began to feel heavy, my eyes closing, sinking down and under, as his arms hooked around my waist.

I remember lying on the sand, his small fists expertly pumping the water out of my throat and lungs. I remember the smell of Christmas.

Finally, Hugo came to see me. The scan showed it was a boy, and he was elated. I swore not to hurt myself or the baby again, and he agreed to keep his promise not to hurt my family.

I only asked for one thing in return: a photo of Diana every year, on her birthday. I wanted proof.

PART XI

1

Gloria hasn't made any noise for ages. I check her pulse again. It's faint but it's there. The dogs stopped barking hours ago, and we can't stay in here forever. The water level is dropping, and I need to get us both out before the jump from the cave becomes a sheer drop. I haven't saved us yet.

Gloria is positioned on the ledge and I'm behind. I've bound my arms and legs tightly around her, shunting us forwards until there is nowhere to go but down. The water is calm now. I say a prayer to God-not-God and lurch us forwards.

My feet hit the rocks almost immediately, and I push us back up, above the water, a trampoline jump, coughing and spluttering. I hold Gloria in one hand and grab for the ledge that juts out of the cliff. The most daring kids walk along that ledge during the day, like those crazy wire-walkers who stroll between skyscrapers.

I think they call this *doggy paddle*, but I'm just trying to keep us afloat. The salt helps. Gloria is quiet, and heavy, but surprisingly buoyant. I creep along the side of the cliff, stopping every thirty seconds to rest my arms, and so I can check that she is still breathing. My lips are numb, my fingers are blue. Finally, when I press down with my toes, I hit sand.

I turn Gloria on to her back and pull her, staggering backwards towards the beach. It's slow but it's the right direction. The sensor jumps under my skin suddenly and I scream in pain. The area around the stitches is hard, and red, and raised, and a red line is creeping up my arm. Then I see them. Two figures running towards us in the dark, sprinting for the water.

Richard reaches us first, and grabs hold of me.

"No, take her," I say, my lips so stiff I'm barely able to speak.

The weight of Gloria is lifted. I collapse, but someone catches me.

"I've got you, darling. I've got you." Aunt Vita carries me like a baby out of the water and across the sand. I look up. Stars shoot across the sky, pulled by angels.

I am passed gently into the back of the truck, and Richard's arms. I hold onto him as tightly as I can, my fingers still shaking. My body shivers violently, and I hear the crack of my teeth against each other. A blanket is draped over and around me. One of Richard's arms holds me firmly in place, while the other strokes my hair.

"Don't let me go," I say to him. I see the angels again.

Richard rocks me and whispers, "I thought we'd lost you."

Someone else lifts up my hand and turns it over. "It's infected and spreading. And she's got hypothermia."

I hear Gloria moan loudly from the front of the truck.

"Drive faster," Susan says to someone. "I'm losing her."

2

The warmth of the sun on my face wakes me, and I open my eyes. The world is shrouded in a white haze. It feels like someone heavy is sitting on my chest.

A figure appears at the foot of the bed.

"Go back to sleep darling," Aunt Vita says, pushing heavy strands of hair from my forehead.

My hand throbs. My throat is completely dry. "Is everyone okay?" I whisper.

"Go back to sleep," Aunt Vita says.

I close my eyes, and drift away.

~

I'm alone in a small bedroom that's covered in blue and white cornflowers. I sit up, take a deep breath, and cough until I'm almost sick. My lungs feel like burst balloons. My hand feels odd, and I lift my arm to look. My palm is bandaged up like a mummy, twice its normal size. I'm wearing rainbow pajamas, and there are fluffy unicorn slippers by the door. Framed on the wall is a quote: 'They sicken of the calm, that know the storm'.

I manage to whisper, "Bullshit."

My legs feel weak as I walk into a large, dark, old-fashioned kitchen that smells of fresh bread and roast chicken. I shuffle the unicorns across the floor to the door and out into the light.

I'm in the garden of an old farmhouse. Endless fields of yellow surround us. There isn't another house for miles. The borders of the garden are bursting with roses, lavender, cornflowers, and huge, fat, purple-headed hydrangeas. A large wooden table sits proudly on the grass under a vast, white umbrella. Two small puffs of cloud are the only interruption in a bright blue sky, and the sun is fierce and high.

Aunt Vita is drinking coffee and reading a newspaper in an old wicker chair in the shade of an apple tree, her glasses half way down her nose. Howard is asleep on her feet. When she sees me she drops her paper.

Richard walks around the corner of the house carrying a pile of wood. "You're awake," he says, as Howard launches himself at my knees.

"Finally," Aunt Vita says as she reaches us.

We sit in the shade of the umbrella sipping tall glasses of cucumber water.

"Byron is in an induced coma," Aunt Vita says. "He had a lot of pressure at the top of his spine. His left arm is broken in multiple places. He'd been stabbed in the abdomen and had a ruptured spleen, but he's so bloody strong. Susan will repair him."

"Where is Gloria?" I ask, watching their faces intently, but they don't look down or away, or do any of the things I was dreading because then I'd know I'd failed.

"She's inside," Aunt Vita says, "but there were complications, Diana. She lost a lot of blood. She's not awake."

"But she's alive," I say, feeling like my heart is going to burst. I want to scream and jump and shout but I don't have the energy to do any of those things.

"Did she lose the baby?" I ask.

"No," Aunt Vita says.

"She's still pregnant?" I say, incredulous. "But we were in that cave for so long?"

374

"Hypothermia is far worse for the mother," Aunt Vita says, "and she was nearly full term. Gloria has a baby girl."

At that moment Susan emerges from the darkness of the kitchen, dressed all in white.

"Diana, I'm so happy you are awake," she says.

"Did she take her bottle?" Aunt Vita asks as Susan leans on her shoulders.

"She did. She fed really well. She's asleep now. I'll go back in, I just wanted to say hello to Diana."

"Where are we?" I ask.

Richard is staring at me, but I can't meet his eye.

"Rose Cottage," Aunt Vita says. "Susan's grandparents' old house. There's no Wi-Fi and no phone signal. We are off grid, for now at least."

"Does the Mayan know where we are?" I say, shivering despite the heat.

"We don't think so," Richard says. "We turned all the phones off before we left town. Unless he physically followed us, he should have no way of tracking us here. I'm sure he'll find a way eventually, so we can't stay this close to Lattering forever."

"How long have I been asleep?" I say, eyeing up the cucumber in my glass. I'm starving.

"Six days," Aunt Vita says. "You managed to get hypothermia, darling. You kept talking about fairies, and angels, and grandmothers falling off cliffs. Your hand is a bit of a mess, unfortunately."

I shrug. It could be worse. We sit quietly for a moment, before Susan stands.

"I should get back inside to our little princess," she says.

I stand up too. "Please can I see her?"

～

In a cot by the side of Aunt Vita and Susan's bed is a tiny bundle of brown limbs, in a yellow vest covered in lemons. Her head is smothered in thick, dark curls. I can't get past how *big* she is. She's a proper person, and she's long, and her feet are huge, and she was all squished up inside of Gloria until a week ago.

"I'll get us some water," Susan says, and leaves us alone.

I want to touch her tiny little hand, but I'm scared. As if she knows, she opens her eyes, and yawns.

"Hello," I say formally. "I'm Diana."

Her pupils are vast, and almost black, and fill most of the white in her eyes. Her hands are balled into two tiny fists, and she's desperately trying to put one in her mouth. She makes all these strange gurgling noises as she twists her little limbs around.

"That's Susan," I say, pointing at a picture of her and Aunt Vita beside their bed. "She's taking really good care of you, but she's not your mummy. You'll know your mummy when you see her. She is beautiful, and fierce, and she's not very well at the moment, but don't be scared. She'll definitely be okay, because she'll want to meet you."

I wipe away my tears with my non-bandaged hand.

∾

Aunt Vita makes me a soft sandwich, but every gulp hurts my throat.

"How are you feeling?" She asks, pressing her hand against my forehead for the tenth time.

"I'm just tired. I might go back to bed. Where's my dad?"

She picks at my sandwich as she answers. "He's in a psychiatric hospital in Yorkshire. I have a friend there, a doctor. He's looking after him. While he's there he's safe."

"Can I speak to him?" I say, and she winces.

"I'm sorry, Diana, not from here. But soon, I promise. I do have something for you though."

She pulls a piece of paper out of her pocket and passes it to me, but I won't take it, so she places it on the table instead. "No more secrets," she says.

∾

I sit in Aunt Vita's wicker chair, under the apple tree. A bee is buzzing by my ear. A plane flies somewhere nearby.

My mother's handwriting is neat and precise, and much better than mine.

I take a deep breath, cough uncontrollably, then begin to read.

My Darling Tom,

I have to leave you both tonight. I'm so sorry. I made a terrible mistake this summer. I met someone and invited him into my life. Now he refuses to leave, so I must go instead. He took Diana, and he had you arrested, but he only really wants me. I'm staking my life on that.

His name is Hugo Beltrome. He is very powerful and very dangerous. Please keep Diana away from him. Hate me, but don't let me leave for nothing, and please, don't tell Vita. She'll want revenge, but revenge won't help. Tell her I loved her. Being her sister makes me so proud.

If I'd told you, you would have convinced me to stay, and none of us would be safe. Even now I feel lucky, that I met you, that we loved each other, that we had our beautiful, brilliant daughter. Love her with everything you've got, Tom. Love her enough for me too, please.

It won't hurt. I am relying on the ocean to take me gently away. Thinking of Diana in bed upstairs, my heart is broken. I want to curl up behind her forever, but this is the only way I can protect her, now.

Please make sure she knows I loved her, more than anything.

Lana x

3

Richard is standing by the kitchen door, a large gym bag squashed full of clothes at his feet. He's wearing a short-sleeved T-shirt. His arms are covered in tiny scars, but there are no new plasters.

Aunt Vita is hugging him goodbye.

"I'm going to check on Gloria," she says, and Richard and I are alone.

"Where are you going?" I say, the words forcing their way out around the lump in my throat.

"I have to find Ralph," he says.

"But we don't even know where he is."

"I asked Jamie, that night at Thetis. He thinks they've taken him to the estate in Scotland."

"But why would they even keep him alive?" I say.

It sounds terrible, but it's true.

"I don't know. But I have to try, Diana."

"I could come with you," I say.

What I really want to do is barricade the door and not let him out.

He smiles, no tomatoes, no blushing. "I wish you could, but I'll be better on my own. I'll just hang around and make myself invisible. I'm good at that. You're a little too conspicuous." He touches a strand of my hair.

"But what about your exams, and Durham?"

He takes my hands.

"Things have changed. I have to change with them."

"But I saw your baby at the house Richard. He looked just like you."

"Ridiculously handsome?" he says, straight-faced.

The first tear spills out onto my cheek. He reaches up and brushes it away gently with his thumb.

"The baby is safe, but Ralph isn't. Okay, I'm going to go," he says finally, letting go of my hands and snatching up his bag. He opens the kitchen door.

"Richard, wait," I say.

He turns around and I kiss him. He drops his bag and kisses me back, lifting me up off the ground, holding me close, pressing his heart against mine. It's completely different to last time, because *we* are completely different to last time.

He lowers me back down to the ground and takes my face in his hands. "I know I'm not the obvious choice," he whispers, "but I do love you."

He grabs his bag and walks out.

4

I get up before dawn and leave a note on the kitchen table. It feels like autumn and I zip up Richard's hoodie. It's far too big, and my hands are hidden halfway down the sleeves, but it smells of him.

I find the bike in Susan's ridiculously tidy garage. It's not Snoopy of course. It's newer, and better, and cleaner. It's got a basket, and gears, and no rust. I don't love it.

I follow the signs to the coast. I already know I can't go back to Shalimar. He'll be watching. The sun comes up as I see the first signs to Lattering.

I use the back roads to get to the beach path. I pull up outside Mandalay, and stare. There are boards at the windows, and a wire fence has been erected around the garden with 'CONDEMNED' signs pinned to it, and 'BUILDING DANGEROUS, DO NOT ENTER'.

I look up at the deck sadly and remember the first night I met Byron there, the lights, and the conversation, and the odd tasting drinks. My fear that I wouldn't fit in. I was scared of everything then.

I hear a familiar bark and I whistle softly, clicking my fingers. Bartlett pokes his head out from behind the barbeque. He looks

380

skinny and dishevelled and dirty. I call his name, and he doesn't hesitate.

$\sim$

I'm hiding beneath my hood, by the bins behind Seagulls. I stand astride the bike, in case I need to make a quick exit. Bartlett sits happily in my basket, greedily nipping at my fingers for more of the biscuits I've been feeding him every few seconds. He's starving.

After about fifteen minutes the door opens, and Felix walks out, in a cerise shirt covered in monkeys and bananas. He's carrying two big bags of rubbish, but he stops when he sees me.

"All I wanna know is are you both okay?" he says.

"We are, kind of. I'm so sorry, Felix."

"I got two new girls and they'll do fine. They aren't you and Glo, but they are good, and they are picking it up. I'm guessing you ain't coming back?"

I shake my head.

"And your aunt?"

"I don't think she's coming back either. At least for now."

He nods and dumps the bags in the bin. "Well you tell 'er from me, anything she needs, I'm always 'ere. And you too, of course."

"Thank you, Felix. I wanted to say goodbye."

"You're most welcome. Take care of yourself, Diana. There are some nasty sorts about."

The door closes behind him, and I turn my bike around.

I ride out to the beach path. I'll cycle down past Mandalay, and then back out of town without passing Shalimar, or going anywhere near Beach Road. It's still early, but I pull my hood forwards around my face, as Bartlett sits in my basket, tongue lolling behind him in the wind.

A solitary figure is walking towards me on the path. I'd have to stop the bike and turn around to avoid them, which will look too suspicious. I slow up a little, and see that it's a girl, her long hair plaited over one shoulder. It's too late by the time I realise it's Virginia.

"Diana," she says, surprised. I'm not used to her using my real name. It doesn't sound like me.

Her eyes are red from crying, and she wipes them hastily. She's standing in the middle of the path, I'll have to push her to get past. I stop my bike.

"Don't tell anybody you've seen me, Virginia, I swear."

"I won't, I promise. I'm so sorry, Diana. For all of it. Audrey is out of control."

"You did it too."

"I know I did. But I promise, at school, it will be different now. Audrey's gone too far this summer, some really weird stuff. She's fucked in the head."

"I've got to go." I say, moving my bike around her.

"I saw Jamie just now, on the beach. He's on his own, by the lifeguard post."

I spot him, sitting on one of the dunes, his Thetis hoodie pulled up to protect him from the sheets of sand whipped up by the wind. I stop on the path and give Bartlett a biscuit. He gobbles it up greedily and barks for another, and Jamie turns around. I take off my hood, shaking out my hair. He stands and starts to walk along the beach, away from town. I know where he's going.

He's already standing in the main room at Brizo when I arrive.

"I thought you weren't coming," he says.

"I had to go back down onto the road, so I didn't pass Shalimar. And I had to tie Bartlett up, too. He's outside. I can't stay long."

We stand on either side of the room. His eye is black, and his lip is split.

"The Mayan did that?" I say, but he shakes his head.

"No, Dad did that. He doesn't know exactly what happened, but he has his suspicions."

"Then why do you stay?" I say desperately.

Jamie shrugs. He is still so beautiful, even with his bruises.

"I've got nowhere else to go, Diana. I don't have any money of my own. I don't have a bank account, I've never had a job. All I know is Thetis, Dad makes sure of that. Where would any of us go, even if we wanted to?"

"You could come with me?" I say.

He smiles sadly, but his eyes widen, and he starts to shake his head in horror and disbelief.

"What? What is it?" I say, stepping forwards.

"Diana!" he shouts, running forwards, grabbing me and throwing me behind him.

I fall on the ground, dazed. In front of Jamie, in a dark hoodie and jeans, is the man in the bird mask.

5

second figure pushes through the plastic sheeting. Thinner, in a black hoodie and tight jeans, wearing a second mask, identical to the first.

"What's going on?" Jamie says, looking from one to another.

"We knew you two wouldn't be able to stay away from each other for long," the bigger one says. We both recognise that voice.

"Fucking Romeo and Juliet," the slimmer one says.

"Josh, what the fuck?" Jamie says, grabbing for the beak of the mask

Josh bats him away, but raises it himself, sneering.

Audrey lifts hers at the same time.

"What the hell is wrong with you?" I say to her, incredulous, but she just laughs.

"Did you get the scares, Pound Shop? Did you piss your poor pants?" Audrey smirks at Josh, but he's just glaring at Jamie. She has no idea what's she's caught up in.

"You're a psycho," I say, snatching her mask. I'm not scared of her anymore.

Josh lunges and grabs my arm. I scream, and Jamie rushes forwards, dipping his shoulder, rugby tackling his brother to the floor.

Audrey grabs my hair and yanks it, and instinctively I punch. My fist meets her nose, and I hear the bone crack beneath my knuckles. She's screaming as blood pours through her fingers. I see the large rubber hammer lying on the floor, forgotten by the builders, and I grab for it, holding it in front of me for protection.

Audrey steps back and catches her heel on one of the loose floorboards, tumbling backwards. Her head smacks the bottom step of the staircase with a loud thud. She lies motionless on the floor in front of me, silent, blood trickling from her nose.

"We have to call an ambulance!" I shout, but the boys are scuffling behind me.

Jamie is on top of Josh, pinning him down, but Josh jerks his body and Jamie falls off. Josh reaches into his boot and pulls out a flick knife, lunging towards Jamie's heart.

I raise my arms and hit him across the back of the head with the hammer, as hard as I can.

He falls to one side, and the knife falls to the floor, but it's already covered in blood.

Jamie stands up weakly, touching his side, holding up his fingers in front of him. They are red and wet.

We stagger across the room, as Josh groans.

"I know where your mother is, you stupid bitch," Josh whispers through clenched teeth.

"Drop your phone, let him call for help," I say to Jamie, and he does.

"Fuck you, brother!" Josh shouts. "When The Mayan finds you he'll kill you both!"

6

Howard starts barking on cue, and Aunt Vita runs down the path towards us. She practically catches Jamie as he slips off the bike behind me.

"He's been stabbed," I say. "I bandaged it as tightly as I could, but…"

Jamie's hoodie is wrapped around his middle and soaked in blood. Richard's hoodie is draped around his shoulders, and wet on one side, too. I peel off my T-shirt, and the back is wet with Jamie's blood.

"Susan!" Vita cries, holding him up.

❧

I sit with my aunt at the kitchen table, sipping fresh mint tea, as Howard throws Bartlett evils and Bartlett just eats.

"I never want to read another note from you again, do you understand me?" she says. She is furious.

"I'm sorry," I say.

"I don't know what the hell you were thinking." She storms back to the counter, throwing a spoon into the sink like it's contagious.

"Don't worry?" She says, grabbing the note from the table, reading it aloud. "Don't worry?!"

Susan walks in and takes her hand.

"How is he?" I say.

"He's lost some blood, but it looked worse than it was. He's sleeping now, but he'll be up in time for dinner."

"And then what do we do with him?" Aunt Vita says, raising her eyebrows pointedly at me.

~

The baby is asleep in a sling on her front, as Susan dishes up Swedish stew.

Jamie pushes the vegetables self-consciously around his plate, as Vita stares at him. "I'm so sorry, it's really delicious, but I'm not that hungry," he says.

"Just a little, for some strength," Susan says, smiling.

"Stop glaring," I whisper to Aunt Vita, reaching for a slice of bread. She makes a clicking noise with her tongue against the roof of her mouth and drums her fingers on the table.

I look to Susan for support, but she shakes her head softly.

Jamie forces a forkful of fish into his mouth.

"Do you know where my sister is? You know that she's Diana's mother I assume?" Aunt Vita says, pushing her plate away.

Jamie swallows hard and puts down his fork.

"Dad's wife lives in our house in Geneva. I know she's called Lana, but I've never met her. She's Gulliver's mum, he's my little brother. He has a photo of her in his room. He's the only one allowed a photo of his mum. I realise now that she looks like Diana. And you, too. It hadn't occurred to me before."

"No shit," Aunt Vita says, and walks out of the kitchen.

"I'm sorry, Jamie," I say, as Vita walks back in.

"Byron is awake," she says.

He is propped up in bed, his dark brown chest strikingly thin against the pale blue of the sheets. His arm is in a sling, his eye is practically open, and he's even smiling.

"How are you?" I say, sitting down on the end of his bed.

"Hey, I knew what I was doing," he says, with a wink, then a wince.

"We've got someone to see you," I say, and Vita walks in carrying Bartlett. The dog goes absolutely nuts. Byron's eyes are full of tears.

"Jamie Beltrome is here," I say, as Bartlett finally stops licking Byron's face and curls up on his lap to sleep. "Hugo beat him up, Josh stabbed him, and he's run away."

Byron nods, still smiling, stroking his little dog. "It's not their fault. They are just kids."

"Was it The Mayan who got you?" I say, and he nods.

"Yeah, he just appeared out of the water, I didn't even see him coming. He drugged me before he beat me, every time, so I wouldn't feel it. He kept apologising, kept saying 'I'm sorry'. Then I'd wake up and my arm would be even more broken, or my eye would be swollen shut, or I'd been stabbed. He's a fucked up little dude."

7

I stand in front of the mirror, staring at my reflection. My nose is longer than I remember. My eyes are different shapes. I start to count the freckles on my cheeks but give up. I hold up a thick strand of my hair with one hand, and a pair of scissors in the other. I cut, without thinking, without sadness or remorse. I'm so different now.

My bare feet are covered in the ropes of my hair. I look back in the mirror. Angry red tufts stick out at weird angles across my head. I rifle through the cabinet, until I find what I want. It's brand new, I think Susan bought it for Byron, and I pull it out of the box, plug it in, and flick the switch. The buzzing tickles as I press it against the top of my head and start to push. It reminds me of my Dad cutting the lawn in our back garden.

"You have to do it in straight lines," he always says, "like Wembley."

~

A big, white, cardboard box sits on a coffee table next to Gloria's bed. The baby is inside, having a kick.

"You've put her in a box?" I say to Susan, who looks up at me. Her eyes widen at my lack of hair, but she doesn't say anything.

"It's designed for it, Diana. We give them out at the refuge, to pregnant women. It's a Scandinavian thing."

"Is it safe?" I say.

"Of course, if you use it properly. I try and let her sleep in here with her mummy as much as possible. I'm going to make a cup of tea."

Gloria looks thin. Susan says she's opened her eyes a couple of times, but she never says anything, and closes them again pretty quickly. I haven't been in the room when she's done it. Diana Ross is playing in the corner. I read our horoscopes out loud when the local paper comes, but she doesn't wake up.

"Hey," I say, sitting by her bed in my usual spot, taking her hand. "I've had a haircut. I think it looks cool. You should definitely see it…"

The baby gurgles and dances on her back in the box.

"We need to give her a name, but we are waiting for you to wake up. We can't call her 'the baby' forever. Susan and Vita keep suggesting weird stuff, but I don't know how much longer I can fight them off, and then she'll be Germaine, or Boadicea. And the thing is…I've got to go away, Gloria, for a bit, so I just wanted to say thanks. For giving me your red sunglasses, obviously. And for letting me sing the harmony to Touch Me in the Morning sometimes, even though I know it's your favourite bit. And thanks for, you know…"

I try to swallow the tears in my throat, but I can't speak.

"Please wake up, Gloria," I whisper, squeezing her hand. "You have a daughter, and she needs you. I do too."

∿

The mornings are getting colder now. Dew sparkles on the grass as the sun rises over yellow fields, and I stamp my feet to keep warm.

The baby is wrapped tightly in her blue blanket, as she sucks the crook of Susan's little finger like a dummy. The flat expanse of her eyelids is framed by dark curls. She still doesn't have a name.

Byron is wearing jeans and a fleece from some random old man brand, which looks odd, but they are the only clothes they could find in the hiking shop nearby. He's holding his coffee with the fingers poking out of his sling.

Jamie ducks his head as he walks out of the front door. Without any lenses he has been wearing Aunt Vita's glasses, and they steam up every time he sips his tea. He is wearing exactly the same jeans and fleece as Byron.

Aunt Vita walks back up the driveway, her boots crunching on the gravel.

"His car is passing the wind farm now. He'll be here in a few minutes."

"How long will you stay at the cottage?" I ask Susan, as she rocks the baby gently.

"A couple more days, I think. I won't move Gloria until I have to, but we can't stay out here on our own. It's not safe. We'll leave when the boys do."

We all hear the engine in the distance. Aunt Vita rests her chin on Susan's shoulder, her arms around her waist.

Byron puts down his mug and pulls me in for a hug with his good arm. "Hey, it's all going to be okay you know, Diana?" I wonder if that's true.

"Where are you going?" I ask him.

"Well, first we are going to find Julie Peters. Then I thought we might try and find Jamie's mum."

I turn to face Jamie, and it's weird. I don't even know this new version of him. He looks lighter but different.

I hug him goodbye. "Thank you for helping us," I say into his ear. "I'm sorry I screwed up your life."

"I didn't want that one anyway," he says, as his lips brush my cheek.

～

B yron and Jamie open the gate for the car.
"I wouldn't let you go with anybody else," Aunt Vita says. "I promise you'll be okay, if you do exactly what he says. I mean it, Diana. Do *exactly* what he says."

She holds my hand as we watch an old, black man in a patterned red shirt and a fedora walking up the path, with his arm around Byron's shoulder.

"That's Byron's dad," I say.

Aunt Vita runs to meet him, and they hug like father and daughter.

"So, you do still travel sometimes, then?" Aunt Vita says, studying his face.

"Only for you, Vita."

"Yeah, he won't come and see me anywhere," Byron says. They look identical, plus or minus thirty years.

"And this must be Diana," he says, turning to face me.

"Hello Mr. Clarke," I say, holding out my hand.

"It's very nice to meet you, Diana," he says, shaking my hand. "You can call me Mr. Clarke if you want, but my name is George. Are you ready for our little adventure?"

I turn to face Aunt Vita. She is swiping angrily at the tears spilling out of her eyes.

"I wish I could stay with you," I say, clutching onto her like she's the only float in the ocean.

"You'll be safer this way, darling, for now at least, and George will look after you. I'll find her for us, Diana, I promise. I'll bring her to you."

"Please be careful," I say. "And please tell her..." I pause. Tell her what? "Tell her I understand."

She strokes my shaved head. "It's time to go."

8

Half way down the motorway I turn on my phone, and a message bleeps straight away: 'Diana. You have stolen something that belongs to me, and I want it back.'

I type: 'You stole something from me first.'

I press send and throw my phone out of the window.

"It's time for your blindfold now, Diana," George says. "It's better if you don't know where we are going."

I put it on, and lean back, but the knot is too tight, and it's digging into my scalp. I sit on my hands, pressing my palms flat into the leather seat beneath me. I could just reach up and untie it, but I don't.

AFTER

A man stands by the side of the motorway at night. He hacks at the undergrowth with a machete, as occasional cars speed by.

Suddenly he stops, drops to his knees, and begins to dig with his hands.

Standing up, shaking off the dirt, he turns the phone over gently in his fingers, surveying the scratches and the sparkly case.

He plugs it in to his car and waits patiently for it to surge back to life.

Finally, a light appears, and he taps in a code.

A photo appears through the cracks, of two teenage girls lying on a beach, their heads pressed together, one with a mane of red curls, the other with a dark plait and a shaved stripe of black scalp, dyed pink.

Best friends.

Juan smiles. "Good evening, ladies," he whispers. "I'll see you both very soon."

COMING SOON...

The Devil's Sons
Book 2, The Girls & Monsters Trilogy

"We can't hide forever. We have to fight."

Three months after the most important and dangerous summer of her life, Diana is still in hiding, shielded from The Mayan and his hunt for vengeance. As Christmas approaches, and her friends fan out across the globe in search of the victims of Thetis, Diana receives devastating news. Sad, angry and desperate to see the ones she loves - decides to take matters in to her own hands. Even if it's the last thing she'll ever do...

ACKNOWLEDGMENTS

My heartfelt thanks go to Claire Jennison at Penning and Planning for being an incredible editor and an amazing source of knowledge about the self-publishing journey. Thank you to Georgina Kamsika for helping me with the sensitivities of this book, which walks a fine and difficult path. Huge thanks to Jem Milton for their beautiful illustration and for bringing Gloria and Diana to life.

Thanks so much to Christina Starmans from the Department of Psychology at the University of Toronto for responding to my clumsy requests for information on what, it transpired, was 'motivated reasoning', and the nature of being an ally. And a big thank you to everyone who read the book in one of its early stages including: Kelly Weekes, Clare Bradshaw, Katherine Rhodes, Katie John, Megan Long, Sanna Mansson, Kelly Bartlett, Harriet Gray, Elise Fergusson, Gracie Heskin, Samantha Haycock and April Holden.

I am incredibly grateful to the heroes in my life who told me to carry on with this book when I thought about giving up. Bethan Newell, my amazing niece, my Diana inspiration and chief reader for many MANY early versions; Amy Kean, my very talented sister, who always helps me remember my dreams, and tries to help me get there; Laura Kean, my trusted advisor in everything life; Andrew Wood, my love and my strength and the most intelligent man there is; and of course my Cecily, for helping me understand what is important, every single damn day. I love you always, Parsley.

ABOUT THE AUTHOR

Lulu Wood is a creative consultant from Essex. She lives in London with her family and their shouty cat. This is her 5th novel.